WARRIORS OF THE NORTH

By

H A Culley

Book Two about the lives and times of Oswald
and Oswiu, brothers who were Kings of
Northumbria, famous warriors and Saints

Published by

Orchard House Publishing

Second Kindle Edition 2018

Text copyright © 2016 H A Culley

TABLE OF CONTENTS

List of Principal Characters

(In alphabetical order)

Historical characters are shown in bold type

Acha – Widow of Æthelfrith and sister of Edwin, both kings of Northumbria

Æbbe - Acha's only daughter. Later Abbess of Ebchester and founder of Coldingham Priory.

Æthelfrith - King of Northumbria who was killed in battle in 616 AD. The father of Eanfrith, Oswald, Oswiu and their other siblings

Aidan - An Irish monk and missionary. Later Abbot and Bishop of Lindisfarne, he is credited with converting Northumbria to Christianity

Cadwaladr – Cadwallon's son

Cadwallon ap Cadfan – King of Gwynedd

Cewalh – Cynegils' eldest son, King of Wessex from 642

Congal Cláen – Nephew of Eochaid. King of the Ulaidh in Ulster

Cyneburga – Cynegils' daughter, later Queen of Northumbria

Cynegils – King of Wessex until 642

Dòmhnall mac Áedo – High King of Ireland, a member of the southern Uí Néill

Domnall Brecc – King of Dalriada

Domangart – Domnall's eldest son

Dudda – Eorl of Norhamshire and one of Oswald's counsellors

Dunstan – Oswald's horse marshal and a member of his gesith (bodyguard)

Eanfrith – Oswald's half-brother, King of Bernicia in 633 AD

Edwin – Acha's brother who usurped the throne of Northumbria. Killed by Penda and Cadwallon in 633 AD

Edwy – A Mercian boy and Oswald's current body slave

Eochaid Iarlaithe mac Lurgain – Son of the late King Fiachnae of the Ulaidh, close friend of Oswald's

Eowa – The elder brother of King Penda; lord of Northern Mercia

Ethelbald – Sometime custos (garrison commander) of Bebbanburg.

Fianna – The daughter of a farmer on Bute who Oswiu took as his lover

Beorhtwulf – A young warrior who became one of Oswald's gesith

Hengist – One of Oswald's gesith, later Sub-king of Lindsey

Hrothga – Eorl of Eoforwīc

James the Deacon – A Roman Catholic missionary in Deira; later canonised

Jarlath – A captured Irish boy; now one of Oswald's gesith, later its captain

Keeva – Jarlath's sister, Oswald's mistress

Kenric – A member of Oswiu's gesith, later Eorl of Dùn Barra in Goddodin

Œthelwald – Oswald's son; later King of Deira

Offa – Oswald's youngest brother, a monk and an anchorite

Osguid – Oswald's next eldest brother

Oslac – Another of Oswald's brothers, later his chaplain

Owain map Belin – King of Strathclyde

Oswald – Second son of Æthelfrith of Bernicia and eldest son of Acha of Deira. King of Northumbria. A noted warrior and ruler who, with Aidan, spread Christianity throughout Northumbria

Oswiu – One of Oswald's younger brothers who became King of Rheged, Bernicia and Northumbria in turn. A devoted Christian who established a number of monasteries

Penda – King of Mercia, a pagan

Peada – His son, King of Middle Anglia as his father's vassal

Raulf – Ethelbald's son and Oswiu's body slave

Rhieinmelth – Princess of Rheged and heiress to its throne.

Ròidh – A Pictish prince who became Aidan's acolyte

Rònan – A captured Pict who became one of Oswald's gesith

Ségéne mac Fiachnaíhe – Abbot of Iona

Sigbert – A captured Deiran boy

Place Names

(In alphabetical order)

I find that always using the correct place name for the particular period in time may be authentic but it is annoying to have to continually search for the modern name if you want to know the whereabouts of the place in relation to other places in the story. However, using the ancient name adds to the authenticity of the tale. I have therefore compromised by using the modern name for cities, towns, settlements and islands except where the ancient name is relatively well known, at least to those interested in the period, or is relatively similar to the modern name. The ancient names used are listed below:

Bebbanburg – Bamburgh, Northumberland
Bernicia – The modern counties of Northumberland, Durham, Tyne & Wear and Cleveland in the North East of England. At times Goddodin was a subsidiary part of Bernicia.
Berwic – Berwick upon Tweed
Caer Luel – Carlisle in Cumbria
Caledonia - Scotland
Cantwareburg – Canterbury, Kent, England
Dalriada – Much of Argyll and the Inner Hebrides
Deira – Most of North Yorkshire and northern Humberside
Dùn Add – Dunadd, near Kilmartin, Argyll, Scotland. Capital of Dalriata.
Dùn Barra - Dunbar, Scotland
Dùn Breatainn - Literally Fortress of the Britons. Dumbarton, Scotland

Dùn Èideann - Edinburgh
Dùn Phris - Dumfries, south-west Scotland
Eoforwīc - York
Elmet – West Yorkshire
German Ocean – North Sea
Gleawecastre – Gloucester, England
Goddodin – The area between the River Tweed and the Firth of Forth; i.e. the modern regions of Lothian and Borders in Scotland.
Gwynedd – North Wales including Anglesey
Hamwic – Southampton, Hampshire, England
Isurium Brigantum - Aldborough in Yorkshire
Legacæstir – Chester, England
Lundenwic – London
Maserfield – Oswestry in Shropshire, England
Mercia – Roughly the present day Midlands of England
Northumbria – Comprised Bernicia, Elmet and Deira. At times it also included Rheged and Goddodin
Oxenforda – Oxford, England
Pictland – The confederation of kingdoms including Shetland, the Orkneys, the Outer Hebrides, Skye and the Scottish Highlands north of a line running roughly from Skye to the Firth of Forth
River Twaid – The river Tweed, which flows west from Berwick through northern Northumberland and the Scottish Borders.
Rheged - A kingdom of Ancient Britons speaking Cumbric, a Brythonic language similar to Old Welsh, which roughly encompassed modern Lancashire, Cumbria in England and, at times, part of Galloway in Scotland
Wintan-ceastre - Winchester, Hampshire, England
Weorgoran-ceastre – Worcester, England

Glossary

Ætheling – Literally 'throne-worthy. An Anglo-Saxon prince.

Birlinn – A wooden ship similar to the later Scottish galleys. Usually with a single mast and square rigged sail, they could also be propelled by oars with one man to each oar.

Brenin – The Brythonic term by which kings were addressed Wales, Strathclyde, Rheged and the Land of the Picts.

Bretwalda - In Anglo-Saxon England, an overlord or paramount king accepted by other kings as their leader

Currach - A boat, sometimes quite large, with a wooden frame over which animal skins or hides are stretched and greased to make them waterproof.

Custos – A guardian or custodian, the word was used in a variety of contexts including to mean one left in charge in the absence of the lord or king.

Cymru - Wales

Cyning – Old English for king and the term of respect by which they were normally addressed.

Eorl – A noble ranking between thegn and members of the royal house. In the seventh century it meant the governor of a division of the kingdom. Later replaced by ealdorman, the chief magistrate and war leader of a county, and earl, the ruler of a province under the King of All England; for example, Wessex, Mercia and Northumbria.

Gesith – The companions of a king, usually acting as his bodyguard.

Hereræswa – Military commander or general. The man who commanded the army of a nation under the king.

Mile Castle – A Roman fort built at intervals of one mile all along Hadrian's Wall.

Seax – A bladed weapon somewhere in size between a dagger and a sword. Mainly used for close-quarter fighting where a sword would be too long and unwieldy.

Thegn – The lowest rank of noble. A man who held a certain amount of land direct from the king or from a senior nobleman, ranking between an ordinary freeman and an eorl.

Ulaidh - A confederation of dynastic-groupings that inhabited a provincial kingdom in Ulster (north-eastern Ireland) and was ruled by the Rí Ulad or King of the Ulaidh. The two main tribes of the Ulaidh were the Dál nAraidi and the Dál Fiatach.

Uí Néill – An Irish clan who claimed descent from Niall Noigiallach (Niall of the Nine Hostages), a famous High King of Ireland who died about 405 AD.

Settlement – Any grouping of residential buildings, usually around the king's or lord's hall. In 7th century England the term city or town normally referred to former Roman conurbations and village had not yet come into use.

Síþwíf - My lady in Old English.

Witan – The council of an Anglo-Saxon kingdom. Its composition varied, depending on the matters to be debated. Usually it consisted of the Eorls and the chief priests (bishops and abbots in the case of a Christian kingdom), but for the selection of a king or other important matters, it would be expanded to include the more minor nobility, such as the thegns.

Villein - A peasant (tenant farmer) who was legally tied to his vill.

Vill - A thegn's holding or similar area of land in Anglo-Saxon England which would later be described as a parish or manor.

SYNOPSIS OF THE FIRST BOOK - WHITEBLADE

Woken in the middle of the night to flee the fortress of Bebbanburg on the Northumbrian coast, the twelve year old Prince Oswald escapes his father's killer, Edwin, to establish a new life for himself on the West Coast of Scotland. He becomes a staunch Christian on Iona and trains to be a warrior.

He makes a name for himself in the frequent wars in Ulster and in a divided Scotland, earning himself the nickname of 'Whiteblade' and establishing himself as the greatest war leader in his adopted homeland. However, he is beset by enemies on all sides and is betrayed by those he should be able to trust the most.

After playing a leading role in deposing the treacherous Connad, King of Dalriada, he helps his successor to extend Dalriada to include the Isles of Skye, Arran and Bute. When King Edwin is killed in battle and those who try to succeed him are also killed by Cadwallon and his invading Welsh army, Oswald decides that his moment of destiny has arrived; he sets out with his warriors to confront Cadwallon and win back the throne of Northumbria.

CHAPTER ONE – THE BATTLE OF HEAVENFIELD

June 634 AD

Oswald had anchored his left flank on the cliff face known as Brady's Crag and the right against the old Roman Wall. Satisfied that he couldn't be outflanked he stood and studied the opposing army. Cadwallon with his three hundred Welsh tribesmen and a hundred battle-hardened Mercian warriors had occupied the low ridge to the east, blocking his route into Bernicia.

'What do you make of them?'

The speaker was his brother Oswiu who, at twenty two, was nearly as experienced a fighter as Oswald. Both had learned their trade in the service of the King of Dalriada on the west coast of Caledonia and in Ulster fighting for the Ulaidh against the Uí Néill.

'They outnumber us but few of the Welshmen have any armour; not even helmets. They have fewer archers too. Against that, the hundred Mercians are all wearing either chain mail byrnies or thick leather jerkins and helmets. I suspect that all of them are trained warriors. However, our men from Dalriada are hardy fighters and have fought with us before. Against that, the Ilesmen and the men of Rheged are more of an unknown quantity and they amount to half our numbers.'

'The men from Rheged are also unarmoured and look little different to the Welsh,' Oswiu added.

'They and the Welsh are both Brythonic tribesmen. Thankfully our men don't paint their bodies with those peculiar blue whorls or lime their hair, otherwise we'd have trouble telling them apart.'

The speaker was another of Oswald's brothers, a monk from Iona called Oslac. He and another brother called Osguid had accompanied Oswald with a few of the warriors who protected the monastery on Iona. They had erected a large wooden cross at the centre of the line and had just finished blessing the army to inspire them.

'Well, it doesn't look as if Cadwallon is going to make the first move,' Rònan observed.

He was the son of a Pictish King from Lewis who had been captured as a boy and had been Oswald's body slave for a time. Now freed and trained as a warrior, he was one of the dozen close companions who formed Oswald's gesith.

'No, I think you're right. Well, if he's not going to attack first voluntarily, we'll have to provoke him into doing so. Take up your positions, I'm going to send the archers forward.'

'You'll need your helmet then.'

Jarlath, another of the gesith who was the brother of Oswald's mistress, Keeva, handed him a prime example of the smith's trade. The crown was made from a single piece of steel to which a chain mail aventail had been attached to protect the neck and a piece of metal with two holes had been riveted to the front rim to protect the eyes and nose. It was decorated with a circlet of gold around the rim and a crest of gold running fore and aft.

The two smiled at one another. Jarlath was another former body slave, this time from Ireland, who continued to serve in that capacity despite the fact that Oswald had freed him some time ago and, at sixteen, he'd just completed his training as a warrior. He too was part of Oswald's gesith.

Oswald put on his helmet and then took his shield from his eleven year old son.

'Thank you, Œthelwald, now go to the rear where the baggage train is and wait there until I send for you.   Do you understand?'

'Why can't I stay and fight by your side, father?'

'Because you have yet to be trained to fight and you know you can't start that for three years yet, when you'll be much bigger. Now go, you're distracting me from the battle.'

Jarlath gripped the boy's shoulder. 'I'll come with you to make sure you get there safely.'

A year ago Œthelwald would have told Jarlath rudely that he didn't need him to look after him. He had despised the youth for being a former slave, but he had matured somewhat since then and instead he nodded his thanks and went with Jarlath.

'Don't kill them all; leave some for me. I'll be back as quickly as I can,' the latter called over his shoulder as he followed Œthelwald towards where the pack animals, horses, livestock and carts were housed in and around one of the old mile castles on the Roman Wall.

Twenty of the older men had been detailed to protect it, as well as the men from Rheged who were the drivers of the carts and drovers of the livestock which had been brought along to feed Oswald's host. Jareth handed Œthelwald over to the man in charge and ran back towards the battlefield.

When he got there he saw that the archers had advanced to within eighty yards of the enemy line and were pouring a steady stream of arrows into them. Some aimed directly at the front rank and others sent theirs at high trajectory into the rear ranks. The enemy archers were responding but there were far fewer of them and Oswald had sent a warrior forward with each archer to protect him with his large round shield. By comparison the Welshmen carried much smaller shields, called targes, which did little to protect them. Only the Mercians in the centre had shields similar to those carried by most of Oswald's men.

Finally the irate Welshmen had had enough and a whole section of them broke the line. They ran towards their tormentors in a disorganised mass. The archers beat a hasty retreat and the line of warriors opened up to allow them through, then closed ranks and brought their shields into position so that they overlapped it with that of the man next to them. This left only their eyes and lower legs exposed. However, the Welsh thought that they had a surprise in store for them. A yard of so from the shield wall half of them knelt down on one knee with their backs bent and head tucked in and the rest, all armed with daggers and seaxes, used them as spring boards to leap high in the air and come down several ranks deep into Oswald's army.

As they landed on the Dalriadan men they tried to poke out their eyes or slit their throats. A few succeeded but many were spitted on swords or spears as they landed. The front rank took two steps forward and cut the kneeling men down as they clambered to their feet. Very few of those who had charged down the slope made it back up again.

What the Welsh didn't know was that it was also a favourite tactic used by Irish tribesmen and many of his army had fought with Oswald in Ulster. The rest had been quickly warned by those in the know as soon as the charge had begun.

Cadwallon cursed and sent his son, Cadwaladr, to the rear.

'I've lost at least eighty men so far so we no longer have the numerical advantage. I'm going to have to charge en masse and hope that they break. In case it doesn't work, I want you to make your way back to Gwynedd. If I die you must seize the throne.'

'No father, I can't desert you. I'll wait at the rear, but with your horse so that we can escape together, if necessary. God go with you and grant that your charge is successful.'

With that Cadwaladr turned and made his way back to the Welsh baggage train.

His father gripped his battle axe, settled his helmet firmly on his head and gave the signal. Over two hundred Welshmen and a hundred Mercians charged down the slope at the stationary line of their foes. The momentum of the charge drove Oswald's men back and broke the shield wall. However, even whilst they drove the latter back, the front rank of the Dalriadans and their allies used their swords and spears to kill the leading rows of their opponents.

Oswald banged his shield into the face of a man with limed hair arranged in spikes, breaking his nose, and then thrust his sword into his neck. The man fell away gurgling as his life blood spurted from his neck, only to be replaced by another half-naked man wielding a large two-bladed axe. He brought the heavy axe down on Oswald's shield, splitting the bronze rim and driving deeply into the lime wood, where it stuck. The man was now without a weapon. Oswald drove the point of his sword deep into the man's belly, twisting it as he pulled it out so bloody, grey ropes of intestine were pulled out with it. The Welshman screamed and fell to his knees vainly trying to stuff his guts back inside him.

He was kicked out of the way by a heavily armoured Mercian armed with a sword and a large shield. Oswald

17

dropped his own shield, now rendered useless by the axe, and pulled his seax from his scabbard. He aimed a blow at the Mercian with his sword which the man knocked aside with his shield whilst cutting at Oswald with his own sword. Oswald parried it with his seax, then swept his sword low, aiming at the man's legs. The blade bit deeply into the Mercian's left calf and came to a jarring halt as it bit into bone. The man's leg collapsed and Oswald thrust his seax into his neck as he fell. During a brief respite Oswald grabbed the Mercian's shield and, sheathing his Seax, pulled the shield close to his chest as he prepared to meet the next attacker.

Further along the line the two monks and the warriors from Iona saw the Welsh trying to uproot the wooden cross. It had stood in line with the front rank at the start of the battle but it was now ten yards away. Furiously Osguid and Oslac, armed only with cudgels, drove forward with the Iona men to stop them. Seeing them battling their way forward, Eochaid yelled for his men to support them and fought his way towards them. His men and those from Rheged followed him and the whole left flank surged forward pushing the Welsh back.

By some miracle Oslac reached the men trying to uproot the cross and laid about him, crushing the skulls of three before the rest of Eochaid's division reached him and took up position in front of the cross. It was then that he realised that Osguid wasn't with him. It was only later than he found his body with four dead enemy around him.

Oswiu was also beginning to push the Welsh back on the right flank. He was hindered by the bank of dead bodies in front of his men, indicating just how many of the enemy had fallen vainly trying to break his line. Once they had clambered over this obstacle, they encountered less and less opposition as the enemy started to flee the field.

The Mercians in the centre refused to be routed, however, and Oswald's own centre found themselves hard pressed to hold the line against them. It was only when Oswiu's division attacked them in the flank that they started to make a fighting withdrawal. When the Welsh were routed on the left as well, Eochaid swung his men through ninety degrees and laid into their other flank. The Mercians were now all but encircled but they made a brave last stand until, when their numbers were down to about thirty, they surrendered.

By then the routed Welshmen were streaming away to the west. Oswald saw Cadwallon's red dragon banner held aloft in the middle of small group of mounted men as they turned to join the retreat. He watched in despair for a moment; if Cadwallon got away he would continue to threaten Northumbria. Then he pulled himself together and yelled for someone to fetch the horses.

By the time that enough horses had been brought forward from the rear, Cadwallon was over two miles away. Oswald and Eochaid mounted with the former's gesith and another dozen men and, leaving Oswiu to mop up the last resistance and take care of both the wounded and those captured, Oswald set off in pursuit. It was only after they had gone a mile that he saw with alarm that one of those riding alongside him was his son, Œthelwald. He realised that he must have been one of those who brought the horses forward. He was about to order him back to the baggage train but he realised that a lone boy on a horse would be very vulnerable to a defeated enemy desperately trying to escape.

As if to emphasise this, they overtook a lot of the enemy fleeing on foot but Oswald ordered his men not to cut them down. He didn't want any delays in his effort to catch up with Cadwallon. Oswald was determined that the wretched man had to pay for the treacherous way that he had murdered his half-brother. Of course, that had left the throne of Bernicia vacant for Oswald to occupy, but that wasn't the point. The King of Gwynedd had invited Eanfrith to discuss peace and then had killed him and his escort during dinner. It was not something that could ever be forgiven.

They eventually caught Cadwallon as his retreat westwards was blocked by the North Tyne River and the Welsh had been forced to head north to the ford at a settlement called Chollerton. The water came up to the horses' chests and the ford was too narrow to allow more than two horses to cross abreast. Cadwallon had sent Cadwaladr across first with a small escort but he and ten men were still on the east bank when Oswald arrived.

They fought bravely to allow time for a tearful Cadwaladr to make his escape, but they died to the last man. Oswald's only regret was that another man had killed Cadwallon before he could get to him. He had left his son behind with Jarlath and Rònan to protect him when he charged so he was amazed to see Œthelwald ride up to a Welshman and, ducking under the sweep of the man's sword, stick his seax into his side. He berated Jarlath and Rònan later but, as they pointed out, his son had suddenly ridden off before they could stop him. They were there to protect him, not imprison him. He made his displeasure known to his son as well, but secretly he was very proud of him for killing his first man in battle at eleven.

20

With Cadwallon dead, he let Cadwaladr go. He suspected that the boy was too young to succeed his father and his assessment proved correct. The news of the king's death reached Gwynedd before the returning Cadwaladr and by the time he got back a man called Cadafael ap Cynfeddw, who was unrelated to the royal house, had seized the throne. In time Cadafael was to prove a real nuisance to Northumbria.

It wasn't until Oswald returned to the battlefield that he learned from Oswiu and Oslac about the death of Osguid. The news robbed Oswald of the elation he was feeling over his great victory and, instead of joining the others in feasting to celebrate, he and his brothers spend the night in prayer over Osguid's corpse laid out under the wooden cross. Even the rain, which started to fall shortly after midnight and continued until dawn, didn't drive them from their vigil.

~~~

Oswald and his two brothers halted on the top of the last rise before Bebbanburg and gazed at their birthplace. The long outcrop of basalt dominated the small settlement to the west of it and the German Ocean beyond it. The vertical face of rock facing them rose two hundred feet from the level ground below it and two steep paths climbed upwards from the settlement towards the two gates, one to the north and one the south. The palisade atop the rock stood twelve feet tall and Oswald knew that the two entrances were protected by double gatehouses. Even if you managed to capture one, there was a fifty foot long approach to the second gatehouse which was dominated from above. Either approach would prove to be a killing ground to an enemy.

However, today the gates to the north stood open and a welcoming delegation of Bernician nobles waited patiently to greet Oswald. Of course, they had all sworn loyalty to Edwin after Æthelfrith had been killed and his family had been forced to flee to Dalriada. Those nobles who had fled with Queen Acha and her children seventeen years ago had all died during the seventeen years of exile, some of old age but many fighting for their adopted country.

Over a dozen of those riding at Oswald's back were the sons of those nobles and they expected to recover the lands in Northumbria that used to belong to their families. Their loyalty had to be rewarded but those standing in front of him ready to welcome him back and elect him as their king would hardly give up their lands willingly. It was to be Oswald's first challenge as king.

But he wasn't king yet, as he found out when he reached the delegation waiting to greet him.

'Greetings, Oswald Ætheling. Welcome home.'

Oswald had been about to dismount, but he remained sitting astride his horse as he glared at the rather rotund nobleman smiling up at him.

'Ætheling? Yes, I am that, but also your king.'

The man looked confused and glanced behind him at the other nobles and the two druid priests who formed the rest of the welcoming party. They merely looked uncomfortable and no-one came to his aid.

'Lord Oswald, it is the prerogative of the Witan to decide who should be King of Bernicia.'

'Yes, I'm well aware of that. Why hasn't the Witan met to confirm my position as your king. I had assumed that they would have done that as soon as word of the defeat and death of Cadwallon reached you.'

The man looked even more uncomfortable, if that were possible.

'Not everyone believed your messenger, Lord Oswald. In any case, the proper selection progress has to be undertaken and there are other æthelings to be considered.'

'Other æthelings? Who?'

'Would you like to dismount and accompany me into the fortress where we can discuss these things in more convivial surroundings?'

'Very well.'

Oswald dismounted and signalled for his two brothers and his son to do likewise.

'Dunstan, take the men to Budle Bay and camp for now.'

The man commanding his horsemen nodded and the army followed him back the way they had come to camp by a small river that flowed into the sea about a mile from the fortress. It was the nearest source of plentiful fresh water as both the fortress and the settlement that nestled in its shadow depended on wells.

'These are my brothers Oswiu and Father Oslac and my son, Œthelwald,' he told the delegation.

'I'm Brant, Thegn of Berwic and custos of Bebbanburg,' the man who was evidently the leader of those present told him. He then led the way through the gates without bothering to introduce anyone else.

The rest made to follow but they were prevented by Oswald's gesith, who interspersed themselves behind Oswald and his family and the discomfited nobles. The two druids were left behind, engaged in earnest conversation. No-one else noticed but Jarlath did and he nudged Rònan, walking at his side.

'Those two will bear watching. They can't be happy about the prospect of a Christian king backed up by a Christian army.'

Rònan shrugged. 'What can they do?'

'Well, assassinate Oswald for a start.'

'They'd have to kill his brothers and Œthelwald at the same time. Who would that leave as king?'

'Oswald's uncles, Theobald and Ecgulf? They are both pagans, as Oswald's father was.'

'Hmmm, they must be the other æthelings that fat slob Brant was talking about.'

Although the two were talking softly, the Thegn of Berwic must have had acute hearing because his face turned a deep shade of pink as he tried to hold his anger in check.

Oswiu was desperate to talk to his brother alone. He felt, correctly, that Oswald had got off to a poor start in Bernicia. He needed the nobles onside if he was to gain the throne and re-unite Northumbria. He'd already heard rumours that Goddodin in the north was trying to re-assert its independence and there was no guarantee that Deira and Elmet to the south would accept Oswald. At least they could rely on Rheged after his betrothal to the pretty Rhieinmelth. He was still trying to work out what he could say to Fianna, who he had been living with as man and wife for several years.

When they reached the great hall they found several other nobles waiting for them.

'I thought that you said that the Witan had yet to assemble?' Oswald asked Brant.

'Some came without being summoned,' the thegn replied tersely. He was still angry after overhearing Oswald's men calling him a fat slob.

24

Oswald looked at him sharply for a moment. It was obvious that the man was fuming about something, but he had no idea what. He shrugged and took a seat at the high table, gesturing for his brothers, son and Brant to join him. Oswiu signalled to a servant hovering nearby and asked for some mead or ale and bread and cheese. It had been some time since they had eaten.

'Well, who are these other æthelings who want my throne?'

Brant had been about to order some refreshments himself and the fact that Oswiu had beaten him to it didn't help his mood.

'Your father's brothers, Theobald and Ecgulf and the latter's sons, Edward and Edgar.'

Oswald looked surprised. 'My uncles must be in their fifties, if they're still alive. The last I heard they were both in Wessex and Theobald was a monk. I wasn't aware that Ecgulf was married.'

The last sentence was said with something of a smile. Even at the age of twelve he had known that Ecgulf was a misogynist who avoided the company of women like the plague. Acha had always suspected that he preferred young men as his bedfellows but, if so, he had been remarkably discreet about it.

'Yes, he married a young girl related to the King of Wessex – a distant cousin. I believe that she was only eleven at the time.'

'When was this?'

'Um, about ten years ago, I think.'

Oswald laughed. 'So Edward and Edgar are still small boys!'

'Er, yes. Seven and five I believe.'

'And you think that they would be seriously considered by the Witan?'

'Well, perhaps not at the moment. But there is still your brothers and your son who are eligible.'

Both Oswiu and Oslac looked amused at the idea but Oswald noticed to his dismay that Œthelwald seemed to be taking the idea seriously. His face had lit up and he was looking at Brant intently. Oswald glared at his son and the boy must have been aware of his disapproval because he looked down at the table and refused to meet his father's eye. Oswald was well aware that his son had a tendency to be arrogant; now it seemed that he was ambitious too.

'Very well. When can the Witan congregate?'

'I'll arrange for the messengers to leave tomorrow. It will take them a week to get to the furthest nobles. Shall we say in three weeks' time?'

'I can't wait that long. Most live a few days' ride away at most. They must have heard about Heavenfield and will be expecting the summons. Shall we say in ten days' time at Yeavering?'

CHAPTER TWO – THE WITAN AT YEAVERING

Late August 634 AD

Yeavering was the old summer palace of the Kings of Bernicia. It lay under the hill fort constructed by the Britons before the coming of the Romans about fifteen miles west of Bebbanburg and was therefore more central.

Because Bebbanburg was a better defensive location, Yeavering had been neglected during the recent troubled times and Oswald got his men to repair the palisade and renew the turf roofs of the king's hall and the huts. His army had shrunk in size since Heavenfield. The men from Rheged, Iona and Fergus' Ilesmen had all gone home with their share of the plunder taken from the dead. Oswald was left with one hundred and twenty warriors, excluding those badly wounded who were expected to recover. They were still at the old Roman fort at Corbridge until they either died or had recovered sufficiently to be moved.

On the appointed day for the Witan to meet, eight of the eleven eorls – the chief magistrates and military commanders of the regions into which the kingdom was divided – were present along with over forty of the sixty thegns. Those who were missing were either from Goddodin or thegns who lived too far away. King Royth of Rheged, his bishop and Rhieinmelth, Oswiu's betrothed, were also present but they kept themselves apart from the rest. Eochaid had no reason to be there and so he had volunteered to take his birlinn, the Gift of God, back to Arran to collect Oswald's mother, Acha, and both Keeva and Fianna, the concubines of Oswald and Oswiu respectively.

Dudda, the Eorl of Norhamshire, being the senior, presided. Oswald noted with some displeasure that there were also fifteen druid priests present. Oswiu leaned across and whispered in his brother's ear.

'Don't protest the presence of the pagan chief priests, Oswald. We can banish them once you're firmly established as king.'

'I hate them too, but Oswiu is correct. Bite your tongue, brother,' Oslac muttered quietly.

Their elder brother sighed. 'You're right. Much as I detest them and their kind, we must build a united kingdom before we can convert it to follow the true faith.'

At that moment Dudda called the Witan to order and those attending stopped chatting in small groups and went to sit in their appointed places. Being a fine day in early September, the place of meeting was outside the king's hall where benches had been placed in a circle for the senior members to sit. The thegns had to be content with standing behind them. Dudda took the one and only chair and Oswald and his family took the bench to one side of him. The other seven eorls took the next few benches and the druids sat next to them. Royth and Rhieinmelth came next, together with the Bishop of Rheged. The last bench was taken by a man and two boys who Oswald hadn't seen before.

'Welcome to the Witan of Bernicia. I regret that the three eorls of Goddodin and their thegns have seen fit to ignore the summons, but that will be a matter for our new king to deal with. We are here today to elect the man best suited to be crowned.'

He was going on to say more but he was interrupted.

'Why is the King of Rheged here; and why is he accompanied by a girl and a bishop of the Christians? They have no place here.'

The speaker was the stout thegn, Brant. Several of his fellow thegns shouted their agreement. Oswald got his feet before either Dudda or Royth could reply.

'They are here at my invitation, Brant. Rheged was instrumental in our defeat of the detested Cadwallon and, following the engagement of my brother Oswiu to Princess Rhieinmelth, Rheged is once again part of Northumbria. The princess is here as the heir of her father and is therefore a member of their witan, and by extension, this one too.

'But we are not the Witan of Northumbria, but of Bernicia,' one of the eorls objected.

'You note the absence of the members from Goddodin, which was a separate kingdom before it became part of Northumbria, but yet question the inclusion of Rheged? Is there not something of an inconsistency here?'

There were a few mumbles in response but no-one spoke out against Royth's attendance again, or of that of his daughter.

'Good. My apologies, King Royth. I'm sure that Brant didn't mean to be discourteous to you or your daughter. Now perhaps we can proceed. We have a lot to decide today.'

With that Oswald sat down again.

This time it was one of the chief druids who got to his feet.

'That's all very well but what is that Christian priest doing here? He is an abomination!'

The man he was referring to was the Bishop of Rheged but this time it was Oslac who got to his feet.

29

'I am an ætheling yet that man has dared to call me an abomination in front of the whole Witan!' Oslac had many qualities and one was the ability to speak loudly and resonantly when he wanted to. The druid who had spoken looked at him mouth agape.

'It wasn't you I was referring to, Lord Oslac, but that man there,' he quavered, pointing to the bishop.

'But I am a Christian priest. When you call a fellow priest an abomination I must infer that you are referring to all Christian priests. And what of my brothers Oswald and Oswiu? They are also Christians. Are they also abominations? I challenge you to defend your offence in a fight to the death. Let us see whose god is the stronger.'

By now the druid, who was quite elderly, was opening and closing his mouth in terror. This time it was Oswiu who spoke.

'Trading insults is getting us nowhere. I'm sure that the druid will apologise to you, Oslac; then perhaps we can get on.'

'Yes, yes. I'm sorry, my lord. I meant no insult to you or your brothers,' the druid gibbered and sat down.

'Good. Now I call for those present to nominate those who they wish the Witan to consider for the throne of Bernicia,' Dudda said quickly before there were any more interruptions. 'Would those who are ætheling and therefor eligible to be considered please stand.'

Oswald stood, as did the old man and the two boys on the bench next to Royth and Rhieinmelth.

'Why aren't you standing, Oswiu, Oslac and Œthelwald?'

'I do not wish to be considered. I am content to support my brother,' Oswiu said with a smile. 'And I am a priest; it would not be possible for me to be king and remain a churchman. The king needs to be a warrior.'

Œthelwald slowly got to his feet. 'I will stand. Although I too support my father, I feel that I should at least be considered.'

Oswald and both his brothers were shocked. They hissed their disapproval at him but he continued to stand until Oswiu got hold of him and roughly pulled him back onto the bench.

'You will never be king whilst I live, boy. You are a traitor,' he spat into his ear.

'Then, let's hope that your death comes soon,' the boy retorted.

'Be quiet, Œthelwald. I'll deal with you later.'

The boy gave his father a resentful glance, but then subsided and remained quiet.

'Well then, it seems that we have four contenders for the crown of Bernicia; Oswald son of Æthelfrith, Ecgulf son of Æthelric, Edward, son of Ecgulf and Edgar, son of Ecgulf. All are descended from Æthelric, son of Ida, the first King of Bernicia. Each contender must state now his case.'

Ecgulf, being the elder by a fair margin began.

'I am the senior of all the æthelings of Bernicia present and as the brother of the last true king in the direct line of descent from Ida, I claim the right to succeed to the throne. Edwin was of the house of Deira and Eanfrith's short reign must be discounted as he tried to betray his country to its enemies. I have been in exile in Wessex since the murder of my brother, Æthelfrith, where I have made many important contacts amongst the Saxons of the south, not just in Wessex, but in Sussex and Kent as well. They will prove to be useful allies to Bernicia in the future. I ask the Witan to acknowledge my right to succeed my brother.'

Edward stood up as soon as his father had sat down and confidently faced the Witan.

'You may consider my father to be too old to lead Bernicia, if that is the case, and only if it is, I offer myself as contender for the throne in his place. I may only be nine years old but I have started my training to be a warrior recently and, with your guidance, I offer myself for election as your king.'

His younger brother stood up next but did so rather hesitantly. He looked around him but said nothing until his brother jabbed him in the side.

'I am Edwin, son of Ecgulf, son of Æthelric. I'm too young to be considered for the crown but I wish to support the claim of both my father and my brother.'

With that he sat down, looking relieved and rather pleased with himself. Œthelwald snorted in derision. Then the latter's father climbed to his feet. All the others had spoken from where they had been seated but Oswald walked to the middle of the floor in front of Dudda's chair.

'Few of you know me, as indeed is the case for my uncle and cousins. But I suspect that you may have heard of me. I am known as Whiteblade, a name men call me because of my success in battle. I have fought more of those than I care to remember in the past seventeen years and I have killed more men than I can count. These are no boastful words but the truth; ask any of those who have known me during my time in exile.'

'It is not something I am proud of; indeed I would prefer to be a man of peace. My desire is to build a strong, prosperous country where even the poorest have enough to eat and which can resist any who seek to plunder our wealth. And by country I don't mean just Bernicia, but Northumbria, including Goddodin - who need to be brought back into the fold without delay - Rheged, Deira and Elmet. I say this, not because I wish to enhance my kingdom for some egotistical reason, but because a strong Northumbria can withstand those who seek to harm us. Don't forget that, whilst Cadwallon may be dead and his army decimated, Penda still rules Mercia and could invade at any moment.'

'You may choose Ecgulf because he is a learned man but he is no warrior and a warrior king is what we need now. Even if he were, age takes its toll. Furthermore, were he to live longer than most and remain in the best of good health, you would be convening again to elect his successor not many years hence. We need continuity to build a strong Northumbria.

'Edward spoke well but he is younger than my own son and it will be a decade or more yet before they are old enough to be considered for such a demanding role. Many may hesitate because they don't know me, or because I am a devout Christian whilst they are pagans, but I submit that I am the best hope that Bernicia, and Northumbria, has for the future.'

Oswald sat down amidst silence. Then an excited babble of voices broke out and it was five minutes or more before Dudda could restore order.

'Do any of the eorls wish to question any of the contenders?'

'Yes, I'm not convinced that we need to revert to unity with Deira. They are awkward neighbours at the best of times, and I should know because my shire is bordered by the River Tees, to the south of which lie both Deira and Elmet. Cadwallon is dead, thanks to Oswald and Oswiu, and Penda has both internal problems and is also in dispute with Wessex. We are not threatened any longer, contrary to what Oswald says, and we need a king who will make us prosperous once more. I'm convinced that man is

Ecgulf. Hopefully his sons will grow to manhood before we have to consider one of them ….'

Oswald's eyes had narrowed dangerously whilst he'd been speaking and gradually he'd become aware of the venomous glare being directed at him. The eorl was shocked by the animosity Oswald managed to convey and his voice faltered to a stop. He wondered if he'd been wise to express his opinion in such a direct manner. By now another eorl was on his feet.

'I'm not so foolish as to believe that, just because one of our despoilers is dead, there is no threat from another. Penda is a ruthless man, and one whose power is growing. Wessex, Kent and East Anglia on his other borders are all ruled by weak men who are no match for him. The petty Welsh kings to the west of Mercia fear him or are his allies. Only Northumbria can stand against him. To do that we need an equally warlike king. I say that Oswald is that man.'

There was a murmur of agreement from the thegns before the next man stood up. This time it was one of the druids.

'Oswald and his brood all follow the false god, the White Christ. Our king must be of the old faith. Otherwise the true gods, the gods of our ancestors, will desert us.'

'It is your gods who are false. There is but one God and Jesus Christ is his son. Your gods don't exist, so how can they help you? It is the Christ, under whose symbol we fought and won at Heavenfield, who can aid us in the battles to come, and only him,' Oswald roared back in reply.

The druid looked affronted and then, seeing the belligerent look on the face of the man who was likely to be the next king, he subsided back onto the bench, muttering to himself and giving Oswald and his family dark looks.

'Does anyone else wish to say anything? No, good. Then it's time for the vote.'

Dudda looked relieved that the discussion was over. At one stage he had feared there might be bloodshed. The casting of votes was a simple matter. Everyone stood and the four contestants ranged themselves either side of Dudda facing the rest. One by one each of those present went and stood behind the man or boy they wanted to be king. Only a few nobles went and stood behind Edwin and none at all behind his younger brother. The druids all sided with Edwin though, presumably because they thought that they could control him. Most of the eorls lined up behind Oswald but the man who had opposed unity with Deira chose Ecgulf. The thegns were more equally divided.

'Forty five support Oswald, twenty nine Ecgulf and eighteen Edwin. Edward and Edwin are therefore eliminated and their supporters must now choose between Ecgulf and Oswald.'

The druids moved en masse to stand behind Ecgulf, together with Edwin and Edward. That gave him forty six votes, but the three thegns who had chosen Edwin stood undecided. They conferred in whispers whilst the rest waited impatiently. Then all three went over to Oswald, giving him a majority of two.

'I declare that Oswald wins by three votes as I too support him as our king,' Duddo declared with a smile. 'Do those who chose Ecgulf abide by the decision of the Witan?'

In answer Ecgulf immediately went and knelt in front of Oswald to pledge him his loyalty; his two sons followed suit and gradually everyone else did the same. However, by the time that the last thegn had knelt, the fifteen druids had disappeared without giving their new king their support.

'Send men after them at once,' he whispered to Oswiu. 'I want them to disappear.'

His brother nodded and called Dunstan to him. A few minutes later the latter and twenty five of his men led their horses away from where they had waited just inside the gate in the palisade that surrounded Yeavering. Once outside they mounted and quietly trotted along the track towards Bebbanburg. Dunstan had watched the druids leave, taking Brant with them. It was fairly obvious that they planned to seize the fortress on the coast and instigate a revolt against Oswald amongst their pagan followers.

CHAPTER THREE – GODDODIN

September 634 AD

The druids were mounted on the small horses that were bred in Bernicia, whereas Dunstan's men had a mixture of the smaller Welsh ponies captured at Heavenfield and the much larger horses given to them by King Royth of Rheged. Leaving the fifteen men who were riding ponies to follow on as best they might, Dunstan led the other ten after Brant and the druids.

They caught up with them at the crossing over the River Till below an old abandoned hill fort. The druids were bunched up waiting to cross as Dunstan appeared. Brant and six of the druids were already across and one more was in the middle of the river, which came up to the horse's belly. The remaining eight turned to face the oncoming horsemen whilst Brant kicked his heels into his horse and rode off eastwards.

A few druids were carrying spears and some cudgels. However their weapons availed them nothing against the highly experienced warriors. Although they were unused to fighting on horseback, they knew how to use their shields and warded off the druids' blows whilst thrusting their own spears and swords into the priests' unprotected torsos. Within five minutes it was all over. Dunstan left one of his men who had a minor flesh wound behind to tell those following on to bury the bodies and the horses' tack in the old hill fort. He then released the horses to run wild before splashing across the ford after Brant and the remaining druids.

The latter had hesitated, obviously debating whether to return to aid their fellows or flee. As soon as it became obvious that the fate of the men still on the west bank was sealed, they rode off to the east.

The water only came up to just above the knees of the larger horses and so Dunstan and his nine men were able to cross swiftly. They had just started out on the pursuit again when one of his men called out to Dunstan.

'The one in the lead had taken a different path,'

'Where?'

'Just beyond that second old hill fort, he turned onto a path leading north but the others are still heading due east.'

'Well spotted.'

'I think that the man with the druids is that fat man who greeted Whiteblade at Bebbanburg,' another man told him, somewhat breathlessly as they cantered uphill.

'What the Thegn of Berwic? That makes sense. Berwic is a settlement on the estuary of the Twaid. It must be where he's heading.'

'Should we pursue him?'

Dunstan shook his head.

'No, our job is to stop those druids from stirring up trouble when they reach Bebbanburg. If Brant takes refuge in Berwic I doubt that it's anything like as impregnable as the fortress on the rock. We can deal with him later.'

They had nearly reached the place where the army had camped by Budle Bay before they caught up with the druids. By that time Dunstan was becoming worried. Oswald's instructions had been clear: the druids weren't just to be killed, they were to disappear. If they didn't overtake them before they crested the next ridgeline they would be visible from the top of the watchtower in Bebbanburg.

He decided he had to take a chance and ordered the four men with bows to dismount and aim for the leaders. They were at extreme range and, as the six remaining horsemen tried to close with the fleeing druids, the archers shot at high trajectory over their heads. The first arrow fell short but it hit the rump of the rearmost horse. It reared up in pain, depositing its luckless rider on the hard ground where he lay winded. Dunstan dropped the point of his spear as he neared the prone druid and jammed it into his abdomen. He wasn't dead but he would be incapacitated enough to keep him where he'd fallen.

The other three arrows reached further into the mass of mounted druids. One struck a man at the junction of the neck and upper back. Again it wasn't fatal but he fell off his horse and lay screaming in agony. The other two hit the horses of the leading druids and brought them down, spilling their riders into the dirt. The horses immediately behind them ran into the two collapsed animals or their winded riders and they too came crashing down. Only one druid was still mounted but he was too busy trying to control his panicked steed to get away.

Dunstan and his men tore into the shambles and stabbed and cut at the surviving druids until they were all dead. They then dispatched the two wounded men before dragging the bodies into the undergrowth. One of the horsemen did his best to cover up the spilled blood but then, mercifully, it started to rain and the red stained grass gradually turned pink before all traces were then washed away.

Dunstan chose a place in the centre of a large patch of shrubbery and his men dug a communal grave with their seaxes in which they buried the druids and the two dead horses before covering them with rocks to prevent animals digging them up again. Finally they covered the rocks with the earth they had dug up. It left a mound of earth, but that couldn't be helped. In time it would settle.

They had thrown the tack from the surviving horses into the communal grave and now they set them free. The wounded ones would either heal or die. Either way there were no brands, or anything else, to connect them to the missing druids. With a final glance around the men set off back to Yeavering in the, now torrential, rain.

~~~

Oswiu arrived outside the settlement at Berwic just as the weak autumnal sun reached its zenith. Behind him marched the army consisting of his own mounted gesith, a war band of two hundred professional warriors, of whom only thirty were mounted, and another thousand from the fyrd, all on foot. He was leading them into Goddodin to bring the rebellious Angles who lived there to heel. However, his mind was far away from military matters at the moment. The arrival of Fianna and his son, Aldfrith, had reminded him that he hadn't yet told her of his betrothal to Rhieinmelth. Before he had parted from the princess and her father at Yeavering he had promised to come to Caer Luel, the capital of Rheged, for the wedding as soon as he returned from Goddodin.

They had crossed the River Twaid at Norham, a few miles upstream from Berwic. The settlement lay on the north bank of the estuary, where it ran into the German Ocean. The original people of Goddodin had been Britons who spoke Brythonic. Forty years previously they had been defeated at the Battle of Catraeth and had been subjugated by the

Angles, who incorporated the former kingdom into Bernicia. Now it appeared that the Angles who had settled north of the Twaid wanted independence from Bernicia. However, both the Picts to the north and Strathclyde to the west were itching to invade and absorb Goddodin. Unfortunately the three eorls who ruled the area from Berwic, Dùn Éideann on the Firth of Forth, and Dùn Barra in the north-east, didn't seem to realise this.

The eorl at Berwic ruled the southern half of Goddodin but Brant, the thegn, was the owner of the land, termed a vill, which surrounded the settlement. Oswiu began his campaign by pillaging Brant's estate and taking away his store of grain and his livestock. His people were now in danger of starvation this coming winter.

'How are you going to winkle him and the eorl out of there, lord?' Kenric, one of Oswiu's gesith, asked him.

Oswiu studied the settlement carefully. The eorl's hall stood on a small hill high above the Twaid whilst the huts sprawled down the slope on the far side. There was a six foot deep ditch and a twelve feet high palisade around the whole place. It was too difficult to take by direct assault without losing a lot of men. A wooden dock had been built on piles sunk into the river bed at the far end of the settlement where several fishermen's currachs, a few merchant ships, called knarrs, and three birlinns were tied up.

'Tonight we set fire to the merchantmen whilst we steal the three birlinns. We'll use them to cut off any escape by sea. When the men come out to fight the fire you and a few men will slip in through the open gates. Make your way up to the other gates next to the eorl's hall and open them so the rest of us can enter. There's only a low palisade between the hall and the settlement, meant to keep out the curious

41

and animals, not for defence, so we'll take the hall and wait for dawn.'

Kenric grinned and nodded.

'Who'll be in charge of the fire party and the crews to cut out the birlinns?'

'All in good time, Kenric. For now we need to find a place away from this road where we can lay low until dark.'

That night the new moon was obscured by clouds half the time so Oswiu's men were able to move into position in stages; creeping forward slowly and steadily so as not to make any noise in the near complete darkness and hugging the ground when the clouds parted to bathe the area in pale moonlight. Finally, after about three hours, everyone was in position. There was no way of communicating so they then had to wait until a glow appeared from the dock as the pile of oil soaked rope and wood caught light on the first of the merchant vessels.

Fortunately, there were only two or three men on watch on each ship and they were either drunk, sound asleep or absorbed in a game of chance. Their throats were slit before they knew what was happening. Oswiu's warriors had brought a small barrel of oil to soak the cordage and wood they found in abundance on each ship, but it wasn't needed as one ship had several urns of olive oil amongst the goods waiting to be unloaded.

As the blaze took hold on each ship the arsonists ran to take cover amongst the rocks that littered the shoreline. Once men came running to try and douse the flames, they came forward to join them, running to fill empty buckets from the sea. Then they slipped away amongst the growing chaos and, whilst most made their way to the birlinns, the rest ran through the dark alleys of the settlement making for the north gate.

The cut-out crews were challenged, but the explanation that they had been told to move the birlinns away from the fire was readily accepted. Ten minutes later they anchored line abreast at the mouth of the estuary.

Berwic was like any other Anglo-Saxon settlement at the time. The huts had been built with no thought as to the layout; consequently the narrow alleys twisted and turned until Oswiu's men lost any sense of direction and came to the conclusion that they were lost. The ground underfoot was a mixture of urine soaked mud, faeces, bones and offal. Flat stones had been put down in a futile attempt to pave the major alleys but most had sunk in the mire, sometimes with an edge poking up so that all they did was make the going even more treacherous. After one man had tripped and fallen, breaking his leg, the rest were forced to slow down as four of them at a time took it in turns to carry him.

Not unsurprisingly, he had screamed in agony but one of his companions had knocked him out, breaking his jaw to add to his misery when he awoke, to shut him up. A few minutes later they arrived at the northern gates into the settlement and opened them for Oswiu and the rest of his men. They made their way to the palisade running around the hall, which was barely six feet tall, much to everyone's relief. There were two men guarding the outer gate who were quickly disposed of, but not before they had shouted out in alarm.

It didn't matter though. Everyone inside the palisade was awake anyway, concerned about the ships burning below them. However, most of them were unarmed, having rushed out of the hall where they'd been sleeping. They were therefore quickly overwhelmed by Oswiu and his men, who had experienced little difficulty in helping each other over the low palisade.

'Why didn't you attend the Witan when summoned?' Oswiu demanded when the eorl was dragged before him.

The man spat at Oswiu before replying, which earned him a punch in the kidneys from one of the warriors holding him.

'Goddodin is an independent country. Oswald's father took that away from us but Edwin's death enabled us to break free of the Bernician yoke. Not only that, he's a Christian and no-one is going to impose a false religion on us.'

'Very well. You have a choice, old man. Either you submit or you will be executed as a traitor and your family will be exiled.'

'If I submit, do I remain as eorl?'

'So you can renege on your oath of loyalty as soon as we depart? No, of course not. You will be stripped of your lands and become a villein.'

'Become a serf? But I'm an Anglian noble, not a Brythonic peasant.'

'You should have thought of that before you rebelled against King Oswald.'

'Then I ask to be exiled with my family.'

'Very well. I can accept that. Where will you go?'

'Mercia.'

'How apt. That pagan devil Penda is welcome to you. I will arrange for an escort to make sure you and your family get there safely.'

Oswiu had a feeling that it might have been better to execute the elderly former eorl, but that would have shocked the rest of the Anglian nobles in Goddodin and he needed to get them on side, if possible. The next man to be brought before him was Brant, the thegn who had held the vill immediately surrounding the settlement. He'd been wounded in the shoulder and had managed to kill one of Oswiu's men in the fight for the hall.

'Brant, you are a traitor. You did at least answer the summons to the Witan, but then you tried to raise the banner of revolt against my brother.'

'You have no proof of that!' Brant replied defiantly.

'No? Why then did you flee with the treacherous druids towards Bebbanburg? You only changed your mind and fled north to Berwic when you realised that we were hot on your heels.'

'Berwic is my home. I was merely returning there after the Witan.'

'Without taking the oath of loyalty to the king? That doesn't ring true.'

'Goddodin isn't part of Bernicia. I didn't need to take any oath.'

'By holding those views you are condemned out of your own mouth. You will be hanged at dawn.'

'But the eorl was allowed to go into exile!'

'You're not an eorl and, furthermore, you were appointed as custos to look after the fortress for the king. You are therefore doubly a traitor. I will allow your family to remain at Berwic as villeins, but that's all I'm prepared to do. Goodbye Brant.'

Oswiu then sent for Kenric and Lucan. They were the sons of Hussa, one of the nobles who had accompanied him and his family into exile. Hussa was now dead, as was his wife, but his two young sons had become two of his closest companions and now members of his gesith. Hussa had been one of King Æthelfrith's eorls and Oswald had decided to reward both of them, and as many of the other sons of nobles who had fled into exile with his mother and siblings, with land in Goddodin. Not only would it reward their loyalty, but it would also ensure the subjugation of the region.

'Lucan, I want you to stay here as Eorl of Southern Goddodin. I can't afford to leave many men with you but I'll let you choose the men to form your own warband. I'm appointing another member of my gesith as the new Thegn of Berwic in place of the wretched Brant. He can recruit a few of my warband to help him take control of your new vill. Kenric, you'll also become an eorl but you'll have to wait until we've conquered more of Goddodin.'

When the two brothers tried to thank him he held up his hand to stop them.

'It's the least Oswald and I can do to show you how much we appreciate your loyalty and service, and that of your father before you. If it hadn't been for Hussa's quick thinking and bravery at Stirling when we were fleeing from the Picts we'd all be dead.'

The next day dawned dull and chilly. The sky was grey and so was the sea; so much so that it was difficult to determine where the one ended and the other began. Brant was pulled from the hut where he'd been held overnight and he protested feebly as the rope was placed around his neck, thrown over a convenient branch, and tied to one of the horses. It was led away slowly so that the portly former thegn kicked and struggled as he was slowly strangled, his face turning a deep purple as he was asphyxiated. It was a much more unpleasant death than dropping into the void on a proper gallows. There at least a man died instantly when his neck snapped.

The army moved on northwards into the increasingly dense sea mist, leaving Brant swinging from the branch of the tree near the gates into Berwic. As a warning to others it would stay there until the birds had picked the corpse clean of flesh and the bones fell to earth.

The previous night Oswiu had given the Anglian warriors who had been captured at the eorl's hall the option of serving him or hanging alongside Brant. Predictably they all opted to serve him. He was therefore able to add forty men to his war band, where he could keep an eye on them, and left a corresponding number of volunteers from his original warband to garrison Berwic.

His next target was Dùn Barra. He knew from questioning the men from Berwic that capturing it was likely to prove a much more difficult proposition. The settlement itself presented no problem, but the hall was built on a small rocky outcrop surrounded on all sides by the sea. The small islet was linked to the mainland by a narrow wooden bridge just wide enough to take a cart. Oswiu had absolutely no idea how he was going to take the place.

~~~

Eochaid was relieved to have reached Iona safely. Sailing around the top of Britain in October was risky because of the autumnal gales. They had been hit by two nasty squalls and they had to make repairs to the rigging on a deserted beach in the Orcades, but otherwise the journey there had been uneventful. His mission was to ask the Abbot, an Irishman called Ségéne mac Fiachnaí, to send a bishop to Northumbria to convert the people to Christianity.

'King Edwin became a Christian but his people remained pagan,' Eochaid began to explain.

'Yes, I know all about the apostate, Edwin, God save his soul. Come to the point, Eochaid, I don't need a history lesson.'

'I'm sorry, father abbot, of course. Oswald is convinced that the secret is not just to convert the nobles, but to concentrate on the people. He needs a bishop who is charismatic and who will work tirelessly with him to make all of Northumbria true believers.'

'And is Oswald now King of all Northumbria?' Ségéne asked sceptically. 'The last I heard he had been accepted by Bernicia but not by Goddodin, Deira or Elmet.'

'You know Oswald; he'll not rest until he is king of everywhere that his father ruled. When I left his brother, Oswiu, was preparing to bring Goddodin back into the fold. You'll be aware that Rheged is already allied to him and that Oswiu is betrothed to its heiress. Effectively it's a client kingdom.'

'Why doesn't Oswald appoint his brother Oslac as bishop?'

'Oslac is very loyal and devout, but he is hardly compelling as a missionary. He is quiet and cautious around strangers. He makes a good chaplain for the king and priest for the vill of Bebbanburg, but he is not the man to convert the whole of the North of England.'

'No, I suppose you're right.'

Ségéne sighed. 'My problem is that most of my best monks have already become bishops in the Land of the Picts. I have a lot of novices under training and monks who are content to live out their lives worshipping God here, but precious few who would make a good missionary bishop.'

'What about Aidan?'

'Yes, I agree that he'd be ideal, and he's a friend of Oswald's so they'd work together well. The trouble is, he's away in Strathclyde trying to convert the pagan Britons there. You may not have heard but Belin died last year and the new king is his son Owain. He's very young, only sixteen I believe, and an unknown quantity. I fear for Aidan's safety, and that of Brother Ròidh, who's with him.'

'I see. If he's alive and willing to come to Northumbria would you be happy to consecrate him as bishop?'

'If you can find him and persuade him, yes.'

'Thank you Abbot Ségéne. My immediate task is to convey the Lady Acha and the families of those warriors from Dalriada who have remained with Oswald back to Bebbanburg, but I'll return and seek out Aidan and Ròidh when I return. It will probably not be until the spring now as by the time that I get back to Bebbanburg it'll be almost winter.'

'In the meantime I'll do my best to find out Aidan's whereabouts,' Ségéne said with a worried frown.

~~~

Oswald was enjoying himself. To celebrate his accession to the throne the first fair since Penda and Cadwallon had invaded was being held at Bebbanburg. Traders had set up a market on the beach - as it was easier for them to set up stalls there to sell what they had brought by sea. A horse and livestock auction was taking place in the paddock on the other side of the fortress and various competitions were taking place in another area. These included archery, wrestling and fighting with blunted swords.

Although Yeavering was where he would normally base himself from spring to autumn, winters in the Cheviot Hills could be severe and roads became impassable. He had therefore decided to spend November to April at Bebbanburg. He'd moved there slightly earlier this year as he was expecting Eochaid to return soon, bringing his mother and the families of his warriors from Dalriada. They would arrive in four birlinns, which would form the nucleus of the small fleet he intended to form to protect Northumbria's coast.

Eochaid had taken a protesting Œthelwald with him to be educated on Iona. Oswald was ashamed to have felt relief when his son had left. He felt that he ought to love his son, and he had tried to do so, but he was an unattractive character and Oswald knew, even at the age of eleven, that the boy wasn't the one to succeed him. The more he thought about it, the more convinced he became that that person should be Oswiu.

Accompanied by Rònan and Jarlath, he made his way to where horses were being auctioned. He had a small number of horses from Rheged but most of his mounts were the small hill ponies that the Picts and the Welsh used. He wanted to mount all the warriors in his gesith on good quality stallions. He knew that they would be spending a long time in the saddle before he could relax knowing that Northumbria was secure, if ever.

'Where do these horses come from? Do either of you know?' Oswald asked, casting a critical eye over the horseflesh on offer.

Rònan disappeared and came back a few minutes later with Dunstan.

'Cyning, the larger horses are war horses originally bred by the Romans from those that the Britons used to pull their chariots. They prized them as cavalry horses and even sent some over the German Ocean to improve the blood-stock in Gaul and Italy, or so the story goes. The next size down are cart horses, then the smaller ones with a sheen to their coat are riding horses and then pack-horses. There are quite a few hill ponies as well, of course.'

'Dunstan, you are a surprising mine of information. How did you learn all this?'

The man shrugged. 'Talking to the breeders and the traders who have come here to buy or sell.'

'I'm not sure we need war horses, we always fight on foot in battle and I suspect that they're too slow for the pursuit. We need some riding horses for the gesith though, together with quite a few cart and pack horses.'

'Horses are useful for moving warriors into position quickly too, Oswald, even if their riders then fight on foot. There isn't much demand today for the war horses; perhaps we could pick up quite a few cheaply.'

'Very well, you seem to know what you're talking about, Dunstan. However, I don't want to be seen bidding; traders always seem to push the price up if the buyer is thought to be wealthy. I'll watch whilst you go and do the trading. Don't go wild though; we don't need more than a hundred all told.'

'Very good, Cyning, but that's a quarter of what's here. Can I take one of these two with me to spread the bidding?'

'Good idea. Take Jarlath. And Dunstan.'

'Yes, Cyning?'

'I'm going to appoint you as my horse marshal. From now on all the horses and ponies I own will be your responsibility, as will teaching my gesith to ride. You'll rank as a thegn.'

'Thank you, Cyning.'

As he walked away Dunstan had a broad grin on his face.

On the second day of the fair the lookout on the tower inside the fortress sounded the alarm bell. Oswald rushed up to see what the sentry had seen whilst his warriors donned their armour. The traders started to pack up in a hurry and the men, women and children who had come from far and wide rushed towards the gates into the fortress.

As soon as Oswald arrived at the platform on top of the tower he called down that all was well. He'd recognised the distinctive sail of Eochaid on the leading ship and the other three birlinns displayed the yellow and red stripes of Northumbria.

'You did the right thing by sounding the alarm if you were uncertain,' he told the hapless sentry, who was a youth of sixteen, 'but you need to recognise friendly sails.

'Yes, Cyning, sorry.'

Seeing how contrite the boy was, Oswald clapped him on the shoulder.

'It's not your fault. I'll make sure that the custos teaches all the garrison to recognise sails; it's important.'

Oswald was about to descend and make his way to the beach to greet Eochaid and his mother when he turned back to the sentry.

'What's your name, boy?'

'Beorhtwulf, Cyning.'

'And are you bright, my little wolf?

'Hardly, Cyning, or I wouldn't have sounded the alarm.' The boy smirked at him. His name meant Bright Wolf.

Oswald laughed and left Beorhtwulf to his lonely task.

He was waiting on the beach when his mother was carefully lifted down from one of the ships. The first thing that struck him was how grey her hair had become. It had been streaked with strands of silver when he'd left six months previously, but now there was no other colour left in it. He splashed through the small waves breaking on the shoreline and hugged her to his breast. He was surprised how light she seemed. She had always been a well-built woman; now she seemed almost frail.

'I'm so proud of you,' she whispered in his ear, 'and so would your father have been. Now let go of me; it's unseemly.'

'And proud of Oswiu too, I'm sure you meant to add. I couldn't have done it without him,' he rebuked her mildly as he released her.

'Perhaps,' was all she'd said. She and Oswald's younger brother had enjoyed a fairly tempestuous relationship in the past. He felt a little guilty when he realised that he was glad that Oswiu was away in Goddodin at the moment. He didn't want the family reunion spoilt by an argument. Just then Oslac arrived and embraced his mother briefly and somewhat diffidently, not sure if that was becoming behaviour for a priest. She returned his hug perfunctorily.

'I was upset to hear about Osguid. He would have been a great asset to you in bringing Christianity to these heathens.'

She didn't seem to notice how much her thoughtless words had hurt Oslac. He'd always been the quiet one – though not as quiet as the youngest brother – Offa – who now lived as an anchorite on Iona. Osguid had ever been the extrovert and introverted Oslac had always suffered by comparison to him.

'I have Oslac to help me at the moment and I had hopes that a monk from Iona will be sent as bishop, however I don't see anyone on the beach.'

Acha shook her head. At that moment both Keeva, Oswald's concubine and Fianna, Oswiu's, came and joined them. Acha waited impatiently for her son to stop hugging and kissing his lover, then apologising to Fianna for his brother's absence.

'Ah, here's Eochaid,' she said with some relief. She wasn't a women who was much in favour of outward displays of affection. 'He might be able to tell you more. He certainly hasn't said anything to me though.'

Eochaid joined them and the two old friends embraced, slapping each other heartily on the back, before walking with Acha and the other two women up to the gatehouse and into the fortress.

'I've put you in your old bedchamber, mother.'

'No, that's the king's chamber. It's yours now.'

'I'm happy enough in the smaller chamber we slept in as boys for now, and I know that Keeva won't mind. It'll only be for a day or so anyway. We need to talk about Deira. I want to consolidate my position as King of Northumbria, not just Bernicia, as quickly as possible and that means getting the Witan in Eoforwīc to accept me before they appoint some other idiot to succeed the inept Osric.'

Osric had been the last King of Deira who had besieged Cadwallon in Eoforwīc the previous year with a larger army. However, he had been foolish enough to divide his men into three camps. Cadwallon had defeated each third in turn, then caught the fleeing Osric and killed him.

'Oswald, I need to tell you about Aidan,' Eochaid told him as soon as the women had left them.

'Aidan? Is he the monk that Ségéne has selected to be my bishop?' Oswald asked thoughtfully. 'He'd be ideal. Why isn't he with you?'

'Yes it's to be Aidan, but it's not as simple as that. He's somewhere in Strathclyde and there's been no word of him, or his acolyte Ròidh, for several months now.'

The two looked at each other and a smile slowly grew on Eochaid's face.

'You want me to go and find him, don't you?'

Oswald laughed briefly.

'It seems that you can read my mind.'

~~~

Beorhtwulf had felt a fool when he'd sounded the alarm but the king had been very understanding; not so Ethelbald, the newly appointed custos, who gave him a week of extra sentry duty. The man was a noble who had remained at Bebbanburg to serve Edwin and his appointment was more of a sop to those whose loyalty Oswald now needed rather than because of any particular qualities in the man. In fact, Oswald didn't like him much. He was too much of a cold fish who never smiled.

Thankfully Beorhtwulf's first night of extra duty was in the warm and not up on the parapet where the cold wind from the east froze your hands and face now that winter was approaching. It would be even worse once the snow and ice appeared in a month or so.

Although Bebbanburg was a large fortress by comparison to most of the duns of other kings, its layout was similar except in one important regard. Most kings and their families lived in a chamber off the main hall where the single warriors ate, caroused and slept. Those men with families generally built themselves their own hut but often joined their younger companions to feast, drink and listen to heroic tales in the evenings.

However Oswald's father had given in to Acha's complaints about the revellers keeping her and her children awake at night and had built a large hut away from the hall which had been divided into a number of individual chambers: one for him and his queen, one for the children and one for important guests. Eochaid had been given the guest chamber and Oswald occupied his old room.

Beorhtwulf was posted at the door of the chamber occupied by Oswald whilst two more guards were stationed outside the only entrance into the timber building. Whilst he was grateful to be inside, he was feeling tired. He'd already done a stint of six hours in the watchtower and the comparative warmth of his present post was making it difficult to stay awake. He therefore decided to pace up and down to combat his lethargy. He was walking past the leather curtain that divided Lady Acha's chamber from the communal area when he heard the sounds of a muffled struggle.

At first he hesitated and then, when he heard someone say 'bitch' loudly and clearly he pulled aside the curtain and peered into the darkened room. He could just make out someone struggling with someone else on the pile of furs that served as a bed when the moonlight coming in through the open window glinted off a knife blade. The assailant was about to stab the person on the bed, presumably Acha.

Without thinking, Beorhtwulf thrust his spear into the neck of the putative assassin and the man dropped his blade, which clattered harmlessly to the floor. The man clasped his neck and shrieked in agony as Beorhtwulf pulled the point of his spear clear and, dropping it, he pulled his seax from its scabbard. Grasping the man's long hair, he pulled his head back so that he could cut his throat. Just before his heart stopped beating, it send a spray of blood from the severed carotid artery which covered Acha's body and face.

Beorhtwulf pulled the body off the bed before asking if Acha was injured.

'No, I'm fine, thank you, apart from being bathed in blood.'

56

As his eyes adjusted to the gloom in the room the boy could just make out her face and saw that she was smiling, indicating that the remark had been in jest.

'Yes, my apologies, síþwíf, I didn't think.'

'It was a good job you didn't, or I'd be dead.'

Just at that moment Oswald burst in followed by Eochaid and the two sentries from the external door to the building. Keeva peered around him, uttered a little squawk, and ran back to their bedchamber.

'What's happened?' Oswald asked, standing just inside the room naked and holding his sword in his hand. Eochaid had at least put on a tunic before grabbing his sword.

'This young man had just saved my life, Oswald. I suspect that he thought it was you in this bed not me, good job too knowing how soundly you sleep. By the way I don't know your name?'

'It's Beorhtwulf, síþwíf.'

'You again!' Oswald blurted out. 'Well, Beorhtwulf, you lived up to your name this time.'

Then something occurred to the king.

'If you were guarding the entrance to my chamber, how did you hear what was happening in this room and get here so quickly?'

'Never mind that, Oswald. Just be thankful that the boy has good hearing and reactions to match. Now I think I need to bathe, and some clean furs for the bed would be welcome. If someone could throw this creature onto the midden I'd be grateful too.'

At that moment Ethelbald arrived with several more guards and some torches. When Acha explained what had happened, the custos examined the dead assassin and muttered that he was a druid. It wasn't until much later that

Oswald had realised that Ethelbald hadn't seemed very surprised.

Beorhtwulf had wandered over to examine the window, which was just an open embrasure with wooden shutters to keep out the cold. These now stood open.

'The leather thong that holds the shutters closed has been cut, Cyning,' he told Oswald.

'That explains how he got into the chamber but not how he got into a seemingly impregnable fortress,' the king mused.

'It seems we have a traitor in our midst,' Ethelbald said grimly.

'Well, time for that in the morning. We must get this place cleaned up. Call the servants to heat some water so my mother can scrub herself clean. I suggest you sleep in my room with Keeva for the rest of tonight. We'll get the shutters nailed shut and Beorhtwulf can guard the entrance with one other. I'll share with Eochaid for now.'

Acha was about to protest about being asked to sleep with her son's lover but she bit her tongue. He turned to Beorhtwulf who was nursing the vain hope that his service might be rewarded by being allowed to get some sleep. It was not to be, it seemed.

'I'll not forget this, Beorhtwulf. I'd like you to join my gesith.'

The boy was overwhelmed. He had only just graduated from a boy under training to become a young warrior; all the other members of the gesith were seasoned men with battle experience.

'I'm honoured, Cyning, but I'm worried how the other members of the gesith will react.'

'Hmmm, they may well give you a hard time at first, given your youth, but they'll respect you for saving my mother's life and killing the assassin. However, you'll have to stand up for yourself. I can't help you there. Well, do you accept?'

'Yes, Cyning, thank you.'

'Good, report to Rònan in the morning.'

'Who needs sleep, eh lad?' Ethelbald muttered in his ear. 'Well, done. I'll let you off the rest of your extra guard duties.'

Beorhtwulf was just about to say that the gesith didn't do normal guard duties when he realised that Ethelbald was teasing him. It was so unlike the normally sombre custos that he wasn't sure that he'd heard him correctly.

~~~

Oswiu gloomily studied the fortified hall of the Eorl of Dùn Barra on its rocky islet. It was even more of a problem than he'd been led to believe. The sea broke against the rocks on three sides of the fortress and the narrow channel between the hall and palisade and the mainland was spanned by a wooden bridge with a section at one end that could be raised to the near vertical by two ropes attached to the far end. It was in the up position now. The only positive aspect was that it couldn't be resupplied by sea except on the calmest of days and the two birlinns that had shadowed his march up the east coast could prevent that happening. However, starving the garrison out could take a long time.

He turned from his contemplation of Dùn Barra as Cenhelm, one of his senior commanders joined him. They stood together observing the seabirds dive into the sea and re-appear, usually with a fish in their mouths. As they watched a couple of seals made their ungainly way onto the rocks near the short cliff at the top of which the palisade was built. Once they had found a flat rock they stretched out in the sun and seemed to fall asleep. Suddenly a volley of arrows with thin ropes attached struck the seals and they were quickly hauled up the palisade and over the top out of sight.

'Barbed heads,' Cenhelm muttered.

'We could wait a long time to starve them out,' Oswiu replied.

'Quite. So what do we do?'

'I don't know. Let me think.'

At that moment a group of his warriors mounted on hill ponies appeared in the distance bringing with them a petrified villein from the vill surrounding the fortress, his thirteen year old son, a few sheep and a cart laden with root vegetables.

'Go and stop them, Cenhelm. I don't want them to be seen from Dùn Barra. I think I have an idea.'

Three weeks later, at the start of November, the Bernician war band gave up the siege and even the birlinns patrolling off the coast withdrew. The eorl breathed a sigh of relief. Their food stocks were nearly exhausted and he thanked his gods that the threat of the oncoming winter had persuaded the Bernicians to give up the siege.

That afternoon the eorl sent out a patrol to confirm that Oswiu really had withdrawn but they hadn't gone very far when they encountered a villein bringing two dozen sheep and a cart full of carrots and turnips towards the fortress. He had two boys with him helping him to herd the sheep whilst he drove the ox-drawn cart.

'Where are you going?' the patrol leader asked suspiciously.

'To Dùn Barra,' the farmer replied nervously. 'I saw the war band that was besieging you withdraw south and thought you might be in need of food.'

'Doubtless you thought you could get an inflated price for it too, you dog,' the horseman replied with a sneer.

'A man has to live.'

'These your two boys then?'

The boys nodded without saying anything.

'What's in the cart?'

'Carrots and parsnips.'

The horseman lifted the corner of the oiled canvas that covered it, then dropped it after a cursory glance.

'Right, on you go then. Good luck screwing more than the basic value out of the eorl's wife though. She's a tough old woman and no mistake.'

For a moment the man thought about turning his men around to accompany the villein back to the fortress; they were all starving and the thought of a decent meal was very tempting. No more seals had been foolish enough to sunbathe within arrow shot and provisions were nearly exhausted. However, he still had to check that the besiegers had indeed headed back to Berwic. Ten minutes later he found out that they hadn't. The ambush was effective and the members of the patrol were either killed or captured.

The sentry on the parapet by the gate saw the villein in his cart followed by the sheep and their drovers and yelled excitedly to his comrades that supplies had arrived. The parapet was soon lined with cheering warriors. The garrison had been fifty five men but, with thirty out in the patrol, only twenty five were left to defend the fortress. The custos and the eorl were just coming out of the hall when they saw the drawbridge being lowered. The custos ran forward and got to the gate just as the cart started across the bridge.

'Who ordered the drawbridge lowered?' he bellowed. 'Get it raised again!'

He didn't get a chance to say any more before the cart completed its journey into the fortress and the sheep followed on. It was now impossible to raise it. Before the man realised what was going on, the tarpaulin covering the thin layer of vegetables was thrust aside and ten members of Oswiu's war band leaped out of the cart. The custos was one of the first men to die as the attackers charged into the few men in the bailey. The eorl tried to rally his men but most were still up on the walkway around the top of the palisade.

One of the Bernicians thrust his sword into his neck and he fell to the ground. The men on the parapet tried to descend but the bailey was now full of sheep milling about and bleating piteously. As they struggled through them one of the Bernician warriors reached the gateway and cut one of the ropes by which the drawbridge was raised. Oswiu and his mounted gesith cantered into the fortress and, leaping from their horses, they waded into the fight.

They were followed by Cenhelm and the rest of Oswiu's war band, but there was nothing left for them to do. Those Goddodin who were still alive surrendered and Oswiu did as he'd done at Berwic. As he'd promised, he made Kenric the new eorl and, leaving him twenty men to garrison the fortress, he recruited what was left of the garrison into his war band and marched south, back to Bebbanburg before winter set in. Dùn Èideann would have to wait until next year.

CHAPTER FOUR – THE WITAN AT EOFORWĪC

October 634 AD

Whilst Oswiu was investing Dùn Barra, Oswald and Acha were on the road south to Eoforwīc. He'd left Keeva behind at Bebbanburg with Fianna. Accompanied only by his gesith of sixteen warriors, his brother Oslac, and their respective body slaves, he had resisted his mother's entreaty to take his war band with him.

'I'm going to Eoforwīc as the ætheling claiming the vacant crown, not as a conqueror.'

'You are putting your head into a noose, Oswald,' she told him bluntly. 'There are druids there too, you know. Word has got around about the disappearance of the druids after the Witan at Yeavering and they're not fools. They know you disposed of them.'

'They were traitors. Besides it's worked; most of the druids in Bernicia have either fled or gone into hiding.'

'Yes, and a lot of them have fled to Deira!'

'I'm the son and the grandson of previous kings so I've the best claim to the crown, along with Oswiu and Oslac here, of course. I'm sure the Witan will give me a fair hearing and they are hardly likely to try again to kill me, not after the last time.'

'No, perhaps not, but others might.'

'Well, I'm not taking my war band into Deira; that would send entirely the wrong message.'

For late October the day was unseasonably pleasant. The column of riders and three baggage carts made its way down Glendale, which ran between the bulk of the Cheviot Hills to the west and the somewhat lower hills between the valley and the coast. Although Oswald had now imposed his rule on Bernicia, he still had enemies; not only the druids but desperate men who'd lost their livelihoods during the depredations of Cadwallon's Welshmen and Penda's Mercians and a few pagan thegns who didn't want to be ruled by a Christian king. He therefore sent three warriors off to each flank to make sure that they weren't riding into an ambush and another two scouted ahead.

The other eight guarded the baggage carts and rode behind him. He noted with amusement that Jarlath and Rònan insisted on riding closest to him. They were Irish and Pict by birth but there was no-one he would trust more with his life. They had both been his body slaves when they were boys but they had long since been freed and were now two of his best warriors. His present body slave was a surly Mercian boy of twelve who'd been captured after the Battle of Heavenfield. He was called Edwy which was singularly inappropriate as it meant rich warrior; the boy was neither.

They camped for the first night beside the River Breamish some eight miles into the wide valley called Glendale. It had been a long day. They had set out just after dawn but were forced to travel slowly because of the oxen-drawn carts, who could move at three miles an hour if the going was good. It had therefore taken them seven hours and darkness was barely an hour away.

Once the leather tents had been set up the three carters, Edwy, and the two boys who served the gesith went into the nearby wood to collect firewood. Just as darkness fell fires were lit and the three boys and one of the carters started to

64

cook the evening meal. Meanwhile four of the gesith moved silently outside the perimeter of the camp keeping watch. They knew better than to look into the camp, where the fires would rob them of their night vision, and they kept stealthily on the move. They were well aware how vulnerable a stationary sentry was.

Each group of four only did two hours on watch so that they remained fresh. In the middle of the night Jarlath was woken for his turn and he made his way slowly and carefully, so as not to make a sound, to the west of the camp. This was probably the most likely direction for an attack as the wilderness of the Cheviots lay on that side.

As he moved from shadow to shadow he heard a twig snap. It might have been an animal but Jarlath didn't think so. He was in two minds. If he was certain that there was a person or persons out there he should go and wake the others, but if it was an animal he'd look a fool, and be unpopular for waking everyone unnecessarily. So he decided to investigate further first. He moved a little further into the wood and then stood still, waiting. It was darker here than nearer the camp but most of the leaves had now fallen so some light penetrated the gloom. Slowly his eyes adjusted and, just as he heard some more leaves rustling, he saw the outline of two men creeping forward. He waited to see if there were more but the pair seemed to be on their own.

From their vague silhouettes they seemed to wearing helmets and had swords in their hands, but no shields. Jarlath was fully armoured and had both. The nearest man was no more than five yards away now and he must has sensed something because he turned to face him. Jarlath didn't hesitate but leaped forward thrusting the point of his sword at the other man's neck. The intruder tried to raise his own sword to ward off the lunge but he was only partially successful. The point missed its intended target – his throat – but pierced his eye instead. He screamed briefly before the blade entered his brain, then he dropped like a dead weight.

Unfortunately Jarlath's sword was momentarily trapped in the dead man's skull as the second man went to swing his seax at Jarlath's neck. He raised his shield and the blow glanced off it harmlessly. The second attacker came in again and this time Jarlath punched his face with the boss of his shield, causing the man to yelp as it broke his nose. He abandoned his efforts to drag his sword free and pulled out his seax instead. By now he could hear some of his companions crashing through the wood calling out his name.

His assailant realised that it was time to leave and turned to flee. In doing so he tripped over a dead branch and went sprawling, losing his seax. Barely a second later Jarlath knelt in the small of his back and pressed the point of his own seax against the nape of his neck. Jarlath thought that his opponent was rather small for a warrior but it wasn't until they had dragged him into the camp and built up the fire so that they could see him more clearly that they realised that he was a boy of thirteen or fourteen.

'Why were you spying on us? Who sent you?' Oswald demanded.

The boy glared balefully at him but said nothing. Oswald sighed.

'We can do this the hard way if you prefer. Jarlath has already broken your nose. I expect it hurts, but that's nothing to the pain you are going to experience if you don't tell me what I want to know. Is that what you want?'

The boy began to look worried. Then Acha appeared with Oslac.

'I'm sure that the boy will see sense, Oswald. Won't you?' she asked sweetly. 'Let's start with your name.'

The boy debated whether to answer as she waited patiently.

'It's Sigbert,' he said quietly.

'And who was the man with you?'

'My father.'

Then he began to sob, but after a few minutes he started to talk. Once he started he held nothing back.

'A man paid us with a lump of silver to find your camp and report back to him tomorrow. He wanted to know how many you were, what sentries you set, how many and where, how alert they were, that sort of thing.'

Oswald looked at his mother. It sounded as if whoever had hired the pair was planning to attack them at some stage before they reached Eoforwīc.

'What was your father? A villein or perhaps a robber?' Oslac asked.

'No, he was a freeman employed by our thegn as a huntsman.'

'And who is your thegn?'

'Leofwine of Morpeth, but he wasn't involved. The man who came and found father earlier today had been riding hard and had evidently come from a distance.'

Oswald was puzzled.

'If your father was a huntsman, why did he have a sword and you a seax?'

'He was an archer in the fyrd when it was called out, but he had been trained to use a sword when he was younger and he was teaching me. A second sword was too expensive, so we used wooden practice ones.'

The boy broke down again and sobbed for a minute or so before he was able to continue. Oslac put a comforting hand on his shoulder and he gave the monk a grateful glance.

'We only had the one sword but the man who hired father gave him my seax as part of the price he agreed.'

'And where were you to report to this man?'

'There is a tavern at the ford over the River Wansbeck. We were to meet him there at midday tomorrow.'

Sigbert rode towards the tavern nervously. He entered and looked around but the man wasn't there yet. He breathed a sigh of relief and sat down in a corner, trying not to look at four of Oswald's gesith who were drinking quietly on the other side of the room. They were wearing homespun tunics and rough woollen cloaks so that they looked like villeins. As such, they wouldn't have been allowed to carry a sword but each had his seax concealed under his cloak.

Oswald had promised the boy that he would be trained as a warrior and join his war band in due course if he swore loyalty to him and played his part in the capture of the man who'd wanted the camp spied on. The boy was reluctant at first - the killing of his father was still too raw for him to want to join his killers but, as Acha had pointed out to him, what other option did he have?

The orphaned children of freemen normally paid their thegn a fee to inherit their land when their fathers died. If they were too young to work the land they would become bonded to another family. They weren't slaves but they might just have well have been. But, in any case, his father had no land, just a hut and what he earned as a hunter. A tenth of that went to the thegn and the rest had fed and clothed them. But Sigbert didn't yet have the skills to be a successful hunter. The rustling of leaves and breaking twigs that Jarlath had heard was made by him, not his father. So he had eventually agreed.

'You're a bit young to be in here on your own aren't you, lad?'

Sigbert eyed the tavern keeper's daughter warily and ordered a glass of milk. She laughed.

'We don't often get asked for that,' she smiled at him. I'll go and get some fresh from the udder.'

He couldn't work out if she was flirting with him or not but her friendliness lifted his spirits and he grinned at her.

'If it's from your udders don't bother with a goblet, I'll drink it straight from the source.'

'You're a cheeky sod, aren't you? Sorry, I like men, not little boys.'

However, she grinned back at him before going off to get his milk. Despite the fact that she'd slapped him down, the exchange had buoyed Sigbert up and he waited for the man he was there to meet with a little more confidence.

He was nursing the untouched goblet of milk and was lost in thought, so he didn't notice the man until he sat down beside him.

'Where's your father, boy?'

'He didn't make it. He was killed by one of their sentries but I managed to get away.'

The man grunted but didn't say anything in reply to the tidings that the lad's father was dead.

'What did you find out?'

'King Oswald only has his gesith with him as far as warriors are concerned. I also saw his mother and a Christian priest plus the usual number of servants, carters and the like.'

'You saw a lot! How do you know the warriors were his gesith?'

'They had campfires so it was easy to see who was there. The warriors wore chain mail byrnies so who else would they be? I counted a dozen of them but obviously there were others on guard. They were in the woods and moving quietly. That's how my father died.'

Sigbert wiped his face with his sleeve to dry it from the tears that were beginning to flow.

'Stop crying and try to be a man! You'll attract attention to us.' the stranger hissed at him. 'What about the horses?'

'Hobbled and tied to a line near the camp.'

The man sat back and smiled crookedly.

'You've done well boy. Thank you.'

The stranger got up to leave but Sigbert grabbed his arm.

'Where's the silver you promised my father?'

'My agreement was with him and he's not here.' The man shrugged. 'You can keep the seax though.'

'You bastard!' the boy hissed at him.

Suddenly the boy felt the point of a dagger being pressed into his side none to gently.

'Let go of me and stop making a scene or I'll send you to join your father. Now!'

Sigbert hastily let go and the man made for the door. Before he got there the four disguised members of Oswald's gesith got up to intercept him. However, he was too quick for them. He kicked an empty bench at them, causing two of them to stumble. Before they could recover he had reached the door and flung it open, only to find Jarlath, Beorhtwulf and Rònan standing there with the points of their swords at his neck. Moments later he was seized from behind and his arms were piniored to his side.

~~~

Aidan didn't know what to do. He had had a modicum of success in bringing the Word of God to the heathen Britons in Strathclyde until Belin had died. Now his son Owain had succeeded him and he was virulently anti-Christian. Aidan and Ròidh had only found out that he'd put a price on the head of every Christian priest and monk when some men had tried to take them prisoner in the last village they'd visited.

They had walked between the outlying huts and hovels, making for the open area to be found in the middle of most villages when their way had been blocked by a group of men wielding clubs, spears and scythes.

'What do you want here, strangers? We don't welcome visitors.'

The speaker was a large, well-muscled man who was probably the blacksmith. Certainly his weapon of choice, a heavy iron hammer, would indicate this.

'I think they're monks, father,' a youth, who was nearly as well-built as his father, called out.

'Are they indeed? Well, it's our lucky day then. The king will pay us well for every Christian head we take to him, and here we have two of them.'

'Run!' Aidan yelled and ran from the settlement with Ròidh at his heels.

The men had pursued them for a mile or so and had then given up. Later on they'd seen two men on horses searching for them. Ròidh had been impressed at the older monk's turn of speed. Aidan was now over thirty whereas the former Pictish prince was still in his mid-twenties. However, there wasn't an ounce of fat on the older monk. He only ate what he needed to survive and consequently he was light

71

and wiry. Ròidh, on the other hand, was always hungry and ate twice as much as Aidan did, given the chance. He too was fit and far from fat, but he carried quite a few pounds more than his companion did.

'What do we do now Aidan?'

'Well, I think our mission in Strathclyde is probably over for now. You can't convert people who are trying to capture you for the reward.'

'But how do we get back to Iona with everyone's hand turned against us?'

Aidan thought for a long while. He knew that they were not far from the southern coast of the region called Galloway. However, even if they got there safely, they would have to cross the mud flats and waters of the Solway Firth to reach the Christian kingdom of Rheged. That would mean stealing a boat of some sort and crossing at high tide.

The only other option was to pray to be rescued. Abbot Ségéne would soon get to hear of King Owain's crusade against Christians and realise that he and Ròidh were in peril. What he could do about it was another matter.

~~~

Oswiu was not in a good mood, despite the ecstatic welcome that Fianna had given him. In fact it made his frame of mind worse because it reminded him that he was engaged to Rhieinmelth of Rheged and he hadn't broken the news to Fianna yet. The presence of his son, a boy of three, made his feeling of guilt worse.

But even more depressing was the fact that he had been dreading telling his brother that he'd failed to subdue all of Goddodin before the imminent onset of winter forced him to return to Bebbanburg. He had prepared himself mentally for

Oswald's disappointment in him; only to find that the king had left the previous day for Eoforwīc with their mother.

He should have felt relieved that he wouldn't have to report his failure to capture Dùn Èideann, but he just wanted to get it over with, so he resented the fact that he would now have to wait to get it off his chest. Furthermore, he felt angry that Oswald and their mother had gone to the Witan in Deira without him. He expected Oswald to be chosen as king, but he was also an ætheling and had a right to be present as a contender, even if he did intend to support his elder brother.

Making love to Fianna the night of his return, and more than once, had improved his disposition slightly but later, after fretting for a few hours he decided to follow Oswald to Eoforwīc. The king may have only taken his gesīth with him but he was travelling with a baggage train and oxen didn't move at more than three or four miles an hour. If he took pack animals, he and his own gesith could overtake him, even though Oswald had one and half day's start on him. It was over a hundred and twenty miles from Bebbanburg to Eoforwīc and Oswiu didn't expect Oswald's party to be able to cover more than thirty miles a day, if that. With any luck he should be able to catch him up well before he got there.

In the event he hadn't got very far before he had to return to Bebbanburg in a hurry.

~~~

The stranger never did give Oswald his name, but from his accent he was a Mercian. They took him from the tavern to where the rest of the group was waiting further west along the River Wansbeck. He didn't have to tell him that Penda had a spy at Bebbanburg: that much was

73

obvious. How else did the Mercian know that Oswald and Acha had departed for Eoforwīc? At first he wouldn't tell them the name of the person who had betrayed him.

Apart from the traitor's identity, Oswald needed to know the details of the ambush that Penda was planning. The stranger was reluctant to part with this information, but Oswald had a man in his gesith who was an expert in extracting information from the unwilling. He did nothing to him physically but he ordered him to dig a grave.

'Now, you have two choices. Either you tell the king what he wants to know, in which case I'll kill you quickly before putting you in the grave, or you remain silent and you will be buried alive. I'll give you five minutes to think about it.'

The Mercian looked at the grinning faces surrounding him and groaned. His over-active mind could imagine what it would be like to lie there as the earth was shovelled in on him, eventually covering his mouth and nose so that he slowly suffocated. He shivered in fear, his head bowed in resignation.

'If you kill me quickly how will you do it?'

"I'll cut your throat. That way the pain with be very brief.'

The Mercian nodded and told them everything that Penda had told him to do. The original plan had been for the Mercians to attack them at night but for that they needed more information. That was what Sigbert and his father had been paid to provide. When asked about the man in Bebbanburg who had betrayed Oswald, he said at first that he didn't know his name.

'That's a pity. In that case you've broken our bargain,' Oswald told him. 'Right throw him in the grave and start to cover him up.'

'No, wait! I don't know his name but it was the custos. He'd send one of the scullions from the kitchen to let me know anything useful and I'd give the boy gold to take back. Penda told me himself that the man who is now custos has been in his pay since the days of King Edwin.'

'What was the name of the kitchen boy?'

'That I do know. He told me his name was Raulf.'

'Raulf? He's no scullion. He's Ethelbald's son,' Beorhtwulf exclaimed.

'Just so. Jarlath, I want you to ride back to Bebbanburg with Beorhtwulf and wait there for Oswiu. Tell him to arrest Ethelbald and his wretched boy and hold them prisoner until I can try them. He's to appoint one of his men as temporary custos and then catch up with me as quickly as he can. If he brings his gesith and as many mounted warriors as he can and they travel with packhorses he should be able to join us in two days' time. Clear? Then get some rest both of you and leave at dawn.'

'What's are the Mercians likely to do now, when you don't turn up?'

The man shrugged. 'They won't dare to go back to Penda having failed, so I suspect that they will try to ambush you en route.'

'Where are they camped?'

'Near the ford where Dere Street and Watling Street meet.'

He turned to Sigbert.

'Well done boy, I'm pleased with you; you played your part well. Now, I've one further test for you before I forgive you your part in this. I want you to cut this man's throat. Do you know how to do that?'

The boy swallowed nervously before nodding mutely. He took the seax one of the warriors gave him and approached

75

the Mercian, who stood head and shoulders taller that the thirteen year old.

'Kneel down.'

It wasn't so much an order as a quavering request. The man did so and the boy went behind him, grasped his long hair and pulled his head back, exposing his throat. He hesitated and swallowed hard before slashing the blade across the man's neck. Blood spurted out briefly and then the Mercian collapsed onto his side. He had died bravely and, as the sun sunk in the west, the gesith finished filling in the grave before they moved a mile away to camp further along the River Wansbeck.

Sigbert was left shaking and then he rushed away to vomit. He got rid of everything in his stomach and then felt a comforting hand on his shoulder. He turned, spew still dribbling from his mouth, to see Oswald standing over him and smiling down at him.

'You're a brave lad, Sigbert. Not many boys your age could have killed a man in cold blood like that. It's a bit big for you but you can have the Mercian's horse. You'll travel with us and, once we get back to Bebbanburg, you can join the other trainee warriors. They are all older than you but, when they see this arm ring they'll know that you've already been blooded.'

He handed the boy a small silver arm ring and Sigbert slid it and up over the small biceps on his right arm. To his surprise it was a perfect fit. He beamed with pleasure and, if only for a moment, he ceased to mourn for his father. Rònan had told him that the pain of his loss would lessen with time. His grief was still very fresh but he could now see a future for himself.

Jarlath and Beorhtwulf left just before the sun rose so that they could reach Bebbanburg well before dark.

~~~

Oswiu listened to what Jarlath and Beorhtwulf told him when they met on the road and immediately turned back to the fortress. As soon as he arrived he sent four men to arrest the custos and another two to find Raulf. He had listened to Oswald's instruction to hold the man captive until he could be tried but he felt that leaving him at Bebbanburg, where many of the men in the garrison were loyal to him, was foolhardy. He would take him with him and kill him later, leaving his body where no one would find it. Then it would just be a mystery and not a cause for resentment and revenge.

Raulf was a different matter. He didn't want the murder of an eleven year old boy on his conscience. His mother was dead so, once his father was disposed of there was no family to ask awkward questions. He decided to give the boy a choice. Calling the boy forward to ride alongside him, he questioned him.

'Did you know what your father was up to?'

Raulf shook his head. 'No, lord. We weren't close. I don't think he ever forgave me for killing my mother when I was born. He had loved her deeply and her death in childbirth was something he kept blaming me for. He was a pagan, though he kept that hidden, whereas I am Christian baptised by James the Deacon, so we had little in common. I was just a messenger who took a letter and brought back a pouch of gold. If I'd known what my father was up to I'd have told King Oswald.'

Oswiu regarded the youngster sceptically. He seemed to be telling the truth but he could be lying in an attempt to save his own life.

'You say that you were baptised by John the Deacon. When was this?'

'When King Edwin was on the throne, perhaps two years ago when I was nine. He was the acolyte of Bishop Paulinus who had accompanied King Edwin's Christian queen when she came from Kent to marry him. He started to teach the sons of the nobility about his faith and I joined them when I was old enough. My father tried to dissuade me but he didn't want to reveal that he was still a pagan. Then, when Edwin was killed and the queen fled, he abandoned us and went south.'

'So this James the Deacon is a Roman Christian?'

'I suppose so; at least I know that Paulinus was sent by the Pope in Rome. I know that you follow the Celtic Church, lord, but we are all Christians, are we not?'

Despite himself Oswiu was impressed by the boy. He seemed to him to be honest and forthright. He had already decided to give the boy a chance, now he was certain that it was the right thing to do.

'Raulf, you must know that I can't let your treacherous father live?'

'Yes, lord,' he said dejectedly, hanging his head.

'You have a choice. You can die and be buried with him, or you can swear allegiance to me on the Holy Bible that you will be faithful to me. My servant fell ill in Goddodin and died. If you agree, you can replace him and become my body slave.'

'A slave, lord?'

The boy was obviously horrified at the idea of the son of a noble being forced into slavery. Oswiu laughed.

'Come on, it's not that bad. Serve me well and it's a relatively easy life. Prove to be idle, though, and you'll be whipped.'

'Oh, I've no fear of that, lord. I'm no shirker, but I've always wanted to be a warrior.'

Oswiu grunted in amusement and called Jarlath forward to join them.

'What were you when you were a boy, Jarlath?'

'King Oswald's body slave, Oswiu, but you know that,' he said, puzzled.

'Yes, but Raulf doesn't. And what are you now?'

'A member of his gesith,'

'Yes, and a close friend too. Thank you.'

He turned back to Raulf as Jarlath fell back into line.

'It's not who you are, boy, it's what you are. Serve me well for the next three years and I'll think about freeing you when you are fourteen so you can train as a warrior, I'm not promising though. And don't harbour any ideas about joining my gesith in due course. That's only for the chosen few.'

'Yes, lord,' Raulf replied, grinning broadly.

~~~

'Cyning, there's a party of horsemen behind us and they're catching us up fast,' Rònan told Oswald a little breathlessly.

He had been riding as rearguard with one of the other members of the king's gesith when they felt the ground tremble slightly. Rònan dismounted and put his ear to the ground.

'Quite a few riders and coming up quickly. It may well be Oswiu, but best move into the trees, just in case. I'll tell the king.'

There was no chance of hiding the baggage carts so Oswald left them where they were. His men melted into the trees. Being late autumn hiding wasn't an option, but the tree trunks might conceal their lack of numbers.

Oswald breathed a sigh of relief as Oswiu appeared leading his gesith. The two brothers embraced whilst Jarlath and Beorhtwulf re-joined their comrades. Acha rode up to the two brothers and, after a perfunctory greeting, asked whether he'd managed to subjugate all of Goddodin.

Oswiu's face fell. He knew that his mother was trying to embarrass him. They had always been at loggerheads and now it seemed that the rancorous relationship between them had turned spiteful, at least on her part. He glared at her.

'Not quite, no. I shall have to return next year to capture Dùn Èideann.'

'Why didn't you stay and finish the job my son gave you.'

'My son? Am I not also your son?' he almost shouted at her.

'Stop it, both of you. I am ashamed of you, mother. You needled Oswiu deliberately, and you have to learn not to react to her taunts, Oswiu. I love you both dearly but sometimes I'd like to knock your heads together until you're both unconscious.'

'I'm sorry to have disappointed you, Cyning,' Oswiu said stiffly before storming off.

'Sometimes I wish I'd left you on Arran,' Oswald told her furiously.

'Oh, let him calm down. He's always been full of himself.'

'Not without good reason, mother. He's a good man and he'll make an excellent King of Rheged in due course. But I need him more than I need you now,' he told her bluntly. 'Now go and apologise and make your peace with him.'

Acha glared at her son and he realised that she was about to refuse.

'It's not a request, Acha, it's a command from your king. If you don't, then I'll exile you back to Dalriada; I mean it.'

It was the first time he'd called her by name instead of mother and it stunned her. For a moment she stood there, partly furious at the way she was being treated and partly fearful that Oswald would carry out his threat. Eventually she walked off in a huff, not following Oswiu, but back to her horse. She mounted it and waited.

'Oswiu, mother was totally out of line, but we have more important things to talk about right now,' he told the younger man when he found him kicking an inoffensive tree in the woods.

'What? Oh, you mean Penda's bloody ambush. Right; give me a minute to calm down and I'll come and find you.'

'Very well, but don't take too long. Daylight is passing.'

Oswiu nodded and sat down with his back to the tree he'd been kicking. Fifteen minutes later he came and found his brother. Acha had dismounted again and was speaking to him but Oswiu totally ignored her and, grasping Oswald's arm, he led him away.

'What's your plan to deal with this ambush?' he asked when they were out of earshot of everybody.

'We have to cross the River Ure at some point. The usual crossing place is the ford near the ruins of the Roman town of Isurium Brigantum. As the Mercian spy said, it lies at the junction of two Roman roads called Dere Street and Watling Street and from there the old road leads directly to Eoforwīc. There is plenty of old ruins for the ambushers to hide in and we'll be vulnerable as we cross the ford.'

'So do we avoid it and cross elsewhere?'

'We could do, and that would probably be sensible, but I need to teach Penda that we're not people to underestimate. So we're going to annihilate his men.'

'How?'

So Oswald told him.

Oswald and seven of his men, all fully armed and armoured, approached the ford with the baggage carts. The carters were nervous but they'd been told that they could hide in the body of the carts as soon as the ambush had been sprung.

Penda's men had almost given up waiting. Their leader hadn't heard from his spy after he'd sent a messenger saying that they had left Bebbanburg, so he didn't know how many men accompanied Oswald and his mother. Furthermore, he'd expected them to ford the river the day before. He'd abandoned the idea of attacking their camp at night; without the information about the sentries and numbers it was too much of a risk. He had, however, sent his best scout to find out how many men there were with Oswald. The scout found them before Oswiu had caught him up, so he was expecting just the king and his gesith.

He had forty men with him. It should be more than enough to deal with less than half their number, even if they were all experienced fighters - especially if he could catch them whilst they were split in two crossing the river. He didn't care about the rest, it was Oswald that Penda wanted dead. He'd robbed him of a hundred of his best fighters at Heavenfield and he wanted vengeance. Furthermore, from all he'd heard, this Oswald was a formidable warrior, not like the amiable idiots who'd sat on the thrones of Bernicia and Deira recently, and that worried the Mercian king.

'They're coming,' the scout he'd sent across the river to watch the Roman road from the north told him breathlessly after he'd crossed via the ford.

The River Ure was too fast flowing to swim horses across and even at the ford it was two and half feet deep. That meant it came up to the chest of a horse and the waist of a man. Crossing was therefore a slow business. The safe passage was marked by withies stuck in the bank on either side of the river. They indicated that the crossing was no more than six feet wide, just enough for a cart with a reasonable safety margin.

As the Mercians watched from the Roman ruins beside the road on the southern side of the ford, the first riders appeared; there only appeared to be eight of them though. They were followed by two oxen-drawn carts. Instead of crossing the ford, the horsemen halted and dismounted. The carts swung around until they were moving parallel to the bank. When they reached the ford they halted. Boys jumped down from where they were sitting beside the carters, unhitched the oxen and led them away. Then they took the horses from the dismounted men, who came forward to push the carts together to block the entrance to the ford.

The Mercians watched all this in bemusement. The Bernicians picked up their shields again and formed a shield wall across the front of the carts. Suddenly it struck the leader of the ambush party that Oswald was well aware of their intentions and was waiting for him to attack. He licked his lips; eight men, however good they were at fighting, were no match for forty well-armed warriors. He was puzzled about the other eight that his scout had seen but he wanted to get this over, with so he gave the order to attack.

His first wave of twenty men, five across and four deep, were two thirds the way across when it became apparent that the carts weren't there just to block the exit from the water. Four archers stood up in each cart, took aim, and released an arrow at high trajectory at the hapless Mercians. Most had the common sense to raise their shields to protect them from the arrows that rained down on them but the archers sent another arrow seconds later at their exposed bodies.

Most wore a chainmail byrnie or a leather jerkin but at close range they couldn't stop the arrows and five men fell. The archers repeated their tactic of firing at high then low trajectory, catching another three men out. Twenty per cent of the first wave were now dead or badly wounded. The archers' tactics maddened the enemy warriors and they tried to move faster towards Oswald's shield wall, however the waist-deep water forced them to continue at a snail's pace. Another two volleys hit them before the ragged remains of the front rank reached the single row of warriors standing in front of the carts.

Oswald watched as the man directly in front of him emerged from the river and grabbed the top of his shield, trying to pull it down so that he could thrust his sword into the king's neck. Oswald angled his own sword so that he could thrust it over the top of his shield into his opponent's eyes but the man moved his shield up at the last moment. Then the man yelled in pain and slashed down at something on the ground. The momentary distraction was all Oswald needed and he thrust the point of his sword into his opponent's neck. The man fell back into the water and Oswald glanced down to see a grinning Sigbert lying between his feet with a bloody seax in his hand. Evidently the boy had thrust it up into the man's thigh.

'Well done, lad. Now crawl back and next time go for his groin.'

Sigbert didn't have long to wait. Less than a second later a spearman thrust at Oswald but he deflected the point easily with his shield. The next time the man shoved his spear at him, Oswald used his sword to chop off the point. The man threw the useless haft away and drew a seax. Once more the king deflected his attack, but this time the man was close enough for Sigbert to extend his arm upwards under the man's byrnie and into his groin. The Mercian screamed in agony and doubled over, dropping his seax. It took less than a second for Oswald to lop off his head.

By now the Mercians had had enough. They had lost twelve of their original twenty and some of the other eight had flesh wounds. One man lost his sense of direction in his panic to flee and left the ford. He was swept away to be drowned as the weight of his chainmail pulled him under.

As the seven men waded back the archers sent a few volleys into their unprotected backs. Not one man made it back across the river in safety.

The Mercians had a few archers of their own and these were now sent forward, each with a second man with a shield to protect the two of them. However, all the Bernicians did was to retreat behind the carts. The Mercian commander was now at a loss. He had no idea how to attack again without losing all his men. They were demoralised and would probably refuse to launch another frontal attack. However, Penda would certainly kill him, and probably the rest as well, if they went back having failed. Whilst he stood there undecided he was startled to hear a hunting horn to his rear.

To his amazement Oswald now led his gesith forward and started to cross the ford, his archers having swopped their bows for sword and shield. Moments later another sixteen men appeared coming out of the ruins behind him. They dismounted and formed another shield wall. He was trapped. His remaining twenty now faced thirty six of the most experienced warriors in Britain.

He was dead either way so the Mercian commander charged at Oswald in a last attempt to kill him. His weapon of choice was a large single bladed axe. He lifted this over his head so that he could bring it down, splitting the king's skull in two. The blow never landed. Oswald dropped to one knee and thrust up into the Mercian's belly. The axe shot out of his hands, which had opened involuntarily when he'd been stabbed, and landed behind Oswald. A thrust deep into the intestines is usually fatal, but not immediately so. The man lay writhing in agony until Oswald took pity on him and thrust his blade into the man's neck. The rest of his men had had enough and threw down their weapons in surrender.

'Did you have any trouble crossing the river, brother?' Oswald asked as he and Oswiu embraced and slapped each other on the back.

'No there was another ford fifteen miles away, but it's as well that you delayed approaching this one until now or we wouldn't have been in position in time.'

'Oh, I think we'd have managed to hold off another attack or two but the danger was that the Mercians, or what was left of them, would have escaped. Now Penda won't know what's happened to his assassination attempt. I don't know whether to leave him guessing or send the heads back to him.'

'Why don't you hang the bodies from the trees as a warning to others? Word will get back to Penda eventually and you don't have to risk the life of the messenger who conveys the heads to him.'

'And the captives?'

'Sell them in Eoforwīc. Kings always need gold and silver, and it will enhance your reputation as well.'

~~~

Oswald wasn't expecting the Witan to be particularly welcoming, especially after the difficult time he'd had at Yeavering, but he hadn't appreciated quite how hostile it would prove to be. The presiding noble was the Eorl of Elmet. Ever since it had been incorporated into Deira by his father it had been accorded the status of a separate province of Deira under an eorl and this man, called Thurwold, was now the senior noble in the kingdom. His name meant Thor's power – a pagan name – which was not a good sign.

The Witan met in what had originally been built as a church but, since the apostasy of the last king, had become the hall where the young warriors of Eoforwīc lived. It wasn't particularly clean – the rushes on the floor hadn't been changed for a while and the bones of past meals, spilt ale and dog and rat faeces were everywhere; and it stank.

Oswald had also noticed that the roof was in a poor state of repair. When it started to rain heavily just after the meeting had begun, water dripped through the thatch in numerous places.

Acha, as the daughter of King Ælle of Deira and the sister of the late King Edwin, was allowed to attend, but Thurwold's first ruling was that she wouldn't be permitted to speak. Both Oswald and Oswiu immediately challenged that.

'My mother is the last surviving member of the royal house of Deira of her generation,' he began. 'As the only

87

surviving child of Ælle as well as the sister of Edwin, she should have a voice.'

'As one of the surviving æthelings, I support Oswald's proposal,' Oswiu stated as he glowered at Thurwold.

'You are here as supplicants before the Witan and don't dictate how we conduct our business,' Thurwold almost yelled at him.

He knew then that the old man could prove to be serious problem. Oswald joined his brother on his feet.

'You say, Thurwold, that this is the Witan's decision, yet I have seen no sign that this is so, just your opinion. I ask the Witan to vote on whether they wish to hear what the Lady Acha has to say. If the majority do not wish to listen to her then, of course, my brother and I will abide by that decision.'

Both brothers sat down again to a general outbreak of noise as those present discussed the issue. Unsurprisingly Thurwold was furious.

'Silence, silence,' he barked getting to his feet and glowering at his fellow nobles. 'I have made a decision and that is the end of the matter.'

That was a mistake.

'No it isn't. You preside because someone must do so, but you are behaving like an autocrat. Each one of us has an equal voice in the Witan; yours is no more important than mine, or mine than the chief druid's.'

Oswald looked with interest at the speaker; a man named Aylmer, another eorl, this time of an area known as the Wolds. He was young, perhaps in his mid-twenties, and, unlike most of those present, he was clean shaven, making him look even younger.

There was a general murmur of agreement and Thurwold wisely decided not to risk further humiliation by putting the matter to the vote. He waved his hand, indicating that he conceded the point.

'Be that as it may,' he continued. 'There are three æthelings who are eligible to be considered but only one who is the son of our last king, Osric.'

Oswiu was on his feet once more.

'That's not true,' he stated flatly. 'There are four æthelings present.'

He sat down as Thurwold scowled at him again.

'Who is the fourth? I see you and your brother and, of course, Oswine, son of King Osric.'

'You are forgetting me, I think. I'm Oslac, also the son of Æthelfrith, King of Northumbria, and the Lady Acha. There is also a fourth brother, Offa, but he's unable to be present today.'

It was cleverly done. Thurwold had been made to look a fool. He spluttered with rage before he regained his voice.

'But you're a monk, a follower of the false god, Christ.'

'There is no true God but one and Jesus Christ is his Son, but that is not what we're here to discuss today. I am nevertheless an ætheling of Deira, as is Offa, so what you have just stated is untrue.'

'Do you wish to be considered as our king?' Thurwold spat at him.

'That is not the point, and I'm sure we'll come to that. You are required as the man presiding over the Witan to list all the æthelings of Deira. It makes no difference if they are present or not, or whether they are a mewling infant or an old man in his dotage.'

Oslac sat down again. He was conscious of his brothers smirking beside him, but also of the looks of malice directed his way by the four chief druids present. Before Thurwold could continue the door opened and a man dressed like Oslac but without the distinctive Celtic tonsure entered, shaking the rain from his habit.

'What are you doing here? You have no seat in the Witan,' Thurwold barked at him.

'On the contrary, I am here as the representative of Queen Ethelburh and her son Usfrea. As the son of King Edwin, Usfrea is also an ætheling.'

'It seems the list of those wanting to be king instead of you grows by the minute, brother,' Oswiu murmured to Oswald.

'Where is Usfrea? Why isn't he here himself? In any case he is only a young boy.'

'That doesn't preclude him from being king; if you elect him, as you should, his mother will act as regent until he is older.'

'Who is the man speaking?' Oswald asked the thegn standing behind him.

'James the Deacon, the Lady Æthelburh's chaplain,' the man replied, stooping down to whisper in Oswald's ear.

'Ah, so he hails from Kent? Where Æthelburh came from? He must be a Roman Christian then.'

'Just so. He served Bishop Paulinus, who was appointed by the Pope in Rome, until Osric became an apostate. Paulinus returned to Kent with Æthelburh and her brood were sent to Frankia for safety. There were four of them but two of the boys died as infants. There is a daughter too, Eanflæd. As far as I know they are both still in Frankia. James stayed here ministering to those who remained Christian after Osric reverted to paganism.'

He stopped talking and straightened up as he saw Thurwold glaring at him.

'I hope we now have a complete list of æthelings,' Thurwold almost sneered. 'Good. They are Oswine, son of

90

King Osric, Oswald, Oswiu, Oslac and Offa, sons of Lady Acha and Usfrea, son of King Edwin.'

Oswald got to his feet this time.

'Whilst I obviously don't dispute that we are the sons of Lady Acha,' he smiled at his mother as he said this, 'more relevantly we are also the sons of King Æthelfrith, elected by the Witan as King of Deira.'

'He imposed himself on Deira and subjugated Elmet,' Thurwold roared back at him.

'That's your opinion. I say that he was the saviour of both Deira and Elmet. Whilst he reigned over you there was peace. Edwin's usurpation of the throne after he rebelled and killed my father has resulted in nothing but invasion and misery for you and your people. Deira needs a strong ruler who can keep her enemies at bay, not the incompetent son of an incompetent father or a boy who isn't even brave enough to come here himself.'

Oswald's speech brought forth yells of acclamation and howls of protest. Thurwold did his best to restore order but everyone ignored him. In the end the Eorl of Elmet got up and stormed out of the hall into the rain, banging the door behind him.

After a while the clamour died down and they noticed that the chair facing them was empty. Aylmer got up and went and sat in it.

'I think we need to debate this calmly. As Thurwold seems to have found something better to do with his time, we need someone else to preside. I'm happy to do that unless someone else wishes to take on the onerous task?'

He smiled and there was a general murmur of agreement.

'Well then, you have a choice before you. Can I start by asking the æthelings in turn whether they wish to stand for election as King of Deira? King Oswald, you are the eldest, do you wish to stand?'

'Yes, I do.'

'Oslac?'

'No, I support Oswald.'

'What about Offa?'

'He would not wish to be considered.'

'Oswiu?'

'No, I also support my brother,'

'Thank you. Oswine?'

'Yes, I have the better claim because...'

'Thank you Oswine. You will have a chance to present your case in a moment. For now we are merely drawing up the list of candidates.'

'James the Deacon, you represent Usfrea. Before I ask you whether he wishes to stand, may I ask how old he is?'

'He is six years old, lord.'

'And does he wish to stand?'

'His mother wishes him to be considered.'

'That is not what I asked you, James. I asked whether he himself has specifically stated to you, as his representative, that he wishes to be considered as King of Deira.'

'No, lord. I haven't seen him since he was sent to Frankia. His mother is in Kent and it is she who wrote to me.'

'Then he has not claimed the throne himself. Does the Witan agree that Usfrea should no longer be considered?'

After there was a general mutter of agreement Aylmer looked at Acha.

'There is one more ætheling I think. Œthelwald, son of Oswald. Since his father didn't mention him I would like his grandmother to confirm whether he is a candidate or not.'

92

'Œthelwald is an eleven year old boy who is currently being educated at the Christian monastery on the Isle of Iona. He has not been asked if he wishes to stand or not.'

'I see, then I am forced to assume that he is not a candidate, but he should have been listed.'

He paused and looked Oswald in the eye. The other stared back at him stony faced.

'I see. Next I call upon each candidate to make a brief, and I emphasise the word brief, statement in support of their candidature. We'll do it in reverse order of age I think. Oswine you first.'

'Thank you Eorl Aylmer. My case is quite simple. Osric was my father and immediate predecessor as King of Deira. He has no other sons and so, being the only one in the direct line of descent, I should inherit the throne. Oswald's claim stems from his mother and so he is the grandson of a king, not a son. His father only seized the throne through conquest and marriage, he was not freely elected. Moreover he is a warmonger who only seeks his own glory.'

He sat down to some applause and, at a nod from Aylmer, Oswald stood up.

'Oswine's speech was all about his rights, his entitlement to the throne. No word was said of his obligations to his nobles and his people. I don't need to spell out to you the threats faced by Deira. Not only have the recent destruction wrought by Penda of Mercia and Cadwallon highlighted the need for us to be strong, but the expansionist dreams of the East and Middle Anglians makes Deira even more vulnerable on its own. You need a proven warrior to lead you, and one with powerful allies. As king, I will bring you alliances with Bernicia and Rheged. We need to take over the weak Kingdom of Lindsey on your south-eastern border before someone else does, bringing the threat nearer to you. I also

93

intent to forge an alliance with Wessex so that we surround Mercia. That way I will bring not war, as Oswine claims, but peace to Deira and Elmet.'

Oswald sat down to applause from many but shouts of disapproval from others, especially the druids.

'Who wishes to speak in support of either candidate?'

There followed an interminable number of speeches in favour of one or the other. However, no-one seemed to have anything new to contribute until Acha stood up.

'It seems to me that Oswald is the better choice for three reasons. He is a direct descendent of King Ælle; Oswine is not. He is merely his great-nephew. Secondly he is wise, just and fearless. I can't claim to know Oswine but his father was a fool, an incompetent militarily and accepted bribes for favourable judgements. Thirdly Oswald has a proven reputation as a victorious leader in battle, Oswine is an unproven youth.'

She sat down amidst a stunned silence. Then someone shouted out 'Whiteblade' – the name Oswald had been accorded as a great warrior in his early career - and the cry was taken up by most there.

When the hubbub had died down, Aylmer asked if it was the wish of the Witan to appoint Oswald as their king. The roar of approval left no doubt as to the answer.

It wasn't until the eorls and thegns lined up to swear their allegiance that Oswiu noticed that, not only had the druids disappeared, but so had Oswine and his closest followers.

CHAPTER FIVE – THE HOLY ISLAND OF LINDISFARNE

635 AD

Eochaid waited until high tide before taking his two birlinns through the treacherous sandbanks of the Solway Firth. He thought that the best way to find Aidan and Ròidh would be to follow their trail. All the abbot on Iona knew was that they had been taken by a trader to Dùn Phris, a fortress a short way inland from the mouth of the River Nith, so that was the obvious starting point.

In total he had eighty warriors, a few sailors such as the steersmen, and eight ship's boys. It was a sizeable force but he wanted to avoid confrontation with the men of Strathclyde if at all possible. As they approached the dùn, but whilst still out of sight from it, he moored as close inshore as he could get and the majority of his men waded ashore. He hoped that he could now get away with claiming that he was a merchant and he had brought cloth and wool to sell to support his cover story.

In the event his two ships didn't seem to excite much interest and he went ashore unarmed except for a seax. Accompanied by two of his men attired as sailors he made his way through the small settlement that had grown up between the few timber-built warehouses alongside the jetty and the circular palisaded fortress situated on a slight rise above the surrounding land. The man he was looking for was called Aderyn, a contact that Abbot Ségéne had given him. He had no idea if he could help, but he was the only hope he had.

The first person he had asked for directions had given him a strange look and hurried away. Like most of his fellows, he was small, swarthy and dark haired. Ethnically they were Britons like the Welsh and many of the inhabitants of Rheged.

Eochaid wondered whether it was their appearance or because he spoke Cumbric with an Irish accent that he kept getting suspicious looks, but whatever the reason it made him uneasy. Nevertheless, he asked another man for the whereabouts of Aderyn's hut and the man took him there himself. However, he did seem a little nervous.

They knocked on the door as their guide scuttled away but no-one answered. He knocked again and this time a female voice asked him in hushed tones who it was.

'Eochaid, Ségéne mac Fiachnaíhe sent me.'

The door was quickly opened and the three men were ushered inside and then hurriedly shut and barred behind them.

'I'm sorry about that, but it isn't a good time to be a Christian in Strathclyde. What does the abbot want?'

'I was looking for Aderyn,' Eochaid said uncertainly.

'He's not here I'm afraid. He fled to avoid being killed, but he had to leave me behind. I'm his daughter and both my husband and my child are sick. I need to be here to tend to them, but you shouldn't stay in case you catch the sickness.'

Eochaid's opinion of the missing Aderyn took a nose dive. Only a coward would abandon his family like that. He looked around the small hut and at first he didn't see anyone else, then he realised that there was a ladder up to a sleeping platform. He turned back to the woman.

'We seek Brother Aidan and his companion. We know that they landed here in October last year but they seem to have disappeared. Can you help us?'

She nodded. 'Yes, he left here to travel up Nithsdale as far as Kendoon Loch. He said that he hoped to travel on from there through the Glen Ken Hills to the coast opposite the Isle of Arran, but it would depend on the weather. I believe that Glen Ken can be dangerous in winter if they get a lot of snow, but I've never been there myself. He may have had to stay for the winter somewhere in Nithsdale; or, of course, he may have been betrayed and killed. However, if that was the case I think word would have reached us. Brother Aidan is well known. Our evil king would boast about it if he'd managed to lay his hands on him.'

'Thank you, you've been most helpful.' Eochaid handed her a leather pouch containing several scraps of silver. 'This will pay for medicine if you know a healer or a wise woman.'

'Thank you, lord. We have a good healer but he is expensive and we couldn't afford him before now. You are our saviour.'

She babbled on about how grateful she was and Eochaid backed towards the door, eager to leave the hut with its sick inhabitants now he had what he wanted. One of the men with him quickly opened the door and the three left hurriedly. Eochaid was embarrassed by the woman's effusive thanks as well as being worried about catching whatever it was that her husband and child had. All three were glad to breathe in the fresher air outside the hut, despite its overtones of sewage and rotting garbage.

They were nearly back at the quayside when they were stopped by four men, all carrying spears and small shields called targes. Two of them had poor quality helmets on their heads, the others were bareheaded.

97

'Why were you seeking the hut of the Christian scum Aderyn?' one of the men wearing a helmet asked them belligerently.

Eochaid realised that the first man they'd questioned had obviously alerted the soldiers up at the fortress. He studied the four Britons. The two without helmets were little more than boys – perhaps fifteen or sixteen years old – and they were edgy. He could tell by the way that their hands kept grasping their spears tightly and then relaxing their grip. They wouldn't meet his eye, nor would the third man. Only the leader seemed confident of himself.

'Someone owed him money and asked me to take it to him. However, he wasn't there so I gave it to his daughter.'

It was nearly the truth and Eochaid said it with conviction.

'Why does an Irishman owe a Strathclyde Christian money?'

'I'm from Ulster but the man who owed the debt isn't. I happened to be doing business with him in Ayr.'

Ayr was another port in Strathclyde. This time it was a lie and the questioner must have sensed it.

'I don't believe you. You're to come with us. The custos wants to question you.'

Eochaid nodded to his two men and turned as if to accompany the four soldiers. The leader and the other man with the helmet led the way and the two youths brought up the rear. If the man in charge had a modicum of common sense he'd have asked them to hand over their seaxes. It took less than a second to unsheathe them and, whilst his two men slit the throats of the two soldiers in front, Eochaid whipped around and confronted the two frightened youths.

'Now you can drop those spears and walk away or you can die here; your choice.'

The two looked at each other, dropped their spears and shields and ran.

A few minutes later Eochaid was sailing back down the river to re-join the rest of his men. The custos would know that he had left by ship and would send boats after him. However, everyone at Dùn Phris had seen him depart on one ship manned by a few sailors, they wouldn't be expecting two birlinns filled with experienced warriors.

Luckily nothing had appeared by the time that the two birlinns were loaded and ready to leave. Eochaid's men rowed out of the estuary and turned east to wait opposite the sandbank on the other side of estuary. Half an hour later three boats called pontos - based on a Roman design with eight oars a side and a square mainsail - sailed into sight crammed with armed Britons. Eochaid's ships were the only ones with oars in the water; the Strathclyde ships having raised their sails and shipped their oars to take advantage of the westerly wind.

The two birlinns sprang forward and the archers in the bows concentrated their efforts on the leading ponto. One of the first to be killed was the steersman and the ponto slewed around out of control until it gybed and the mast snapped. Few of the men on board her were wearing chainmail or even a leather jerkin and many were killed or wounded by arrows before Eochaid's ships swept past her. The first enemy ponto wouldn't be going anywhere soon.

The other two ships tried to get their sails down and put their oars in the water. They succeeded – just – but they hadn't picked up any speed by the time that Eochaid's birlinns reached them. Each of the two pontos had twenty men on them, less than half the number of the opposing vessels. Eochaid's birlinn came alongside one of them just after his archers had rained a volley of arrows down on the crew. Half a dozen of the twenty were killed or injured and the morale of the rest had sunk to rock bottom. Eochaid jumped over the gunwale down into the belly of the smaller ponto spearing a man with his sword as he did so. He sprung up from the crouching position in which he had landed just in time to parry the sword of a large man dressed in a chain mail byrnie with an expensive helmet with a faceplate. As the man swung his sword at him again Eochaid knocked it away with his shield. His adversary didn't have a shield but wielded a seax in his left hand. He now used this to stab at Eochaid's throat. The Irish prince knocked it away with his own sword, which left his opponent's belly exposed. He brought the sword back quickly and thrust it at the large paunch.

The links of the chain mail were well made, but not were strong enough to resist the sharp point of a good sword. Several of them parted and the point burst through, cut through the thick leather jerkin underneath and lodged in the man's intestines.

He howled in pain and furiously tried to slash at Eochaid's neck. The Irishman jerked his head back out of harm's way and rammed the bronze rim of his shield up into the man's throat, bruising his windpipe badly. He man gasped for breath then fell to his knees in agony as the fatal wound to his innards incapacitated him.

Once his men saw that he was dying the heart went out of them and the few survivors surrendered. The other vessel had already surrendered, but the leading vessel had now sorted itself out and was making for the entrance to the River Nith as fast as it could go. However the wind was against it and so it relied on rowers, of which there weren't enough left to man every oar. Eochaid left ten men behind to secure the ship he had just captured and the remaining thirty grabbed an oar and put their backs into it. It soon became apparent that they were overtaking the smaller ponto quite quickly. They had no chance of reaching the entrance to the river, let alone the safety of Dùn Phris and so they stopped rowing and surrendered.

~~~

Eochaid and fifty of his men moved quietly through the mucky alleys of the settlement below the fortress of Dùn Phris. He had learned from the captives that the man with the paunch who he'd killed had been the custos and a virulent anti-Christian. Quite a few of those who had surrendered had claimed to be Christians who had denied their faith when the pagan Owain had come to the throne. They were only too happy to tell Eochaid what they knew in the hope of avoiding slavery or death.

He had left thirty men, the boys and the wounded with the five ships and the prisoners at a sheltered spot on a bend in the river, whilst he took one of the captives as a guide and set out to capture the fortress. He had reluctantly decided that he couldn't leave it behind in enemy hands whilst he ventured into the interior.

'Godwine,' he said, calling forward one of the most experienced scouts in his crew. 'I need to know all you can find out about the sentries.'

The man nodded and, beckoning one of the other scouts to join him, the pair set off at a lope towards the settlement. Eochaid's crew were a mixture of Irishmen from his own clan of the Ulaidh in Ulster, where his nephew, Congal Cláen, was king, and Angles who had joined him when

101

they all lived on the Isle of Arran when Oswald was its thegn. Godwine was one of the latter.

Whilst he was waiting for Godwine to return Eochaid found himself thinking about the future. He had left Ulster when Congal had betrayed his own grandfather, who was also Eochaid's father, on the battlefield and seized the throne of the Ulaidh for himself. Eochaid had vowed never to return but recently he'd been asked by Domnall Brecc, King of Dalriada and Congal's supposed overlord, to help him in the growing conflict between the Ulaidh and the High King of Ireland. A similar plea had gone to Oswald but he'd wisely ignored it. He had enough problems trying to re-unite Northumbria without getting embroiled in the complex politics of Ireland.

Eochaid didn't find it so easy to disassociate himself from the land of his birth. Although he'd been Oswald's friend and comrade in arms since they'd first met on Iona when he was fourteen, he was beginning to think it was time for him to become his own man. The days when they'd been close and did most things together had passed. Increasingly he felt that they were growing apart now that Oswald was a king. By the time that Godwine had returned he'd made his mind up to respond to Domnall's call for assistance just as soon as he'd completed his current mission.

'They are obviously alert, Godwine told him. 'We saw sentries patrolling in pairs around the circular palisade. I can't be certain but I think that there are three pairs. There are four more on the walkway by the gates. The palisade is more than twice the height of a man with a ditch perhaps five feet deep in front of it except, of course, at the gates.'

'Thank you, Godwine. Very concise and helpful. Did you manage to see what is inside the palisade?'

'It's on the top of a rise with no high point from which to see over the palisade. We could see the roof of the hall and several huts though.'

'What is the roofing material: straw, turf, timber?'

'It was thatched with straw.'

Eochaid smiled. 'Good. As we haven't had any rain in the past few days, it should burn nicely.'

He had several archers amongst his men. When they lit a fire outside the palisade the sentries became agitated but the gates remained firmly shut. When the first fire arrows arced into the night sky and lodged in the thatch of the hall and two of the huts there was a lot of shouting, and then panic as the water chucked from leather buckets failed to reach far enough up the roof to make any difference to the flames. These had to be filled from the well and it took time for them to haul the water up to the surface. It was a fruitless exercise and before half an hour had passed the inside of the fortress was blazing furiously. It became too hot for the soldiers to remain in the confined space and the gates suddenly swung open.

'Here they come. Spare the women and children but kill the men,' Eochaid yelled, more to salve his conscience than in expectation that he would be obeyed.

The women and children emerged first. One or two were killed by the inexperienced warriors high on adrenalin before their first fight, but most were allowed through the circle of attackers and disappeared into the settlement. The garrison tried to charge the waiting warriors in a wedge but most were suffering from smoke inhalation and a few had serious burns. They stumbled and weaved about trying to suck in the relatively clean air away from the burning buildings and that destroyed the cohesiveness of their charge.

103

Eochaid had positioned himself in the middle of the two ranks of the shield wall. He saw a large Briton wielding an axe come straight for him and he crouched down waiting for the man's attack. Unlike most of his fellows, this man was protected by a byrnie and a simple round helmet. He swung his long axe in a circle as he neared Eochaid, threatening to cut in half the men on either side of him as well. Eochaid ducked and held his shield up, hoping that the axe head would glance off it. It never reached him, getting stuck in the torso of the man to his left.

He stepped forward and thrust the point of his sword into the throat of the large Briton as he struggled to free his axe. The man gurgled and fell to his knees, struggling for breath. Eochaid's sword had severed his windpipe but hadn't cut any vital blood vessels. He rectified that by pulling out his sword and slashing it into his neck, half severing his head from his body. It flopped sideways in a spray of blood and the man toppled sideways.

When they saw him go down, the fight went out of the rest of the Britons. They fought on but, as more and more of them were killed, the remainder surrendered.

'He was their lord,' Godwine told him later.

'How many did we lose?'

'Only three, plus a few more wounded. When we counted their dead there were over forty of them.'

'Wounded?'

'None. I fear the men killed them rather than be bothered with looking after them.'

Eochaid nodded. 'Not very Christian but they would have been a problem for us.'

He suspected that Godwine had given the order to slaughter the wounded. He wasn't happy about it, and certainly wouldn't have ordered it, but it did solve a problem. They couldn't have sold them as slaves in that condition and they couldn't have gone in search of Aidan with a dozen or more wounded enemy warriors in tow.

'How many captives?'

'Seventeen; a mixture of old men, young warriors and boys.'

'Boys?'

'Yes, slaves who worked in the kitchens, stable boys and the like. There are five of them.'

'Bring them here.'

When they were brought before Eochaid he could see that they ranged in age from ten to perhaps fifteen. None looked like the small, swarthy dark haired Britons who inhabited Strathclyde.

'Are any of you Angles or Saxons?' he asked in English.

The youngest and the eldest stepped forward, declaring that they were both Angles. Another was from Dalriada and the two with red hair turned out to be twins from Ulster. Unfortunately for them they claimed to be from the Uí Néill clan, the enemies of Eochaid's people – the Ulaidh.

The two Angles and the Dalriadan were given the option of slavery or becoming ship's boys and serving Eochaid. It wasn't a difficult decision for them to make. The two Irish boys were returned to the rest of the captives. Eochaid would take them up the Solway Firth to Caer Luel in Rheged the next day with the men they'd captured earlier to sell them as slaves. Then they could make a start on the journey up the Nith to find Aidan and Ròidh.

~~~

Ròidh peered out from under the bush where he was hiding and, now certain that there was nobody anywhere near him, he darted out from concealment to check on the trap he'd set the previous day. He was in luck. A large hare had been snared and it was the work of moments to kill it and take it back to the cave where he and Aidan had taken refuge.

They had been extremely lucky. When they had been warned about King Owain's campaign against Christians, Aidan had decided to head for Ayr on the west coast of Strathclyde and try to either hire or steal a fishing boat to travel across to Brodick on the Isle of Arran, which was in Dalriada. Oswald had been Thegn of Arran and Bute and it should then be a simple matter to find someone to take them back to Iona. The problem was firstly to survive the coming winter and then travel all the way up Nithsdale and Glen Ken without being discovered.

God had been smiling on them because halfway up Nithsdale they had found an isolated hut. The previous occupants had obviously succumbed to some sort of illness because there were five bodies in the hut: a man and woman and three children. Aidan and Ròidh buried them and then proceeded to burn the beds in which they had lain, replacing them with furs they had found stored in the loft. The man had evidently been a hunter and fur trader because they also found a hunting bow and quiver full of barbed arrows together with a long skinning knife.

When he was a boy living in the crannoch on Loch Ness Ròidh had been taught how to fish, to hunt and to trap; skills which now proved invaluable. Thankfully the winter proved to be wet but not too cold, apart from a couple of periods of ice and snow. There had been some salted meat, cheeses and flour in the hut and Ròidh supplemented this with small animals he managed to trap, the odd deer and trout from the river.

Luckily no man troubled them but the wolves were a different matter. They were forced to stay in the hut for two days during the first blizzard of the winter in mid-December. Fortunately they had enough supplies stored so that Ròidh didn't have to go hunting. In particular there was a young doe in the shed attached to the hut, hanging until the venison became tender. After a week a pack of wolves had ventured into the clearing where the hut stood and scrabbled at the door to the shed. Perhaps unwisely, Ròidh went outside with his bow to scare them off.

His first arrow took a large wolf in the shoulder and it immediately yelped and turned to face its attacker. The rest of the pack joined it in growling menacingly at the young monk. He sent another arrow towards the big wolf and hit it in the side of its chest. Again, It wasn't fatal as the head of the arrow bounced off the animal's ribs. It gathered itself and launched itself at him. Ròidh stood there petrified and would have undoubtedly been killed had Aidan not stepped in front of him and buried the skinning knife deep in the wolf's chest. The wolf struggled briefly then dropped to the ground. It twitched once and then lay still.

The rest of the pack howled their dismay at the killing of the alpha male – all except one who had been waiting for an opportunity to challenge the dead wolf. He now growled and tried to induce the rest of the pack to attack the two men, but the alpha female knocked him to one side. The alpha male and female jointly led the pack and she was letting him know that she would choose her next mate.

Whilst the wolves milled around in confusion Ròidh sent another arrow winging towards them. This one hit the young challenger just behind the ribs and tore into the animal's small intestine. It yelped in pain and tried to tear the arrow out with its teeth. Being barbed, this just made the wound worse and, after a minute or so, it collapsed onto its side.

The rest of the pack had had enough and, led by the alpha female, they disappeared back into the trees.

'That was close. Thank you for saving my life Aidan.'

Aidan sat down heavily on the ground as the energy imparted by the adrenalin that had been coursing through his veins left him weak and light headed. He shook his head to clear it, then smiled.

'I wonder what wolf meat tastes like?' he mused. 'The skins will be useful too. Come, let's get them inside and skin and butcher them. You can take the offal well into the woods and leave it there for the pack. Perhaps that'll keep them from our door until this cold spell ends.'

By mid-March the weather had improved sufficiently for them to continue their cautious journey north-east up the rest of Nithsdale until they reached a series of small lochs that marked the end of the river and the beginning of Glen Ken. But then Aidan contracted a fever. Ròidh was at his wit's end; Aidan was rambling and was very hot to the touch and then, just as the monk had just about given up on finding shelter, he came across a cave for them to shelter in.

When Ròidh returned with the hare Aidan was sleeping soundly. He skinned and gutted it before chopping up the meat to add to a stew of wild herbs such as yarrow, black elder and meadowsweet to reduce his fever, and wild garlic, bulrushes and wild asparagus to bulk it out.

It took him a long time to feed the stew to his fellow monk but in the end he managed to get quite a lot of it into him. He ate half of the rest himself, leaving the remainder until the morrow. Later he made Aidan some herbal tea and then lay down on one of the wolf skins to sleep.

The next day Aidan's fever broke and he was lucid, at least part of the time. It took a long time for the monk to recover and it was the middle of April before he was fit enough to walk any distance. That first day they covered less than five miles but the next morning Aidan awoke feeling stronger and had more colour in his face. Even so it was a struggle for him to make eight miles. By now they were following a stream up into the hills and they could see Loch Doon below them to the east. Aidan thought that they probably had around twenty five miles to go to reach Ayr.

They had reached another small loch, no more than a tarn in a hollow fed by several small streams, when they found the going too boggy to continue, so they climbed up the side of a large hill. From the summit they followed a small stream that seemed to be heading in the right direction. That night it rained heavily and Ròidh was worried that Aidan's fever might return. Thankfully he seemed alright the following morning and they set off into the mist that covered the land like a blanket.

As the morning wore on the mist dispersed and the sun emerged to dry out their sodden clothing. They made good progress that day and were now walking downhill. It was mid-afternoon by the time that they crested a ridge and came face to face with a party of hunters. There were about ten of them and they were accompanied by four deer hounds.

Aidan and Ròidh still wore their habits, though they were rather ragged by then, but what gave them away as Christians were the wooden crosses hanging from the ropes around their waists and their tonsures. Over the months hair had started to grow again on their tonsures but Aidan had insisted on using the sharp skinning knife to shave it off every week. Although they now exhibited four days' worth of

109

stubble instead of smooth skin above their foreheads, there was no mistaking what they were.

~~~

Eochaid decided to take two of the three pontos with him. Each required sixteen rowers and there would normally be a few more men on board to steer and handle the small mainsail. However, he wanted to take as many men as possible in case they ran into trouble, so he added a few more warriors and a couple of ship's boys to each crew, leaving the remainder behind with the wounded to guard the two birlinns.

At first the Nith was navigable without any problems but as they ventured further upstream they encountered a few shallows, the odd weir and even an area of rapids. To get through them they disembarked and hauled the pontos over the obstacle one at a time. It took time but it was a lot faster than walking along Nithsdale.

After leaving the settlement behind they saw few other signs of habitation. There was the occasional shepherd with his flock high on the hillside and some isolated huts with a few animals and small cultivated areas, but they were few and far between. After passing through three small lochs on the fourth day they found the river impassable by boat and they continued on foot leaving just six boys and two warriors to guard the pontos.

'Are you certain that Aidan will have got this far?' Godwine asked him.

'No, I've only got the vague intention he mentioned to Aderyn's daughter to go on, but if he was making for Ayr he must have come this way,'

110

Godwine nodded and ran off with another warrior to scout the path ahead. Eochaid looked at the hills looming above them on either side of the glen and sent out two more pairs of scouts to watch their flanks.

The sun was at its zenith and Eochaid was feeling more than a little warm when Godwine came running back to say that he had found a cave which showed signs of recent habitation. There was nothing to indicate that the people sheltering there were the two monks but, nevertheless, Eochaid felt that it was an encouraging sign.

By dark they had covered another fifteen miles. They had encountered the boggy area around the source of the river and made their way higher up the hillside and camped in a hollow beside a small stream. That night the nice weather broke and it rained heavily. Eochaid and his men huddled under their cloaks, shivering and wet; no one was sorry when dawn arrived.

At first they couldn't see much around them because of the thick mist but gradually the sun burned it off and by mid-afternoon their clothing had mostly dried out again. Eochaid looked at the rusty state of his byrnie and helmet and wished he'd thought to bring a boy with him to clean it. He was just wondering if there was any sand nearby with which to scour the rust off when Godwine came running back to him.

'There are two monks below us surrounded by a group of Britons on mountain ponies.'

'How far away are they?'

'No more than a quarter of a mile, but they're prodding the two prisoners along with their spears. If we attack they could well kill the monks before we can reach them.'

~~~

As they stumbled along prodded in the back by the huntsmen's spears Aidan kept mumbling prayers whilst Ròidh was desperately trying to think of ways to escape. In the end he thought that their best chance would come that night. He just prayed that they would be camping in the open and wouldn't reach their destination before dark.

The two men riding in front of him spoke quietly to one another, but not so quietly that Ròidh, who spoke their Brythonic language better than Aidan, couldn't hear what they were saying.

'Why don't you just kill them now, lord, rather than go to all the trouble of taking them to Dùn Breatainn. I'm sure that King Oswain would be just as happy with their heads.'

'Well, I'm not. He is likely to give me a greater reward for giving him Aidan, who has caused him so much trouble with the thousands of our people he has tricked into becoming believers of the false god, Jesus Christ, than he is for some head who could be anybody.'

'What about the other one? We don't need him do we? He's just a waste of food.'

The leader of the hunting party thought about that for a moment.

'Perhaps you're right. But we can have some sport with him tonight before we kill him.'

Ròidh sobbed when he heard that but he tried to be brave for Aidan's sake. The two had become extremely close during the decade that they had been together and Ròidh would have given his life to save Aidan. Now he desperately tried to think of a way to protect him, which might cost him his own life, but which might give his mentor a chance. He had almost given up in despair when suddenly half a dozen armoured warriors appeared from behind some rocks ahead and stood across the track, barring their way.

112

Almost instantaneously several arrows thrummed through the air and several of the Britons and their ponies were hit. Chaos reigned as the warriors ran forward and either speared the chests of the ponies in front of the two monks or slit their throats with their swords. As the riders tumbled to the ground they were quickly dispatched. In less than a minute eight of the ten huntsmen were dead.

However, as one of the dog handlers dropped to the ground his two deerhounds attacked Eochaid's men and it took them a minute of two to dispatch the hounds. The other handler released his dogs and tried to escape. Unlike the other hunters he was on foot and hadn't gone more than a few paces when he dropped with several arrows protruding from his back. His two dogs did manage to escape and Eochaid let them go.

The remaining mounted Briton was the one who had wanted to kill both Aidan and Ròidh. With a roar he thrust his spear at Aidan intent on killing him before he died, but Ròidh saw what he intended and stepped in front of his mentor intending to take the spear in his own chest instead. Just as he was about to deliver the fatal thrust the Briton jerked backwards in the saddle with a spear implanted in his chest. Godwine had seen what was happening, picked up a discarded spear, and threw it with all his considerable might at the Briton. Such was the force of his throw that the man was catapulted over the rear of his pony, but not before his own spear had hit his intended target and Ròidh fell to the ground with blood pouring out of his chest.

~~~

'Just supposing that Eochaid is successful in finding this particular needle in the haystack that is Strathclyde, where do you intend Aidan to establish his monastery.'

Oswald looked at Acha with annoyance.

'You seem to have little faith, mother, either in Eochaid's abilities or in Brother Aidan.'

'I don't understand why you need to make this Aidan Bishop of Northumbria instead of giving the honour to your brother Oslac.'

'Because Aidan is a successful missionary and Oslac has no experience in converting pagans. Besides, he doesn't want to become a bishop, he's perfectly content being my chaplain and the priest for the vill of Bebbanburg.'

'But -'

'No mother. We've had this conversation before and I'm tired of you trying to tell me what to do. I appreciate your help in making me King of Deira as well as Bernicia but I'm not a little boy. I don't need your help anymore and I won't put up with your interference.'

He stopped and then held his hand up when his mother was about to respond, her eyes flashing dangerously.

'Not another word before we both say something we might regret.'

He took a deep breath whilst he tried to calm himself down. Thankfully his mother bit her tongue, but she kept glaring at him.

'To answer your question, I've looked for somewhere like Iona, a small island where the monks can be secluded; where they can concentrate on a life of prayer and devotion to God. I think I've found one not far from here. It's one of the Farne Islands.'

Acha frowned. 'But I thought that they are all too small to support a community who will need to be self-sufficient?'

'Most of them are, but the largest island in the north seems to me to be ideal. It's called Lindisfarne.'

'That isn't a true island though. It is at high tide but at low tide you can walk across the sands to it.'

'That's true, but it's the best site that there is on the east coast. Furthermore the thegn has just died without an heir so I can appoint the abbot as the new thegn without upsetting anyone.'

'Have you visited the place to see if it's as suitable as you say?'

He drew his breath in sharply and bit back an angry retort.

'No, I'm going to visit it shortly.'

'I'll come with you just to...'

She got no further, halted by her son's abrupt departure from the room. He turned when he reached the doorway.

'You don't listen do you? You will not accompany me and you will not try to advise me. It's time for you to devote the rest of your life to contemplation and prayer. I'm grateful for your help in the past but I am king and I have other advisors now, if I need them. Men who don't try and control me.'

With that he left leaving behind a furious Acha. She paced up and down trying to think of ways to prevent Aidan becoming bishop, and presumably abbot of this new monastery on Lindisfarne, so that Oslac could take his place. Her best hope was that the wretched monk had died in Strathclyde.

~~~

Aidan was alive and well, however the same could not be said of Ròidh. The spear thrust hadn't penetrated the monk's chest far enough to kill him but it had scored along his rib cage slicing his flesh open for some eight inches. Not only did he lose a lot of blood before the wound could be stitched closed with catgut but it had subsequently become infected.

This put Eochaid in something of a dilemma. He really needed to get back to the boats and sail downriver to Dùn Phris before Owain had the chance to send a sizeable force against him. Those who had escaped from the place would have spread the story of the fortress' destruction and although King Owain's capital, Dùn Breatainn, lay two or three days march to the north and across the other side of the Forth of Clyde, there had to be enough warriors at Ayr and at other settlements along the west coast to give him a problem; and they were less than a day away.

As they hurried back to where they had left the two pontos Ròidh's fever grew worse and the wound turned an angry red and became puffy. It was then that what Aidan always described as a miracle happened. They had camped for the night back at the place where they had left the boats, ready to make a start south at dawn, when an old woman walked into the camp. Eochaid later questioned the sentries as she should never have been able to get past them but they denied having seen anyone until she appeared well within the perimeter of the camp.

She had knelt down beside the delirious Ròidh and Aidan went to remonstrate with her but something told him that she was there to help, not harm, his companion. She had produced a box containing maggots and placed them on the suppurating wound before handing Aidan a small pouch full of herbs.

'Leave the maggots on the wound until they have eaten all the rotten flesh,' she croaked. 'Then bind it with freshly washed bandages each day until it has healed. Make a tisane

116

with these herbs and give it to him every few hours until the fever breaks. You can't move him until then.'

She rose to her feet with difficulty and made her way slowly out of camp. Again the sentries said that she hadn't passed any of them.

Eochaid had said nothing but once she'd gone he told Aidan that they couldn't stay there. It was too dangerous.

'You heard what the wise woman said,' Aidan replied. 'He can't be moved until the fever breaks. God willing that will be soon. Now I must boil some water to make the tisane.'

Eochaid was in a quandary. Aidan wouldn't leave Ròidh and he knew that every day that they delayed made it more certain that they would be trapped there. In the end he decided to stay there for one day and sent for Godwine.

'I want you to send out scouts back the way we have just come and the other way downriver to warn us if any sizeable body of armed men appears.'

'And if they do, as they surely must if we sit here like rats in a trap?'

Godwine wouldn't normally have spoken so bluntly to the Irish prince but he and the men thought it was extreme folly to delay. If Ròidh died, then so be it. They weren't prepared to put all their lives at risk for one monk. The general feeling was that they had come for Aidan and, if necessary, he should be taken with them by force.

'Then I will decide whether to ambush them or flee. Now do as I bid you.'

Eochaid wasn't a fool. He knew how the men felt and he shared their fears. However, he wanted to save Ròidh's life if possible and he certainly didn't want to have to force Aidan to come with them.

'We'll wait one more day, Brother Aidan, but at dawn the next day we will have to depart, whatever condition Ròidh is in, so you'd better pray for a swift recovery.'

Aidan was about to protest but one look at Eochaid's determined face told him that it would be a waste of time. He nodded.

'I understand. But I won't leave him here all alone. We have been through too much together for me to abandon him now.'

Eochaid knew that Godwine was right. If it came to it they would have to take Aidan with them by force, but he said nothing yet.

~~~

Oswald rode across the flat sands that separated Lindisfarne from the mainland. The tide was on its way out so he knew that he had several hours before they'd have to return, unless they wanted to have to spend the night there. The locals had told him that there was normally a window of at least seven hours when it was safe to cross the sands, but the tide came in very quickly once the sea started to return.

He had taken Oswiu and Oslac with him, together with Sherwyn, the thegn of the vill on the mainland opposite the island, and his gesith. There was only one settlement on Lindisfarne and that was the small fishing village on the east coast; the rest of the inhabitants lived in huts dotted about, or so he was told.

The island was shaped like a short axe with the handle pointing due west towards the mainland. Oswald quickly dismissed the handle part as it was essentially sand dunes with marram grass growing on them. It wasn't until they

118

reached the axe head that they saw signs of
habitation. Initially there were a few isolated huts
surrounded by grazing land and a few small areas which were
cultivated. At the eastern end of the island there was a small
settlement with a few fishing boats drawn up onto the
sand. It stood on the southern side of a small cove which
formed a natural harbour.

There were a few more huts to the south of the
settlement but what drew Oswald's attention was the old
thegn's hall at the north east corner of the axe head. It was a
simple building made of wattle and daub with a thatched
roof. There was no palisade but thorn bushes had been
planted around it, presumably to keep animals out rather
than for any defensive purpose. There was a sizeable area of
pastureland around It on which a few sheep and two cows
grazed. Oswald turned to Sherwyn.

'Do you know the extent of the thegn's holding?'

'I believe it is the area between the fishermen's
settlement and the area of arable land over there, which is
owned by the churl who lives in that hut,' he replied pointing
to a small dwelling a few hundred yards away outside of
which two children were playing.

Oswald had been surprised that the inhabitants didn't
seem in the least perturbed by the arrival of a score of men,
armed and mounted, in their midst. When he asked Selwyn
the man explained that he had warned them that he would
be visiting the island and bringing some other men with
him. He hadn't mentioned that one of them was the king
though.

Oswald and his two brothers were comparing the area
available for the new monastery with that on Iona.

'I think the whole island may be about half the size of
Iona,' Oslac said uncertainly.

'Yes, that's about right, but the whole of Iona is devoted to the monastery whereas here you have the fishing settlement and a few churl's smallholding as well,' Oswiu agreed.

Oswald was pursing his lips in thought. Eventually he spoke.

'A lot of Iona is unused except for a few grazing sheep. The church and the other buildings don't take up much room, it's the cultivated land that provides the monks with their food that occupies the most space. Then there are the beehives.'

He was referring to the small conical huts built of stone in which those monks, termed anchorites, who wished to retire from the world could live in.

'Well, they could build a few on the islands over there.' Oswiu said with a straight face, indicating the plethora of small islets called the Farne Islands to the south of Lindisfarne, little knowing that that was exactly what would happen in the future.

'But is there enough space for the new monastery here?' Oslac brought the king back to the matter at hand.

'I think so. What do you think Oswiu?'

'I think it's the closest you are going to get to a setting like Iona on the Northumbrian coast.'

'Very well. Now all we need is for Eochaid to find Aidan and Ròidh so we can start work to make this a Christian country.'

CHAPTER SIX – THREE WEDDINGS

Rheged and Wessex – 635 to 636 AD

Aidan had spent the night on his knees in prayer and was feeling exhausted. It wasn't surprising that, after the privations they had endured in hiding over the past six months, not sleeping for twenty four hours should have drained him of all energy. When Eochaid's servant arrived with a tisane for Ròidh he found the other monk in a near delirious stupor.

'Lord, come quickly. There's something wrong with Brother Aidan.'

Eochaid had been washing in the stream and immediately followed the youth over to the two monks without bothering to dress.

'Brother Aidan, are you alright.'

He grasped the monk's shoulder in a panic. He hadn't come all this way and risked the lives of his men only to find that the man he sought had lost his mind.

'What's wrong with him?'

The other voice startled him until he realised that Ròidh was awake and lucid. He put his hand on the wounded monk's forehead and sighed with relief. All signs of the fever had gone; it must have broken sometime during the night. At least that meant he could now be moved with care. It would take him some time before the wound healed but the infection had gone.

Hearing his friend's voice seemed to bring Aidan out of his trance and he gave thanks to God for Ròidh's deliverance before allowing himself to be taken on board and made comfortable beside Ròidh so that they could both sleep during the voyage downriver.

~~~

Oswiu took a deep breath and entered the hut he shared with Fianna and his son, who was now four. Telling the slave who looked after them to take the boy outside, he sat down and took Fianna's hands in his. She had just turned twenty and was, if anything, even prettier than when he'd first met her and fallen in love when she was thirteen.

He tried to speak but his mouth was so dry he could only croak. He swallowed and tried again.

'My love I have something to tell you.'

She looked at him expectantly and wondered what could possibly have made Oswiu, who was always so confident, nervous. He cleared his throat and tried again.

'My brother the king wishes me to do something for the good of all Northumbria and I have agreed,' he said in a rush. 'He wants to bring Rheged under his leadership and to do that he seeks an alliance between their house and ours. King Royth's daughter is his only child and there are no other members of his family left alive, so whoever marries the Princess Rhieinmelth will become the next King of Rheged.'

'Yes, I understand. So Oswald will marry this Rhieinmelth? Does Keeva know? She will be devastated.'

122

'No, my love. It's not the king who will marry her; he wants me to do so.'

For a moment Fianna sat there in stunned silence. Then she quietly began to weep. He tried to put his arms around her but she pushed him away.

'What happens to me and our son? Are we to be sent away?'

'If you stayed here as my lover it could be awkward,' he began.

'Do you love this Rhieinmelth?'

'I think I could come to do so, in time.'

It was not in Oswiu's nature to lie but he was not being entirely truthful. He still loved Fianna but the thought of taking the extremely pretty Princess of Rheged to bed excited him more than he cared to admit. He'd fallen in love with her the first time he'd seen her.

'Well, I asked what will happen to us. To me, your ex-concubine, and your bastard?'

Oswiu felt wretched. He hadn't thought further than actually breaking the news to her and had made no plans for her future; nor had he thought about what would happen to his son.

'Do you want to go back to your father?' he asked hesitantly.

'What? Go back to Bute and my family and admit that my father was right about you all along? No, I'd rather die.'

'I'm sorry. I knew that this would be difficult for you; I just didn't appreciate how difficult.'

Fianna got to her feet.

'I think you'd better spend the night in the warrior's hall. I don't want you around us any more, not now you've disowned us. When do you leave to marry your new lover?'

'It's not like -' he started to say, and then realised that it was just like that. 'In two days' time. In the meantime I'll give some thought to your situation.'

'You do that,' she said coldly. 'Now I'd like to be alone please.'

It wasn't until he'd reached the warrior's hall and sent his body slave to fetch his belongings that he realised that Fianna was bound to tell Keeva. She was a bright young woman and she would realise that Oswald, now he was king, would need to make a political marriage as well. He'd better warn his brother.

~~~

Jarlath had long admired Fianna from a distance. He was secretly in love with his sister's best friend but he knew that he had to keep his love secret. If Oswiu found out he'd be in deep trouble. It gnawed away at him but he did his best to ignore it. It was better after they left Arran and he didn't see her every day, but then she'd arrived at Bebbanburg and his longing for her was rekindled.

When Keeva told him that Oswiu had cast Fianna aside he didn't know whether to feel sorrow at her humiliation or joy that she was now free. Thankfully he had the common sense to realise that if he went to see her now and confessed his love for her he would ruin any chance he might have had with her.

However, he was desperate not to let her slip through his fingers. So he confessed his passion for Fianna to his sister. Keeva immediately saw that bringing the two of them together would be an excellent solution but it would have to be engineered carefully. The first thing to do was to ensure that Oswiu didn't pack Fianna and her child off somewhere

124

or, even worse, arrange for her to marry. So she went to see him. Of course she didn't tell him that Jarlath was in love; that would have been stupid.

'Lord, thank you for seeing me. You probably won't be surprised to hear that my closest friend, Fianna, has confided in me. Not unnaturally, she is worried about her future and that of her child.'

Oswiu sighed. 'Thank you for coming to see me Keeva. I'm glad you did. Frankly I don't know what to do. I am happy to acknowledge my son as mine and to treat him as such as he grows up; I'm sure that my wife will understand. However, I can't expect her to tolerate having my mistress around. '

'I suppose that one solution might be for Fianna to marry. That way she wouldn't feel threatened or slighted by Fianna's presence. Of course, her husband would have to be prepared to bring up another man's son.'

'Yes, you may have something there.'

Oswiu saw that this was the obvious solution and immediately accepted the idea enthusiastically.

'I don't suppose you have anyone in mind?'

'Well, my brother is still unmarried. I could have a tactful word with him and sound him out.'

'Ummm, very well. But be discreet. We'll need to think how to get Fianna to accept the idea if Jarlath is willing.'

'Leave it to me, lord. I'll keep you informed, of course.'

Oswiu left for Caer Luel the next morning with a clear conscience. He had every confidence that Keeva would arrange the marriage of Fianna and Jarlath before he returned.

~~~

125

Oswald was surprised to receive an invitation from Cynegils, the King of Wessex, to visit him at his capital, Wintan-ceastre. It seemed that a bishop named Birinus had arrived in his kingdom from Rome and had converted many of the West Saxons to Christianity. Cynegils invited Oswald to be his godfather for the baptism ceremony and to discuss matters of mutual interest. Oswald could only think of one: both their kingdoms bordered Mercia and there was an ongoing border dispute between Mercia and Wessex. Furthermore, both Penda of Mercia and Cynegils were trying to wrest control of Lundenwic from the East Saxons.

Oswald decided to accompany his brother to Caer Luel to attend his wedding and then to travel from there down to Hamwic on the south coast of England by sea. Wintan-ceastre was less than half a day's ride from there. His only concerns were who to leave in charge at Bebbanburg and being intercepted by Welsh or Irish pirates during the voyage from the Solway Firth to Wessex.

He considered making his mother regent in his place but he didn't trust her not to make decisions he wouldn't agree with. In the end he sent for her, his son and Dudda, Eorl of Norhamshire, his senior noble.

'Thank you all for coming. I'll be brief because there is a lot to do before I leave with Oswiu.'

At this both Acha and Œthelwald look surprised. No-one had mentioned anyone from the family accompanying Oswiu to his wedding.

'If anyone should go with my son, it should be his mother,' Acha butted in.

Oswald gave her an impatient look.

'Don't interrupt, mother. Do me the courtesy of listening to all I have to say before you speak,' he told her somewhat

126

brusquely. 'From there I'll be travelling down to Wessex to act as godfather to King Cynegils and, hopefully, making him our ally against the Mercians and the Welsh. I'm likely to be away for some time and will probably have to stay at Wintanceastre for the winter. That means that I will need to appoint regents whilst I am gone.'

He paused whilst those present looked at each other, each suspecting that the king would appoint one of them to act as regent.

'It is a heavy burden and so I have decided that it needs to be shared. Mother, I would be grateful if you would look after the routine administration of the kingdom; Œthelwald, you will be in charge of its defence. However, I am conscious that you are, as yet, young and lack experience so I intend to appoint a hereræswa to command the army and to advise you. Dudda, I would like you to oversee justice and to issue judgements in my name. This means that the three of you will form a council of regency.'

'Wouldn't it be simpler just to make me sole regent,' Acha asked.

Her tone left no one in any doubt that she felt slighted.

'No,' Œthelwald interrupted. 'I'm the king's son and I will occupy the throne after him. This is my chance to gain experience. I should be regent.'

Dudda cleared his throat before mildly pointing out that the succession was not a matter of primogeniture under Anglo-Saxon law. The king's eldest son was merely one ætheling amongst all those who would be considered by the Witan. Œthelwald looked furious but Oswald held up his hand for silence before his son could remonstrate with Dudda.

'This is not a matter for debate. I have made my decision. Dudda, would you stay behind please so that we can discuss who should be considered for the post of hereræswa. Thank you mother, Œthelwald. You may leave.'

Both left, equally unhappy with Oswald's decision.

'Now, who should I appoint, Dudda?'

'Well, Cyning' the old eorl reflected for a moment. 'There's Dunstan, your horse marshal, but it might be politic to appoint Hrothga as the senior eorl in Deira - though I have no idea how good a military commander he is – or Leodgar, the captain of your gesith.'

'Hmmm, I want someone on the spot to keep my son from making stupid decisions, so not Hrothga. I was going to take Dunstan with me, so perhaps the obvious choice is Leodgar. I'll let him and Œthelwald know.'

'Will it be a permanent appointment, Cyning?'

'No, I agree I should appoint a hereræswa; the Lord knows I've enough to occupy my time without commanding the army as well. However, that post will be Oswiu's in due course. I'm not telling you a secret if I say that he would have been my choice as sole regent, had he been here. Even after he is wed, he won't be returning here immediately. He needs to get to know the kingdom he'll inherit one day, and winter is no time to traverse the wild uplands between Caer Luel and here. He'll come back with me when I return.'

'Do you want your mother to move the court from here to Yeavering in the spring?'

'Yes, that's an excellent idea. I'll let her know.'

At dawn the next morning the two brothers set out with their respective gesith and a sizeable baggage train for Rheged. Oslac remained behind to minister to the people of Bebbanburg and to conduct Aidan to Lindisfarne when, or perhaps if, he arrived. Oswald hoped to borrow a birlinn from Rhieinmelth's father to take him south but, as it turned out, that didn't prove necessary.

~~~

It took three days for Eochaid to return to where their two birlinns were waiting. When they came to shallows or weirs where the boats had to be manhandled through or over them, they transferred Ròidh around the obstacle on a stretcher. The infection had cleared up and after two days Aidan removed the maggots as the putrefying flesh had been eaten away, then he stitched the two bits of sound flesh together. Some of the ship's boys used the discarded maggots as bait and caught several fish to supplement the boring diet of dried meat, cheese and oatmeal biscuits.

They passed the settlement with the blackened ruins of its fortress and beached the two boats next to the birlinns and the other ponto. That evening the crews dined on several sheep that those left behind had rounded up, supplemented by herbs and wild plants that they had found. Ròidh was still in considerable discomfort from his wound but he joined Aidan for the feast. The next day they set sail for Caer Luel, using the ship's boys and the extra warriors from the two birlinns to crew the three pontos.

At midday they sighted the Rheged capital ahead of them and this time, instead of stopping short of the old Roman town as they had done before, they went on and moored alongside the jetty under the old Roman stone walls, patched where they had collapsed with timber palisade, which surrounded the town. At first the inhabitants had been confused and a little wary. The two larger ships displayed the red and yellow striped sail of Northumbria but the three pontos carried the plain red mainsail of Strathclyde. Both were evident, although the sails were furled as it had been necessary to row upriver.

129

When Eochaid disembarked he was surprised to be received by, not just the king and his daughter, but by Oswald and Oswiu as well.

'Welcome Eochaid, you're just in time for my wedding,' Oswiu told him with a broad grin.

'How did it go?' Oswald asked after the usual pleasantries.

Eochaid didn't answer but turned and gestured towards the second birlinn where Aidan was helping Ròidh to descend the gangplank.

'I'll tell you all about it later but God and His Son must have been watching over us. It was a close run thing, in more ways than one.'

Oswald congratulated him and went to greet the two monks. If Aidan was surprised to be enveloped in Oswald's arms, he didn't say so, but he did warn him not to do the same to his companion, explaining about his wound.

'You've no idea how pleased I am to see you both safe and well.'

'Well? Ròidh should be dead and would have been if an old woman hadn't appeared as if by magic in our campsite. Ròidh's chest wound was festering and his flesh was rotting. She cured his fever and gave us maggots to eat away the putrefying flesh. I tell you, Cyning, she was sent by Christ himself.'

'No need to call me Cyning. We've known each other too long to stand on ceremony. Did Eochaid explain what I have agreed with Ségéne, provided you are amenable, of course?'

Aidan nodded. 'I am honoured, of course, and I can't wait to get started. Will you be returning after your brother's wedding?'

'No, I'm bound for Wessex and the baptism of King Cynegils.'

'Baptism? Who by? I didn't know that Iona had …. Ah! I suppose it is to be conducted by some Roman bishop?'

'Yes, Bishop Birinus I gather.'

'Not a name I know,' Aidan said dismissively. 'It seems that we and the Romans will soon be vying to convert the English.'

'Well, you're both followers of Christ, even if you don't acknowledge the Pope in Rome or agree on how to calculate Easter. In any case it's irrelevant, it's you I want to convert the North.'

'Yes, of course. I must return to Iona first though. Ségéne is a consecrated bishop as well as abbot and he must lay his hands on me to make me a bishop. Have you had any thoughts about a monastery for me to use as a base?'

'Yes, it's on the Island of Lindisfarne, not far from Bebbanburg. Oslac has seen it and can take you there. He has my authority to recruit labour and pay for materials and, no doubt, he can help you to recruit your first monks.'

'Oswiu will not be returning then?'

'Not until I do next spring. He must get to know his new land once he is the heir. Whilst I'm away my mother and my son, together with the senior eorl form the regency council, but Oslac is the man to help you.'

'Very well. I'll need a ship to take me to Iona and if I can borrow a horse, I'll set out as soon as I return. However, first I must make arrangements for the care of Ròidh until he's fit enough to make the journey east. Will you bring him with you when you return this way?'

'Of course. I'll arrange for a small escort to accompany you too. There is a lot of wild country between here and the east coast.'

Aidan laughed. 'That won't be necessary. If I can survive for a winter in Strathclyde with every man's hand turned against me, then the journey across a largely deserted wilderness should present little problem.'

'Very well; but I will give you a boy to act as your servant.'

'That would be kind. I'm afraid that I've been spoilt; I mean by having Ròidh to look after me.'

~~~

Aidan set off on the eighty mile journey to Bebbanburg as soon as he'd returned from his consecration on Iona. Although it was late summer the weather was cold and a light drizzle soon permeated every layer of clothing. He was missing the company of Ròidh but he soon realised that his new companion was irrepressibly cheerful. The boy was called Garrett and was the son of an Irish father, one of Eochaid's crew, and a Dalriadan mother from Arran. He had just turned twelve and had been a ship's boy for just over a year.

They had got to know one another on the ponto that took him to the Holy Island of Iona and back. The voyage had been uneventful and he'd left again as soon as the abbot had laid his hands on his head and said the words that transformed him from monk to priest and then bishop. He loved Iona but he was impatient to reach his own Holy Island and start his new mission.

Even the drizzle that accompanied them on the road north from Caer Luel failed to dampen Aidan's spirits and, as if in response to Garrett's sunny disposition, the weather gradually improved and by mid-morning their cloaks were gently steaming as the sun dried them out.

Initially the landscape beyond Caer Luel had been flat and uninteresting, but once they had forded the River Esk, they could just make out the hills in the distance. Their route took them due north initially along Ewes Water towards the head of the River Teviot. This took them into Strathclyde for a while but it was be a much shorter journey than following the old Roman defensive wall across to the east coast before heading north.

Once across the Esk Garrett rode ahead to warn Aidan of any habitation, patrols or hunting parties. Recalling his recent escape from one of the latter the new bishop wondered whether he'd been wise to turn down the offer of an escort, but they saw no-one except for the odd isolated farm and a few small settlements. These they avoided by taking to the hills.

It took them two days to reach a settlement known as Haws Wic on the Teviot and Aidan breathed a sigh of relief as he knew that they were now in Bernicia. However, this was border country and the place was protected by a small fortress in which the local thegn lived with his warriors. Aidan had expected to be received as a friend of the king, but he realised that he might not be as welcome a guest as he had supposed when he was shown into the hall and saw a druid standing by the thegn's chair, whispering urgently into his ear.

Garrett had disappeared to look after their horses and Aidan hoped that he would stay away from him for a while. This looked as if it would be his first test as Bishop of Northumbria and the boy could be in danger through association if he mishandled the coming encounter.

'Greetings, lord. I'm Aidan, Bishop of Northumbria and friend of King Oswald.'

Aidan thought that establishing himself as close to the king might persuade the thegn to tread carefully. It certainly made the man sit up straighter and narrow his eyes in speculation.

'What brings you to Haws Wic, Bishop Aidan?'

'I am charged by the king to establish a monastery on the Island of Lindisfarne.'

It was clear that the name meant nothing to the thegn, which was unsurprising given the isolated location of the settlement some forty miles from the east coast.

'It's near Bebbanburg,' he added helpfully.

'So you are merely passing through?' the thegn asked with a relieved smile on his face.

The druid bent down to whisper in the thegn's ear again but the man waved him away.

'I hear that this King Oswald is a follower of the White Christ, so was King Edwin but he soon changed back to the old gods. What makes this king different?'

'He was brought up on Iona, the Holy Island where I was trained. He is a true believer in the one God, not like Edwin who became a Christian for political reasons.'

'And what makes your god superior to those that I believe in?'

'Your gods don't exist, lord, God and His Son, Jesus Christ do.'

'Can you prove that?'

At that moment Garrett entered carrying Aidan's satchel and other things he might need overnight. Aidan beckoned him to his side and took an illuminated book from his satchel.

'This is the Word of God. It tells of Jesus' life on earth and his ascension into Heaven where he sits at the right hand of God the Father after he rose from the dead.'

'Show me the book.'

Aidan did so but, whilst the thegn admired the calligraphy and the illuminations, he couldn't make head or tail of it.

'I can read English, priest, but I don't know this language.'

'It is written in Latin, one of the ancient tongues that was spoken when Our Lord Jesus was on Earth.'

'Pah!' the druid sneered after peering at the book. Unlike the thegn he couldn't read a word in any language. His religion was passed on verbally. 'That could say anything and be written by anyone. It proves nothing. Our gods are Woden, Thunor, Tiw the god of war and Frey, the goddess of virility and prosperity. We offend them at our peril.'

'And you risk eternal damnation. You will be cast down into the fires of Hell if you deny Christ. Do you not also worship the spirits in the air, the water, the earth and the woods? There isn't a multitude of these spirits, as you would have people believe, but one – the Holy Spirit who exists with God and his son Jesus as the Holy Trinity.'

The thegn had looked worried at the mention of Hell but now he appeared puzzled.

'If there is but one God, how is it that there are now three?'

'Christ was begotten of the Father and is at one with him and the Holy Spirit proceeds from the Father and is also at one with him. They are three parts of one entity, not three separate gods. Don't think of them in human terms but as three equal parts which have merged into one.'

The thegn looked interested, much to the druid's concern. He glared at Aidan, who smiled back at him whilst Garrett, hidden from the thegn by Aidan's body, stuck his tongue out at him. Of course, this enraged the druid further, which was the boy's intention.

'This is nonsense, lord. We should drive these two from Haws Wic with stones and clubs.'

'Be quiet. I didn't give you leave to speak or ask your opinion. Leave us if you can't keep quiet.'

The druid drew himself up and stalked out of the hall looking offended. It didn't escape Aidan's notice that a few of the warriors sitting around listening to the conversation sniggered. It appeared that the druid wasn't popular.

He joined the thegn for the evening meal and continued to explain the basic teachings of Christ to the man. He was full of questions, all of which Aidan dealt with deftly. In the end the thegn invited him to stay awhile and preach to the residents of the settlement the next day. In the end it was the druid who was driven out and the thegn, his family and most of the inhabitants were baptised in the River Teviot before he left.

'A monk will visit you as soon as possible to carry on your instruction, but I can't say when. In the meantime call your people to prayer on Sunday mornings and read the prayers I have left for you.'

The man nodded and then surprised Aidan.

'My second son wishes to become one of your monks at this place Lindisfarne. When he is trained he can return to us as a priest to minister to our needs.'

'I'm delighted, though it will be a year or two before he is trained. Where is your son? Will he come with us now?'

A boy of about eight rode forward on a pony and joined Garrett.

'I see. Well, it may be more than a year or two, nearer six,' he laughed. 'What's your name boy?'

'Lucan, Bishop Aidan,' the boy answered clearly in a high treble voice.

'Welcome Lucan. You're my very first novice.'

'What about Garrett?'

At this the other boy laughed.

'I want to be a famous warrior like Whiteblade, not a monk,' he declared with a laugh.

'Whiteblade?'

'It's what King Oswald is called by his warriors.'

With that Aidan headed his horse towards the east and the trio rode out of Haws Wic heading for Bebbanburg.

~~~

Oswald was full of conflicting emotions. He had loved Gytha and now he loved Keeva, perhaps even more than he had his wife. He was well aware that one of the things that kept his son at a distance from him was his love for Keeva. Œthelwald felt that, by taking Keeva as his lover, he had betrayed Gytha's memory.

Now he was walking side by side with his brother into the church at Caer Luel for the latter's marriage to Rhieinmelth, a girl he could have married himself and who he was falling in love with more and more every time he saw her. He felt awful about it. Oswiu had always been there at his side, wholeheartedly loyal, and now he felt that he was betraying him - not in deed, but definitely in thought. It didn't help that the girl kept giving him coquettish looks before looking down demurely. She had definitely been flirting with him ever since he arrived.

Oswiu had solved the problem of his own concubine by marrying her off to Jarlath. That was another of Oswald's problems: whether or not he loved Keeva, he needed to marry and produce an heir; he discounted Œthelwald as he just couldn't see him as a successful ruler. He was now thirty-one and his next son would need to grow up and earn himself a reputation if the Witan was to consider him seriously as a contender. He knew that Cynegils had a

137

daughter, Cyneburga, who was twelve and he had a vague notion of asking for the girl's hand if he could forge an alliance with her father against Mercia.

Of course, this had nothing to do with romantic feelings, unlike Oswiu who was definitely in love with his prospective bride. It was purely political, and it was another reason for his growing jealousy of Oswiu. He sighed. If he continued to think like this he would not only drive himself into depression but probably lose his brother's support as well, something he could not afford to do.

They had only a minute or two to wait until the bride entered on the arm of her father. She was wearing a light blue woollen overdress with short sleeves over her white linen underdress. The neck was trimmed in the fur of an ermine and the cuffs were embroidered with gold and silver wire. Around her neck she wore a gold chain with a cross and, around her waist, a gold embroidered leather belt, worn loosely with the tongue hanging down about a foot or so. As a woman about to be married, she wore a white linen wimple and a circlet of gold to proclaim her royal status. Despite the fact that her long dark hair was hidden, she looked beautiful.

Oswald and Oswiu were dressed more modestly. Both wore light woollen tunics with simple embroidery around the neck, a plain leather belt from which hung a short dagger, woollen trousers tied below the knee with ribbons worn in a criss-cross pattern, plain leather shoes and, in Oswald's case, a circlet of gold around his head. Most of the nobles present were dressed similarly.

In contrast the King of Rheged was dressed as richly as his daughter. His tunic was of crimson linen, embroidered at both neck and cuffs in gold wire, and he wore a bright blue cloak held in place by a large gold and enamel brooch. Contrary to custom, he wore a sword, rather than a small dagger, with a leather scabbard dyed red. The gold circlet on his head was twice the size of Oswald's and it was encrusted with jewels.

'You seem to be marrying a peacock's daughter, brother,' Oswald whispered and Oswiu had difficulty in not laughing.

'In truth, I don't know which is the prettier,' he replied.

The exchange seemed to lighten Oswald's mood and the rest of the proceedings went without too much of a hitch. Of course, there were quite a few instances of drunkenness at the feast that followed but there were few brawls and only one man got seriously wounded.

'How soon can you be ready to leave?' Oswald asked a rather bleary-eyed Eochaid the next morning.

'What? You want to leave so soon? My men and I are just starting to enjoy ourselves.'

It wasn't like Eochaid to be belligerent towards him and he realised that his friend was still drunk.

'I didn't say I wanted to leave now. I asked when you would be ready.'

He too was in a testy mood. He'd had quite enough of watching his brother and his young bride billing and cooing at each other.

'Oh, sorry. I've got a thumping headache and I think I'm going to be sick.'

Oswald sighed. It looked as if it might be a day or two yet.

Four days later the crews of the two birlinns had recovered sufficiently to be able to face the swell of the sea without examining the contents of their stomachs too often. Oswald had asked Alaric, his elderly steersman, to see if he could recruit enough men locally to crew the three pontos and he had gathered enough volunteers to be able to crew twice as many. They were mainly untried youths and old men who wanted to escape their wives for a while and embark on one last adventure.

Oswald didn't imagine that the three smaller boats would be much help if they ran into trouble on the way down past Ireland, the Isle of Man and Cymru, but at least five boats would look too large a naval force for most pirates to tackle. In the event it proved to be a trouble free journey and even the weather was benign. Five days after they had set out they sailed between a large island and the mainland before turning north to enter the wide inlet that led to Hamwic. Oswald was fortunate that Alaric had been here before or otherwise he doubted if they would ever have found the trading port.

The arrival of five fighting ships caused some initial consternation, but fortunately the local thegn had been warned by Cynegils to expect the King of Northumbria. Just as dusk was falling they reached Wintan-ceastre and were welcomed by Cynegils, his rather plain wife, his two sons, Cwichhelm and Cenwalh, and his daughter Cyneburga.

Oswald's heart sank because Cyneburga evidently took after her mother and not her rather handsome father. It was at that moment he decided that, even if he had to marry this girl to cement the alliance, he would keep Keeva as his lover. He couldn't imagine that he'd get much pleasure out of bedding this unattractive infant. It made him even more envious of Oswiu.

~~~

At the feast in his honour that evening Oswald was amused to see that he had been seated between the king

140

and his daughter, rather than his wife – called the Lady of Wessex and not the queen for some reason. She had been placed between Eochaid and the eleven year old Cwichhelm on the other side of the king.

To his surprise he found out that the girl was not only well-educated, but she also had a wicked sense of humour and whispered derogatory remarks to Oswald about most of the nobles seated around them. He decided that he was beginning to like her and started to go out of his way to make her like him too.

Although none of the family had yet been baptised, she told him that she was Bishop Birinus' most diligent student. Cwichhelm wasn't really interested and was becoming a Christian merely to please his father. Cenwalh was too young to really understand what it all meant.

'He really isn't very bright anyway,' she confided to Oswald. 'Mother still treats him like a baby and he behaves like one as a result.'

'And are your parents likely to prove good Christians?' he asked, trying to appear disinterested.

'That's not something you should really ask me,' she replied disapprovingly, 'unless, of course, you intend me to be your wife.'

Oswald was taking a gulp of mead at the time and spluttered, spraying most of it over the table.

'What did you just say?'

'I don't think that there is anything wrong with your hearing, not yet anyway.'

He laughed. 'You're not shy about saying what's on your mind are you? What do you feel about it?'

'I know I won't be allowed to fall in love and marry where I choose; and who would choose a plain girl like me anyway. So I'd rather marry someone I admire and who I think will be my match intellectually; and someone who won't beat me. Father sometimes beats mother when he's drunk you know.'

'No, I have never hit a woman, except in self-defence, of course,' he grinned at her. 'So do I meet your other criteria?'

'Are you fishing for compliments, Cyning? I wouldn't have thought that was in your character.'

'It isn't!' He was beginning to like this young girl more and more. 'I just want to make sure that you would be happy if I asked your father for your hand.'

'I think you know the answer to that. You'd have known by now if I wasn't happy with you.'

'Good. I'll speak to Cynegils in the morning.'

~~~

Oslac watched anxiously as Aidan paced up and down the proposed site for the new monastery. Eventually the new bishop, who would also be the monastery's abbot, returned to where Oslac was waiting with Garrett and Lucan.

'Yes, excellent site. I'm most grateful to your brother, Oslac. It has everything I could desire, including some isolated islets for us to retreat to for days of quiet meditation.'

'Yes, Oswald thought that they would be useful for that. Perhaps he had our brother Offa in mind. He spends weeks at a time in the beehives on Iona.'

'That is an excellent Idea. Perhaps we could induce him to join us here. He could become even more of a hermit on one of the Farne Islands.'

'Yes, it would be good to know that he was so much nearer, and I'm sure our mother would be pleased too. She hasn't seen him since he left for Iona aged twelve.'

142

'Excellent. I need to send a messenger back to Iona in any case. Using the hall we can establish the monastery immediately. I'm sure we can recruit more novices here but I'll need a few monks who are ordained priests and some more to act as Master of the Novices and the other administrative posts.'

'But where will you all live? It will take time to build sufficient huts for the monks, besides you'll need kitchens, storerooms and so on.'

'We'll have to make do with the hall for now.'

'But I thought you'd need that for the church?'

'No, we'll use God's amphitheatre.'

Seeing Oslac look at him still puzzled he explained.

'We'll hold out services in the open for now.'

'But what if it rains, or even snows?'

'Then I'll keep my sermons short,' Aidan said brusquely, bringing the discussion to an end.

Oslac returned to Bebbanburg to send a messenger to Iona. He would have to go via Care Luel and ask Oswiu to arrange for a boat for Iona. He would then bring the volunteers back with him.

'How long will it take?' the impatient Aidan asked him.

'It's September now and no-one in their right mind will sail along the west coast during the stormy season. That normally means from early November to March. That really means you have six weeks at most. It's possible that they will be here this year, but I wouldn't count on it.'

'Very well. We'll leave it in God's capable hands.'

The next day Aidan started his mission to Northumbria by preaching to the islanders of Lindisfarne. He wasn't about to commence his ministry amongst a load of heathens. His first problem was finding somewhere to baptise them. There was no running water on the island. Drinking water came from a

143

number of wells and a cistern in which rainwater was collected. The sea was used for washing both bodies and clothes, though the locals didn't do much of either. In the end he decided that he would either have to immerse them in the sea or fill a font and pour holy water over them from that. After deliberation, he decided on the latter.

Once he'd converted the islanders he began by visiting the vills nearby. Knowing that the king and his family were all Christians he found both people and nobles receptive in the main. By the time that twelve monks arrived, three of them priests, most islanders had become Christians, and had been persuaded to give Aidan a day's free labour once a month for the good of their souls. A simple thorn fence had been constructed around the monastery to keep animals out and work on the timber huts had started. He'd even established a small colony of bees for honey, built a granary to house the wheat and barley he'd been given to see them through the winter and plant crops in the spring, and constructed a dovecote to provide pigeons for the table when it wasn't a day of fasting.

Pleased as Aidan was to see the new monks, he was even more delighted to see who else had arrived with them. Ròidh's wound had healed and he'd recovered enough to accompany the monks instead of waiting until the spring and the return of Oswald.

Garrett was surprised to find that he greeted Ròidh's arrival with mixed feelings. He was now free to return to life as a ship's boy. He couldn't re-join his father's crew as they were down in Wessex but there were other birlinns that patrolled the Northumbrian coast and he was certain he'd be able to join one of them. However, he'd enjoyed serving Aidan and had fallen under the charismatic bishop's spell. He would find parting from him something of a wrench. He finally decided to ask Aidan if he could serve him and Ròidh when they began their journeys all over Northumbria to convert the people. His intention was to do that until he was fourteen and old enough to start his training as a warrior.

Aidan readily agreed. He liked the boy; he was honest, a hard worker and intelligent. He knew how much he wanted to be a warrior; however, he very much doubted that Garrett would leave him when he was fourteen if he stayed now.

~~~

Oswald woke the day after the welcoming feast determined to ask her father for Cyneburga's hand in marriage but his conscience troubled him. He still hadn't found a solution to the problem of Keeva and he wanted to resolve that first. He didn't want to keep her a secret from his new wife; not that it would stay secret for long. The whole of Bebbanburg knew she was Oswald's concubine. He needed to be open about it if possible and he needed to know how Cyneburga would view his current domestic arrangements. The trouble was he couldn't get the girl alone to speak to her in private. It was all very well talking to her quietly at table but, if he asked to speak to her at any other time, her mother would doubtless stay within earshot as chaperone.

He wasn't sure that he could broach the subject at the supper table either, even if he was sitting next to her again. If her reaction was adverse, perhaps vehemently so, she would doubtless draw unwelcome attention to themselves and he would have to explain. He groaned to himself but Eochaid overheard it.

'Is something troubling you, Oswald?'

'Yes, but this time it isn't something you can help with, my friend.'

'You won't know that until you tell me what the problem is, now will you?'

Oswald sighed. 'I want to marry Cyneburga; she's witty and intelligent, despite her youth, and she will make me a good companion. Of course, it will also make Wessex an ally against Mercia. However, I can't honestly say that I find her sexually attractive. Even if I did I don't want to have to give up Keeva.'

'No, she is rather plain isn't she, but she might still be good in bed you know.'

Oswald grimaced. 'It's alright for you. You're happily married to the woman you love.'

'Hmmm, true; even if we aren't together as much as I'd like.'

'I suppose I'm to blame for that. You've been a good friend to me over the years.'

'You thought I was a stuck up prig when we met all those years ago on Iona.'

'Well, you were! But it didn't take me long to peel away the arrogant brat and find the true you underneath.'

'It's a pity you couldn't have had the same effect on my treacherous cur of a nephew.'

'Don't worry. I'm sure that Congal Cláen will meet his downfall soon. He's upset too many people to live a long life.'

'That's what worries me. You know I have no desire to be King of the Ulaidh but I don't think I'll be able to avoid it if Congal dies. As you know, he's only managed to produce one daughter so far and she's still an infant. However, that doesn't solve your little problem.'

'No. Perhaps I should just offer to marry Cyneburga and hope for the best?'

'Perhaps. You won't be the first king to have had both a wife and a concubine.'

'No, I suppose not. But I wouldn't want to upset Cyneburga.'

'You're an enigma, you know. You'd quite happily kill a dozen men on the battlefield, even boys if they're fighting against you, but you're worried about the feelings of a twelve year old girl.'

'That's different. You are fighting for your life and for that of your men on the battlefield.'

'What about those fifteen druids who disappeared on their way back from Yeavering?'

Oswald gave him a sharp look. 'I concede that they were killed on my orders and in cold blood, but it was to prevent an uprising which could have cost a lot of lives. I would rather you didn't mention that ever again.'

Eochaid was surprised by the vehemence with which Oswald said this. He had evidently touched on a raw nerve. Then he became angry.

'We've been close friends for a long time, Oswald, and never once have you spoken to me like that. If you value our friendship don't ever treat me like a naughty boy. I have always spoken my mind to you and you have always appreciated my honesty. I'm not going to start pussy-footing around you now,' he told him coldly.

He stalked out of the room and Oswald realised that he had just compounded his problems. What was wrong with him?

He never had a chance to repair the damage. The following day Eochaid came to him to say that a messenger had arrived from Ulster. King Congal was gravely ill and was asking for him.

'I've sent word to Bebbanburg for my wife and family to travel to Caer Luel. I'll meet them there and travel over to Larne. Naturally, I'll let you know the situation after I get there.'

There was little warmth in Eochaid's words or his demeanour. Oswald went to embrace him but Eochaid turned away and boarded his birlinn.

'Be careful of pirates,' he called after him.

'Only a fool would be at sea this late in the year. I wouldn't be going unless I had to.'

The first of the winter storms had already occurred and there was still a heavy swell, although the wind had died down to a stiff breeze.

'I'll pray for you,' Oswald told him with a smile.

For a second Eochaid smiled in return, then it faded and he gave the order to cast off. It would prove to be the last time Oswald saw his friend.

~~~

To Oswald Whiteblade, the letter from Eochaid to Oswald began, *King of Northumbria, greetings.*

No one regrets the manner of our parting more than I. It seems so petty in retrospect after nearly twenty years of friendship. I said that I would let you know the situation in Ulster. My nephew is slowly recovering but he is still very weak and it's likely to be some time before he'll regain his strength. In the meantime he has asked me to be his war leader, what you Angles would call his hereræswa, and I have agreed.

He is much changed and, although I can never forgive him for betraying my father and causing his death, I am prepared to stay for the sake of my people. I hope that we will be able to work together after he recovers.

The Uí Néill continue to try and encroach on our territory; indeed they seem determined to take over all of Ulster. Domnall Brecc sends us no aid, although officially he is our high king. No doubt he has enough troubles of his own with the warlike Owain of Strathclyde trying to retake Cowal and even Arran. Anything you can do to divert Owain's attention to his border with Rheged and Northumbria would be welcome.

I think you should marry your Wessex princess and tell her that she will have to share you with Keeva. I'm sure she'll understand. You'll be kind to her and look after her, which is a better fate than many royal brides enjoy. I'm told that Penda beats his wife regularly just to remind her that he is her master but, of course, that may just be a tale circulated by his enemies. Heaven knows he has enough of them.

One rumour that I have heard and which might interest you is that he plans to take over the Kingdom of the Middle Angles on his eastern border and place his oaf of a son, Peada, on the throne as his vassal.

Take care my friend and God be with you.
Eochaid.

Oswald felt a great relief that the rift between them seemed to have been healed, but the warning about Penda's plans to expand his kingdom caused him some concern. He decided to go and talk to Cynegils. Not only would the acquisition of Middle Anglia threaten Deira, it would also extend Mercia's border with Wessex. True, there were two buffer territories in the way, the Middle Saxons in the case of

Wessex and Lindsey in the case of Deira, but they were both small and weak. It was likely that Penda planned to take them next.

'Cynegils, good morning. I hope I'm not disturbing you? '

Cynegils was with Bishop Birinus discussing his forthcoming baptism and that of his family.

'Ah, Oswald, it seems we have a little difficulty concerning the ceremony next week. My elder son had just told Birinus that he doesn't believe in Christ and he wishes to remain a pagan. The boy had ever been a concern to me. I'm sure Œthelwald doesn't give you the problems that Cewalh gives me.'

Oswald smiled grimly and waited until the bishop had made his excuses and left them before replying.

'I wish that were true. Œthelwald is ambitious and resents the fact that I don't give him enough responsibility. I have good reason not to. He is a poor leader of men and has little military skill.'

'Do you not wish him to succeed you?'

Oswald wasn't about to answer that question. If he fell in battle he'd want Oswiu to follow him, but that wasn't something he'd want known. It would make his son hate Oswiu even more than he did now.

'It's not my choice; it'll be up to the Witan. On a more important matter, I have just had a warning that Penda is planning to absorb Middle Anglia into Mercia and make Peada its sub-king.'

'Really? How certain are you of this information?'

'It's only a rumour, but it seems fairly widespread in Ireland.'

Cynegils was puzzled. 'Why Ireland? If we haven't heard of it here?'

'Because Penda has been recruiting men there, and in Cymru.'

'Ah, I see. Then that would seem to confirm that he is preparing for war again. What will you do?'

'I'll move into Lindsey whilst he is busy consolidating his position in Middle Anglia.'

'Hmm, won't that provoke him into war with you?'

'Not if you threaten him from the south and I invade Lindsey in force. He lost a lot of his best warriors at Heavenfield, which is why he's recruiting Irish and Welsh ones to replace them, but they are ill-disciplined and poorly armed. He's not ready to go to war with us yet.'

'I hope you're right.'

~~~

Oswald licked his lips nervously. Apart from the noticeable absence of Cewalh, the baptism had gone well and Birinus was making progress with the conversion of the nobility. He seemed to feel, as Paulinus had done in Northumbria, that the common people would follow the lead set by their betters. Oswald was not so sure. Aidan was, he knew, convinced that you needed to convert the country vill by vill, nobles and the people together.

But he had other matters on his mind today. He was about to marry Cyneburga and he still hadn't told her about Keeva. He was ready to do so but they hadn't been alone together since their marriage had been agreed.

He took a deep breath and walked over towards the new stone built church in Wintan-ceastre. The snow crunched under foot as he walked, accompanied by his steersman and the three shipmasters from the pontos. The sky overhead was now blue but there were clouds of steel grey moving in from the west and he fully expected it to be snowing again by the time the ceremony was over. At least the frozen ground, after last night's hard frost, was preferable to the normal mixture of mud, faeces and rubbish that one had to wade through to get from one place in the town to another.

Bishop Birinus conducted the brief wedding service and then celebrated the Roman mass. It was not something that Oswald was comfortable with as it was quite different to the Celtic Church's. However, the interminable sermon was depressingly similar. He was aware that his new wife kept giving him sidelong glances throughout the prayers that followed. He couldn't work out whether she was flirting with him or was just anxious about how he'd treat her. Oswald began to wish he could get up off his knees as they were beginning to ache after long contact with the stone paving. At least in the Celtic Church prayers were said standing up.

As he had expected, it was snowing hard as they left the church and an extra inch or so had fallen. This had been trodden into slush by the feet of the hundreds of well-wishers who had come to gawp at the happy couple, so he was glad that there were two horses waiting to convey them back to the king's hall for the feast that was to follow.

'Thank goodness that's over,' Cyneburga whispered to him once they were seated together next to Cynegils at the high table. 'I thought that Birinus was never going to shut up.'

Oswald had to stifle a laugh. Perhaps marriage to Cyneburga would be enjoyable after all.

After they had been conducted to their bedchamber by a crowd of drunken men and giggling women, they lay naked beside each other. She had become very quiet and nervous and he was equally reticent. He kept thinking of the last time had made love to Keeva and he had absolutely no desire to do the same to this plain virgin with hardly any breasts as yet.

'Has your mother explained what happens now?' he asked after the silence between them had become uncomfortably long.

'Yes,' she whispered back. 'Please be gentle with me.'

He smiled and was about to reassure her that he would be but then realised that the time had come to be honest with her.

'I have something to tell you. I should have said something earlier, but there was never the right opportunity. You needn't worry about me having sex with you yet; you're too young.'

Before he could continue she sat up in bed and turned to him in agitation.

'But you're a man. My mother told me that you need regular sexual release.'

'Sexual release?' He laughed at the quaint phrase. 'I'm sorry, I shouldn't have laughed. It was just the way you phrased it. I hadn't heard it called that before.'

Her face had crumpled when she thought he was laughing at her but now she grinned at him.

'Well, it's what she called it.'

'I'm sure she did. But you don't need to worry about my brutish masculine needs.'

'But I do, I want to be a good wife to you.'

'And you will be. I like you a lot, I admire your wit and your knowledge and I enjoy your company. I'm just not ready to have sex with you.'

'Oh, but isn't that a wife's first duty? Don't you want children?'

153

'I already have one son and, harsh as it may sound, I would rather not have had him. Œthelwald has few admirable qualities and he's inordinately jealous of his uncle, Oswiu, who has all the flair and personality that my son lacks.'

'Oh! But our children may be more like your brother than your son.'

'True, but I still think you are too young for me to ravage you just yet.'

She giggled when he said ravage but they grew serious again when she saw how sombre he now looked.

'Besides,' he sighed, 'I already have someone who I love and who provides me with all the sexual release, as your mother calls it, that I need.'

'Oh, you mean you have a paramour?'

'A paramour? Where did you hear a word like that?'

'It's what my mother calls my father's lover. He is very discreet about her, of course, but he spends most nights with her. Mother says that it's a great relief.'

Oswald was reminded how young she was. All her education about sex between men and women seemed to have come from her mother, who Oswald thought of a something of a prude.

'Then do you mind that I too have a lover?'

'No, not in the least if it means I don't have to put up with you humping me every night. To be honest, I've been dreading it. The thought of submitting to a man's lust made me want to become a nun at first, but then I met you and I thought that sex might not be too bad with you. I'm pleased you don't want to yet, but does that mean that you will never make love to me?'

'No, but not until you are a woman. I mean until your body has finished developing.' He paused. 'So you wouldn't mind me visiting Keeva at night?'

'Keeva? Is that he name? Will I like her?'

'You'd want to meet her?'

'Of course. We have you in common and, if I like her, we may become good friends.'

Oswald started to laugh and Cyneburga looked at him as if he was mad.

'What's so funny?'

'You are, you're priceless. I was so concerned about your reaction to my relationship with Keeva and here you are telling me you want to make a friend of her.'

'Only if I like her; and stop laughing.'

He didn't and she started to giggle. On the other side of the door her mother, who was trying to hear what was happening couldn't make anything out until the sounds of merriment reached her ears.

'Well,' she said to herself. 'That's not how I remember my wedding night. All I remember is pain and indignity.' She walked away feeling jealous of her daughter.

~~~

Jarlath was equally worried about his marriage to Fianna. At first the girl had been heart-broken when Oswiu told her that their relationship was over. Unlike his brother, he had no wish to keep both a wife and a mistress. His conscience wouldn't have allowed it. Furthermore, he knew that if Rhieinmelth failed to conceive reasonably quickly, the fact that Fianna had already presented him with a son would have been a reproach to her.

155

It was Keeva that came up with the solution. She let sufficient time pass so that Fianna had moved on from grief over Oswiu to concern about the future, then she went to see her.

'What will you do now?'

'I don't know. Oswiu said he would provide for me somehow but he has gone off to marry his bloody princess without doing anything. How could he do that?'

'Perhaps he means to do something when he gets back.'

'Huh! He won't want me around like a ghost at the feast.'

For a moment her eyes flashed and Keeva realised that the fiery little spitfire that Oswiu had found on Bute was still there under the surface.

'Perhaps if you resolved your own future it might make him regret not helping you himself?'

'You think so? Perhaps; but how do I do that? Who'd take in Oswiu's cast-off and his bastard?'

'Well, my brother is still unmarried and he was only saying the other day that it was time he settled down and found a woman to look after him. I think he's beginning to find all the lads in the warrior's hall a little infantile.'

'Jarlath?' Fianna said in surprise. 'I hadn't thought of him. He's a good looking lad and he's a member of the king's gesith. But would he have me?'

'I don't know but I can ask him. Of course he's in Wessex with the king at the moment but I can write to him and ask. He knows you well, after all.'

'Yes, would you? You are a true friend Keeva.'

Now Jarlath was back, as were Oswald and his new wife and Oswiu with his. As it was early April, everyone was getting ready for the move to Yeavering. Keeva had told Oswiu that Fianna was now engaged to her brother and, such

156

was his relief, he had rewarded her with a new necklace that he had intended to give to Rhieinmelth. She was pleased, but not as delighted as she was when, much to her surprise, she was introduced to Cynaburga and was told by her that she wanted her to be one of the women who looked after her.

'It's alright,' the girl told her. 'You can carry on having sex with Oswald so I don't have to.'

She couldn't make up her mind whether the young queen was incredibly naïve or was just teasing her. Either way, if it meant that Oswald could keep her as his lover she didn't mind.

Jarlath made his way over to the new church that had just been built at Yeavering and saw a radiant Fianna coming to meet him. She was attended by her five year old son and Keeva. For the first time he saw that her head was encased in cloth, hiding her abundant brown hair, framing her face. It made her look even prettier than she did with her hair unbound as it enhanced her oval face, small button nose and full lips. As she joined him at the altar, her pale blue eyes glanced at him briefly before she lowered them demurely. A second later she looked up again and brazenly made eyes at him before grinning. Whatever the future held for him, Jarlath had a feeling it wouldn't be boring.

CHAPTER SEVEN – THE RISE AND FALL OF KINGDOMS

637 AD

Eochaid sat on his horse beside Congal Claen. Since Congal had recovered his strength in the latter half of the previous year Eochaid had found his nephew more and more difficult to deal with. He was capricious, illogical and prevaricated over every decision. It was a wonder that he had stayed on his throne as long as he had if he was like this before his illness.

Eochaid had roundly defeated the northern branch of the enemy clan and for the moment they had retired to western Ulster to lick their wounds. Instead of consolidating his position in the north of Ireland, Congal had foolishly decided to invade the Kingdom of Meath and confront the High King of Ireland, Dòmhnall mac Áedo, a member of the southern branch of the Uí Néill. There was nothing Eochaid could say to dissuade him.

They had swept into Meath and had nearly reached Tara, the traditional seat of the high kings, before Dòmhnall had mustered sufficient forces to oppose them. Congal had taken fright and had withdrawn until his army was joined by five hundred warriors led by Domnall Brecc, the King of Dalriada and Congal's overlord. They found what both Congal and Domnall Brecc considered a suitable defensive position in the very south of Ulster near a settlement called Moira. They placed their right flank to the east of the boggy ground around Lough Neagh, a large lake, and the left was protected by the extensive woods to the west of Moira.

What neither king had appreciated was the number of cavalry that Dòmhnall mac Áedo had included in his army. Battles were fought on foot; horsemen were only used in the pursuit of a routed foe. However, the high king didn't play by the rules.

Congal had managed to muster four hundred men but, apart from his own bodyguard and a few chieftains, they wore little protection and were poorly armed. Furthermore, they were ill-disciplined. Eochaid had his battle-hardened warriors, many of whom had been with him for years. They were the crew from his birlinn and numbered around fifty. Domnall Brecc's Dalriadans were better armed and disciplined than the Ulstermen, but that wasn't saying much. They were a mixture of trained warriors who at least had a helmet of some sort, a leather jerkin or a byrnie – often much patched – and sword and shield. Some had a seax as well and others carried a spear or an axe. Of the total host of nearly a thousand, just over a hundred were archers.

The army of the high king was as numerous but, in addition to those on foot, Dòmhnall had two hundred horsemen. Eochaid was worried about these and advised the two kings to dig concealed pits in front of their position, but both assured him that they had nothing to fear from the horsemen; they would doubtless dismount and fight on foot as usual.

'Besides,' Congal pointed out, 'very few of the Uí Néill have any armour. Our archers will slaughter them before they get anywhere near us.'

'I hope you're right, nephew.'

There was nothing Eochaid could do but he made sure that his men knew that, even if the rest were routed, they would fight a rear guard action to delay the pursuit for as long as possible.

The battle started when the Uí Néill and their allies moved forwards. For August the day was far from seasonal; it was dull and cold and Eochaid shivered despite his thick padded linen tunic under his byrnie. Sixty yards from the Ulaidh and the other Dalriadans they halted and their archers ran forward. There were only about a hundred of them but suddenly boys appeared from behind the ranks of spearmen with slingshots. Whilst the archers shot their arrows at high trajectory to make the waiting warriors raise their shields, the boys sent pebble after pebble at them, hitting their unprotected bodies. Those wearing armour and helmets escaped largely unscathed - though a few stones broke arms and legs - but the unarmoured majority suffered much worse. Many were incapacitated and quite a few were killed. This enraged them and the whole line was about to charge their tormentors when a roar from Eochaid stopped them.

Ignoring the two kings, who didn't seem to know what to do, Eochaid ordered their archers forward. They concentrated on the slingers, most of whom wore little more than a ragged woollen tunic, and forty or more boys were killed or wounded by the first volley. The rest went to sling another load of pebbles at the enemy archers but the second volley hit them first. Only about thirty boys were left and they rapidly fled, dismayed by the massacre of their fellows. The Ulaidh archers now concentrated on their counterparts on the opposing side. The latter had stupidly continued to send high trajectory volleys at the enemy foot, who could now use their uplifted shields to protect themselves. The first volley from the Ulaidh hit a third of them and they became aware of the danger. Firing one last

160

volley at the opposing archers, they retreated behind the lines of their infantry.

It was only then that Eochaid noticed that the mounted contingent of the Uí Néill had moved over to the left flank where Congal was in command. Either his nephew didn't know what to do or he didn't think they posed a threat. However, they moved into a wedge formation with the point aimed at the extreme left of the line. When they charged they rolled that flank up as more and more of them got between the warriors and the trees.

Congal had grabbed a spear from one of the young warriors standing near him and had tried to spear the horseman charging directly at him. He'd have done better to have stabbed the horse in its chest. The man riding it pulled savagely on his reins and the horse tuned so that he could take Congal's thrust on his shield. Then, sawing on the reins to move his mount the other way, he chopped down at the Ulaidh king, striking him a heavy blow on his shoulder.

The links of his chain mail byrnie parted but the padded leather jerkin he wore underneath prevented the blade from cutting into him. However, it did break his collar bone. He dropped his sword to clutch at his shoulder, letting go of his shield in the process. The horseman grinned ferociously and swung his sword at his neck. Blunted as it was by cutting through the links of chain mail, it was more of a metal bar than a sharp blade. However, the blow to Congal's neck was sufficient to break it and he dropped to the ground unable to move. The damage to his spinal cord was such that, had he survived, he would have been paralysed from the neck down. Although his body guard now clustered around him, it was too late. They were cut down or impaled one by one until one of the mounted spearmen was able to thrust the point of his spear into Congal's eye socket and thence into his brain.

As soon as the cry went up that Congal had fallen, Domnall Brecc and Eochaid knew that the battle was lost. Domnall and his men fled back to Larne as quickly as possible where their fleet of birlinns, currachs, merchant ships and fishing boats waited. He had rounded up every means of sea transport he could find to convey his five hundred men over to Ulster. However, it didn't look as he would need all of them to carry the survivors home.

In contrast, Eochaid did what he had planned and conducted a fighting withdrawal. Much to his surprise, most of the victorious Uí Néill left him alone. Many were engaged in looting the dead on the battlefield and the rest found it less hazardous to chase down the routed Ulaidh and Dalriadans instead of tackling the well-armed and disciplined warriors with Eochaid. Much to his surprise he reached the fortified town of Larne three days later having lost no more than eight men. A few more were wounded, but none too seriously.

He immediately set about the defence of the place whilst Domnall Brecc left him to it, setting sail back across the sea to Dalriada. Unfortunately for him the high king had anticipated this and a small flotilla of birlinns and currachs full of his warriors were waiting for them. The crews of the fighting ships were Irish pirates that called no king master, but Dòmhnall mac Áedo had paid them well to ambush the Dalriadans. Scarcely two hundred of Domnall Brecc's original army of five hundred made it back home again. Not only had he been severely weakened militarily, which left him exposed to attack from Strathclyde, but the reign of the kings of Dalriada over the Ulaidh in Ulster was also at an end.

~~~

To Oswald, King of Northumbria, greetings from Eochaid, King of the Ulaidh,

Oswald sat up with a start when he read the opening line of the latest letter from his friend. He had heard that the headstrong Congal had decided to invade the southern Uí Néill lands but word of the decisive Battle of Moira hadn't yet reached Yeavering.

'What is it, my love? You look surprised,' Cyneburga said as she joined him.

Keeva had walked over with her and went to sit on his other side. The two had liked each other from the start and they, with Oswald, now formed an unconventional trio. In all respects except one the girl from Wessex was his wife and Queen of Northumbria. Oswald had yet to have sex with her, though he slept with her often enough. However, he spent more time in Keeva's bed than Cyneburga's and their relationship was anything but platonic. They were discreet about it and, as Keeva was the queen's constant companion, the situation now caused little gossip. Only Acha openly disapproved. Even Bishop Aidan seemed to have accepted it.

'I've had a letter from Eochaid.'

'What does it say?' Cyneburga asked.

She took a keen interest in what was happening in the world; Keeva was only interested in domestic matters.

'I don't know yet,' he laughed. 'You haven't given me a chance to read it; but the opening line is interesting. It seems that he is now king of the Ulaidh.'

He decided to read it aloud to both of them and even Keeva started to take an interest.

First of all I have to tell you that my nephew is dead. His decision to attack Dòmhnall mac Áedo did not end well. We

163

were defeated at a place called Moira and Congal was killed. If it wasn't for the discipline of my warriors I suspect that I too would now be dead. As it was, we reached Largs safely and we were besieged by the Uí Néill. Domnall Brecc managed to escape but the rumour is that his fleet was attacked on the way back to Dalriada and it is said that he lost over half his army. However, I cannot vouch for the accuracy of these reports. I do know that he lost a lot of men during the battle and afterwards during the pursuit. I suspect that Dalriada has been severely weakened and there must be a danger that Owain of Strathclyde will seek to take advantage of this.

You may be surprised to see that I am now King of the Ulaidh having always said that I had no desire to occupy this, or any other, throne. However, the elders implored me to accept the crown. There is Congal's son, of course, but he is too young and is the son of an unpopular father whereas everyone regards my father's reign as something of a golden era. I felt that I had to accept in order to try and save my clan.

I have decided to try and negotiate a truce with the High King. I hope that by acknowledging him as my overlord I can save the Ulaidh without having to give up too much territory. However, and this is my primary reason for writing, it would strengthen my hand if you could threaten Dòmhnall mac Áedo by giving me your support. I'm not asking you to send me any warriors, just the threat of doing so will give him a reason for agreeing to a reasonable compromise.

I hope that you will be able to help in this way, much as I regret having to ask you.

Your friend always,

Eochaid

'What will you do?'

'I'll do better than threaten Dòmhnall, I shall send Oswiu to go and speak to him. It sounds as if my brother will need to go back to Dalriada to see what is happening there too. If the weakness of Dalriada means that Owain is more powerful by comparison, then both of Strathclyde's neighbours are threatened. He will need to see to the defence of Rheged.'

'If you're sending Oswiu to the west, what will you be doing?' his wife asked, knowing that he would go himself if there wasn't something more important.

'I need to forestall Penda by moving into Lindsey before he does.'

~~~

It was the middle of September before Oswiu reached Larne. He had decided to travel in peace but to prepare for war and so he took three birlinns from Bernicia and linked up with two more from Caer Luel in addition to the three pontos Eochaid had captured from Strathclyde the previous year. In all he had just over three hundred warriors and, although they might not be enough to attack the army besieging Larne on their own, they would be a serious threat when combined to the Ulaidh.

Before he arrived he had sent a fishing boat to reconnoitre Larne from the sea, so he knew that the high king had no more than five hundred men in the besieging force. This wasn't too surprising as many of those who had fought at Moira would have gone home to get the harvest in, or had sufficient plunder not to want to stay for the sack of Larne.

The arrival of his fleet at the entrance to Larne Lough had caused a certain amount of consternation amongst the besiegers. They had a birlinn and four small currachs trying to blockade the port – rather ineffectually if Eochaid's ability to send a message to Oswald was anything to go by – but they disappeared further into the lough as soon as Oswiu's ships appeared. Oswiu sailed into the harbour without any problems and disembarked his men. An hour later he and Eochaid rode out of the main gate accompanied by Oswiu's gesith and three of Eochaid's chieftains. They halted a hundred yards from the gate and waited for someone to come and talk to them. When no-one appeared after a reasonable amount of time, Oswiu rode nearer to the enemy camp and bellowed loud enough for his words to carry at least as far as the high king's tent.

'Dòmhnall mac Áedo, this is Oswiu, Prince of Rheged and Hereræswa of Northumbria. Stop skulking in your tent and come and talk to me and my friend King Eochaid of the Ulaidh. If you are too cowardly to come and face us I and my hundreds of doughty Northumbrian warriors will come and drag you out. Now act like a man instead of a shy girl and come out and face me.'

Oswiu was well aware that calling a man a coward and a girl was a great insult and, as all his men had heard it, not something that the high king could ignore and keep his throne. He appeared a few minutes later leading a glittering array of petty kings, their banner bearers and about thirty horsemen as escort.

'What are you doing sticking your nose in where it doesn't belong, Oswiu. Go back to Rheged or whatever rock you crawled from under or I will send your head back to your brother in a box.'

166

'Brave talk for a man too scared to come to a parley unless it's with twice as many men to protect him as we have. Send half of them back now; you know the rules for negotiations. Each side must have the same numbers.'

'But your men are heavily armoured and well-armed; mine aren't.'

'Well, hopefully we won't need their services. Send everybody back two hundred paces except you and your closest advisers and I will do the same.'

Dòmhnall nodded and waited until everyone except five of his chieftains had reluctantly withdrawn. Oswiu and Eochaid did the same. Of course, as the opposing side were all mounted, they had a distinct advantage over Oswiu's gesith, who were all on foot, but he decided it wasn't worth making an issue of.

'Now, happy?' Dòmhnall asked. 'Has your Ulaidh companion lost his voice or is he allowed to speak? After all, he is my vassal and you have no business being here.'

'I'm here at Eochaid's request, and that of my brother. Now that you have finally had the sense to negotiate properly I'll hand over to King Eochaid.'

'What is it you want, Dòmhnall? If you want me to agree that my nephew was a fool and should never have attacked you, I'll agree. But he's dead and his stupidity is a thing of the past. We need to move on. I'm sure you have more pressing matters that require your attention down south; I know I have a great deal to do here in Ulster.'

'What? You expect me to forget and forgive just because Congal Claen is dead? I need a great deal more from you than an apology. This war has cost me a great deal of money for a start.'

'And it's likely to cost you a lot more, both in terms of money and men, if you prolong it further.'

167

'My men will be happy with the plunder they'll gain when they sack Larne; I won't need to pay them as well,' Dòmhnall sneered.

'Don't be stupid,' Oswiu cut in. 'You will never take Larne now. Eochaid and I won't have to do anything. Now the town has been reinforced, your men will know there is no chance of you taking the place and will start to drift away. In two weeks you won't have enough men left here to even withstand my gesith.'

Eochaid gave him an annoyed look for interrupting but waited for Dòmhnall's answer, however the latter seemed lost in thought.

'Very well. I'll agree a treaty with you, Eochaid, but under several conditions. Your friend here takes his men and goes back where they came from, you do me homage as your high king, pay me one thousand pounds of silver now and two hundred every year from now on and give up the territory disputed between you and my clan in the west of Ulster.'

Eochaid was surprised at how easily Dòmhnall had acceded to his request for a truce, but he supposed that he needed to conclude business in the north and return to Tara before someone else decided to make a bid for the throne. He smiled and made his counter-bid.

'Oswiu will withdraw when you do, I acknowledge you as high king, I'll pay you two hundred pounds of silver now and fifty every year from next year but I won't give up any territory.'

Dòmhnall was about to reply when one of his chieftains moved his horse alongside the high king's and whispered in his ear. He nodded and turned back to Eochaid.

'How old is your son Lethlobar now?'

Eochaid had been expecting Dòmhnall to demand hostages against his future good behaviour and, in truth, he was surprised that the man hadn't mentioned his son before.

'He's nine, why?'

'I'll cut the tribute to five hundred pounds of silver now and one hundred from next year but you'll surrender Lethlobar to me as a hostage. If you break faith with me he dies.'

'If I'm to give up my only son I want to be sure that he is well treated. I also need to be sure you'll keep faith with me. You have five sons, surrender Óengus, your eldest to me in return.'

The other man shook his head.

'No, not Óengus. He's already training to be a warrior. My second son, Fergus Fanát, is the same age as Lethlobar. I suggest that you bring him up for the next five years and I will do the same for your son. When they reach the age of fourteen they will be returned so that they can start their warrior training.'

It was a fair offer and it would be good experience for Lethlobar. However, his wife would probably never forgive him. Although they had three daughters, they had only had one son and she doted on him.

'So be it, but five hundred pounds of silver is more than I can afford. Three hundred pounds now and seventy thereafter.'

'Very well. Meet me here with your son and the silver at Noon tomorrow and I'll have my scribe draw up the treaty now. You can kneel and pay me homage then.'

Eochaid watched him ride back to his camp before turning to Oswiu.

'Thank you, my friend. That was easier than I was expecting.'

169

'There is one thing you seem to have forgotten though. If you acknowledge him as your overlord you'll be breaking faith with Domnall Brecc as you are a sub-king of Dalriada.'

'I know and I regret that, but the sea between us has grown ever wider. We and the Caledonian Dalriadans are all Scotii but that's all in the past now. Ulster is geographically part of Ireland, not Caledonia, and it's time we accepted the political reality of that fact.'

'I see. It's your decision, of course.'

'I'm sorry you don't approve, Oswiu, but I don't have a choice. Domnall Brecc is in no position to support me if I fight on and, to be honest, I suspect he might welcome the break; then he can concentrate on the situation in Caledonia. I'll write to him and explain if you'd be good enough to take my letter with you when you go.'

'Of course. Will you also write to Oswald?'

'Yes, my biggest regret is that he and I are unlike to meet again now. I need to consolidate my position here and I know Oswald faces continuing conflict with Mercia. It's the penalty we pay for being kings I suppose; we are no longer our own masters.'

~~~

Domnall was at Dun Add when Oswiu arrived there. He greeted his former subject warmly and congratulated him on being the heir to Rheged. However his good mood didn't last long and he read Eochaid's letter with a growing scowl.

'Thank you for bringing this, Oswiu. You obviously know the contents. Would you mind leaving me alone for a while? I need to think about this. Someone will show you to a guest hut.'

170

'Thank you, Cyning, but I'll sleep with my men in their camp down by the loch.'

Domnall nodded absently and then asked Oswiu to come and see him again in the morning.

When Oswiu awoke the next day he looked out of his tent to see a grey fog covering the land and the loch but, by the time that he had gone for a swim in the sea and then washed the salt from his body, the grey haze was starting to lift. He went and ate a bowl of gruel with some of his gesith and then made his way up to the fortress as the sun started to burn off the rest of the mist.

Domnall seemed to be in a better mood too. This time his two sons, Domangart and Cathasach, stood by his side and three of his nobles had joined him. One of them, Fergus, King of Islay and the Isles, Oswiu recognised and they nodded at one another. The two boys were twelve and eight respectively and initially Oswiu ignored them. Then he became aware that the older boy was glaring at him. He found it slightly unnerving but told himself that he was being stupid; why on earth would a young boy hate him and what did it matter anyway.

'Ah, Oswiu, I'm glad you could join us.' Domangart snorted in derision, earning himself a sharp look form his father.

'I don't know why you want to associate with a traitor, father,' the boy stated, drawing gasps from the others in the hall at his impudence.

Oswiu was furious. 'What do you mean 'traitor', boy. You're lucky you're so young; men have died for less.'

'Domangart! Be quiet! You're here as an observer to learn what happens in the small council, nothing more.'

'No, Domnall, let the boy speak. He must have a reason to say what he did.' Oswiu's eyes narrowed as he scrutinised the lad. 'But it had better be a good one because, if it isn't, I expect your father to have you flogged.'

The threat didn't seem to impress Domangart.

'My father has never laid a hand on me, and isn't going to on the say so of someone who deserted us when we needed him.'

'It seems to me that, if he hasn't yet beaten you, then he should have done so long before this.'

As the atmosphere deteriorated men started to finger the hilts of their swords. The fact that he was on his own didn't seem to bother Oswiu in the slightest.

'Stop this! At once!' the king's voice cut through the air and his men took a step back.

'Domangart, leave us!'

'A moment please, Cyning. I would be grateful if your son could explain what he is accusing me of first.'

His voice was calm and even but the way that the words were spoken managed to convey the anger that Oswiu was feeling more so than yelling would have done.

'Well, my son? Answer the prince.'

'If he and his brother had stayed here, as they were sworn to do, then we wouldn't have been routed at Moira, we wouldn't have lost three hundred of your best warriors and a quarter of the kingdom to boot. Now, because these two went off to seek glory elsewhere, instead of doing their duty here, we are threatened by the pagan Owain of Strathclyde and by the Picts. We have already lost Skye. It's all his and his brother's fault.'

'You make it sound as if Oswald and Oswiu are better leaders in battle than your father,' Domnall said with some bitterness.

'It's just what all your warriors are saying, father.'

172

'Come here, Domangart,' Oswiu told him, beckoning him with his finger.

The boy's own anger had dissipated when he saw how badly his words had affected his father and he walked towards the Northumbrian with downcast eyes. Oswiu put one hand on his shoulder and lifted his chin with his other hand so they he and Domangart were looking each other in the eye.

'Then your father's warriors don't know what they're talking about. Yes, I know that the battle was lost but it wasn't the first time that Congal Claen had caused his own side to be routed. Oswald and I were at a previous battle when Congal turned his coat and killed his own grandfather. We lost that day too and there was nothing that Oswald or I could have done about it. The defeat wasn't our fault, no more than the debacle at Moira was your father's. As for deserting him, we left with your father's blessing and now, because Rheged threatens Strathclyde from the south and Bernicia from the east, your father can concentrate on defeating the Picts instead of having enemies all around him. Do you understand?'

Domangart nodded and mumbled 'sorry.'

'Good, now you've apologised perhaps we can forget about that flogging.'

The boy wasn't entirely certain whether Oswiu was merely jesting.

'I'm not so sure I'm as willing to forgive you as Prince Oswiu apparently is, Domangart,' his father told him. 'You need to acquire some manners and a little discretion, as well as learning not to listen to gossip.'

He turned back to Oswiu, inviting him to sit, along with his councillors. A chastened Domangart resumed his place behind his father and exchanged a sheepish look with

Cathesach, mouthing sorry at him. The younger boy stared at him for a moment, then ignored him.

'Your son mentioned the fact that Picts have recovered the Isle of Skye,' Oswiu stated flatly.

'Yes, it's no great loss -'

'Maybe not to you, Domnall, but it is to me,' Fergus interrupted. 'It was part of my kingdom after all.'

'What I meant, as you well know, is that Skye provided us with very few good quality warriors, and that is what we need right now. Of more concern is the encroachment of the Picts into Glen Dochart. Of course, this threatens Strathclyde to the south as much as it does Dalriada to the west, but it is a concern. Whilst the Picts were a loose confederation of seven different kingdoms with no one overlord they weren't much of a menace to us, but now they seem to have united under the rule of Bruide, the son of Uuid, things have changed. I don't need to tell you that the western end of Glen Dochart is only fifteen miles from the head of Loch Fyne.'

Oswiu sucked his teeth. If the Picts reached that far they would threaten the whole of Eastern Dalriada. Of course, Domnall was right; they could just as easily move into northern Strathclyde instead.

'What do you propose to do?'

'I don't think they'll do anything further this year. They'll want to consolidate the gains that they've made. I'm expecting them to make a move next spring; by then we'll be ready for them. I want to muster as many warriors as I can in Glen Aray between the head of Loch Fyne and Loch Awe. I'm hoping that you might be able to support me Oswiu?'

'I will if I can but I'm my brother's hereræswa. I have to go where he wants me and, at the moment, his priorities are to prevent the expansion of Mercia and to re-capture Dùn

174

Èideann. This will bring the remainder of the Gododdin territory back under Northumbrian control.'

'I see. Well, I'll pray that he can spare you and your warriors.'

The council proceeded to discuss various plans for dealing with whatever the Picts decided to do and calculating who could supply how many warriors, in which Oswiu only had a passing interest and he began to wonder where Oswald was now. He was jolted back to the present when the council came to an end. He too got up to leave, but Domnall Brecc asked him to stay.

'I'm grateful to you for the way that you handled my unruly son, Oswiu. He seems to respect you now.' He hesitated before continuing. 'I wondered whether you would consider taking him with you and training him as a warrior with your Northumbrian boys?'

To say that Oswiu was flabbergasted would be an understatement. The boy had been deriding him and accusing him of treachery not two hours ago and now Domnall wanted him to take the insolent puppy with him and train him. It beggared belief.

'Why, Domnall? What's wrong with training him here? After all, Dalriada didn't too bad a job of teaching me and Oswald how to fight.'

The king shuffled his feet uncomfortably. Plainly he didn't want to explain why. In the end he decided to be honest.

'It's his mother. She dotes on her first born and she indulges him. I'm afraid he's growing up to be a spoilt brat. You saw an example of what he can be like earlier.'

'Yes, indeed. That explains a lot. Very well, I'll take him with me when I go. I don't envy you having to tell his mother though.'

~~~

Oswald looked around the hall in Eoforwīc. He was pleased that the great majority of eorls and thegns from Bernicia, Elmet and Deira had answered his summons to the war council.

'Thank you for coming. Those who have failed to answer the summons will be called upon to answer for their failure to appear, I can assure you. Now, as most of you know, Penda and his Mercians have overrun Middle Anglia and he had put his son, Peada, on the throne as sub-king.'

Evidently most of them certainly didn't know and uproar followed his announcement. Oswald waited for the hubbub to die down, then held up his hand for quiet.

'What do we need to do to combat the menace of Mercian expansion?' He waited in the tense silence for a moment or two before continuing. 'I believe that Penda intends to invade Lindsey next which would give him access to the German Ocean. That means he can threaten our coastline from the River Humber all the way to the Firth of Forth. I intend to pre-empt him by occupying Lindsey first.'

'What about King Caedbaed? Will you depose him and kill him and his family?' One of the thegns asked.

'No, provided he acknowledges me as his overlord, he can keep his throne as a sub-king. We will however leave one of my gesith as his hereræswa and be leaving a small garrison to train his young warriors to fight as we do, in armour and with sword and shield.'

'Who will you take with you, Cyning?' another asked.

'I don't need too large a force but it needs to be strong enough to dissuade Penda from trying to oppose us. I'll take the warband from Elmet and Deira; seven hundred men should be enough for that.'

Oswald crossed the Humber at Goole, near the border between Middle Anglia and Elmet. Once over the river he was in Lindsey and he advanced towards the king's hall at Wrawby. This involved crossing another river – the Trent – and this time the far bank was occupied by Caedbaed's warriors.

'I have no intention of forcing a crossing, I would lose men needlessly and alienate the people I want on my side against the Mercians,' he told Hrothga, Eorl of Eoforwīc and commander of the contingent from Deira, when he asked him how he intended to attack.

'I want you to find me another crossing place, then we'll send a few hundred men to take up a position behind them and cut off their retreat. When they realise they're trapped I'll give them a choice between dying and joining my army.'

By noon the next day Oswald was across the Trent and marching on towards Wrawby, his ranks swelled by another two hundred. They stood out from the rest of the army though. Whereas Oswald's men were armed with at least a sword and shield and wore body protection of some sort, the men of Lindsey wore just a tunic and in the main carried a spear or an axe. There were a few men armed with a hunting bow and some carried a shield, but they were all poorly equipped and ill-disciplined compared to Oswald's warriors.

King Caedbaed met him before he reached Wrawby. Dunstan, his horse marshal, had been scouting ahead with a small patrol when he saw a group of horsemen approaching along the Wrawby road.

'Can you describe them to me?'

'They were about twenty strong and led by an old man. Another man in his late twenties or early thirties rode by his side. Both were well dressed but weren't equipped for war. The rest looked like those we encountered at the ford over the Trent, except they were all mounted. A few had helmets and all carried a spear and a small round shield. Oh, and they all wore blue tunics.'

'I imagine that it is probably Caedbaed and his son, Bubba. The rest are presumably his gesith. We'll wait for them here.'

When the King of Lindsey and his party appeared, Oswald rode forward accompanied by Dunstan, Hrotha and Hengist, the new leader of his Gesith. Caedbaed halted his group and, calling for his son and two of his escort, he moved forward a little and then waited for Oswald to reach him.

'Why are you invading my kingdom, Oswald?' Caedbaed began without preamble.

'I'm not here as an invader, Caedbaed. I'm here to protect you from Penda and his Mercians. You've presumably heard that they've invaded Middle Anglia and killed the king and his family. Penda's son now sits on the throne. Do you want that to happen here?'

'I told you that the rumours were right, father, but you wouldn't listen,' Bubba hissed in his ear.

'Be quiet, Bubba. When I want you to speak I'll let you know.' He turned back to Oswald. 'I can understand why Penda would want to invade Middle Anglia. It gives him a buffer between Mercia and both East Anglia and the East Saxons, but what would he want with my kingdom?'

'Access to the German Ocean. From your coast he can raid all of Northumbria.'

'Ah, so you're protecting your own interests by trying to oust me.'

'Of course, except I'm not seeking your throne. You are most welcome to carry on ruling Lindsey, but as my vassal.'

'You expect me to pay you tribute? Never!'

'I didn't say that.' Oswald had come to the conclusion that it might be easier to deal with the son, rather than the father.

'Well, what are you proposing?'

'That I become your overlord and you accept one of my men as your hereræswa. I'll leave a few men to help train your warriors properly so that they have a chance against the Mercians if they invade and, if they do, I'll come to your aid.'

'Pah! There's some trick behind this; why would you want to go to all this trouble just to help me against the Mercians? It doesn't make sense.'

'Not to you obviously. If you're not happy with my proposal then perhaps it is time for you to go into a monastery to live out your days. I can tell from his reaction that Bubba sees the mutual benefits of what I've said.'

The young man nodded and looked delighted at the suggestion that his father should spend the rest of his days on his knees praying whilst he took over.

'I think you've got something there,' Hrotha whispered in Oswald's ear. 'The son is itching for his father to die so that he can take over.'

Oswald nodded. The more he thought about it, the more certain he was that Bubba would make the better sub-king; and, because Oswald had put him on the throne, he'd be in his debt.

The old king had said nothing; he just glared at Oswald.

'Very well. I think we're agreed. Caedbaed, I'll escort you north to Lindisfarne where Bishop Aidan will be delighted to welcome a new monk. Bubba, I suggest you leave your father with us for now, then I can start to explain to him my mission to convert the North to Christianity. I'll come to meet you outside the walls of Wrawby at noon

179

tomorrow. You can swear fealty to me then, along with your leading nobles.'

Caedbaed started to protest but Oswald gave him a warning look. He subsided, knowing that he was now dispensable. He was clever enough to know that, provided he went along with Oswald's little game, he'd be allowed to live out his days as a monk. If he didn't cooperate he'd conveniently die on the road north.

'This is Hengist,' Oswald was saying, 'who'll be staying behind to help you. I suggest that he goes with you now so that you can get acquainted. I'll bring the men who'll help you train your warband tomorrow, together with a cart full of armour and weapons.'

Bubba was no fool. He realised that Hengist was being sent with him to make sure he didn't do anything foolish. Of course, he could kill the Northumbrian, but then Oswald would be sure to exact a terrible revenge. No, Oswald had made him king, albeit as a vassal, and he'd just have to make the best of it.

~~~

'Oswald has made a mistake if he thinks that moving into Lindsey before I was ready to do so will prevent me from conquering it,' Penda said furiously to his son.

'What can we do, though? Northumbria grows more powerful by the day and they're now allied to Wessex. You're already in dispute with Cynegils over Hwicce. If you go to war with Oswald it'll allow Wessex to take over Hwicce,' Peada replied.

'Why don't you tell me something I don't know? Do you think I'm a fool, boy?'

'I think you're letting your hatred of Oswald cloud your judgement,' his son replied, not in the least perturbed by Penda's irate response.

Penda paced up and down the king's hall in Stamford, biting his lip and trying to control his rage. Eventually he sat down again next to his son and sighed.

'He's becoming something of a problem, but you're right. Now is not the time to tackle him. Sooner or later he and I are going to find out who's the bretwalda of England though.'

'Is that how you see yourself, as bretwalda?'

Penda glared at his son before replying.

'Yes, if I'm not acknowledged as the overlord by the other kings, then it will be that bloody man, Oswald. I'll never accept that. Already he's spreading his poisonous religion all over the north.'

Peada, who was interested in Christianity himself, said nothing. His father was a pagan and hated the people he called the followers of the White Christ with a passion. Then he thought of something.

'If you hate the Christians so much father, why did you ally yourself with Cadwallon of Gwynedd?'

'Because it suited my purposes at the time. Don't confuse principles with pragmatism. I still need the Welsh as allies otherwise we'd have to deal with constant raids into our kingdom.'

'Yes, I can see that. Will the loss of Lindsey affect your long term aim to take over East Anglia as well?'

Penda looked at his son sharply. 'Who told you that?'

'I heard you talking to Eowa.'

'What I discuss with my brother is private and you shouldn't have been eavesdropping. When I want you to know something, I'll tell you. Is that clear?'

181

'Don't you trust me?'

'I don't even trust my brother. You'll find being a king is very lonely, boy. You need to keep your own counsel and think very carefully before you confide in anyone.'

'What about mother? Don't you trust her?'

Penda snorted. 'Trust Cynewise? You are naïve, aren't you? She thinks a secret is nothing more than a good bit of gossip to be spread around. Don't misunderstand me, I love your mother in my fashion and she's provided me with six healthy children, but I'd never talk to her about anything important.'

'You can trust me, father; I'd never betray you.'

'I know that, but I've learned to keep my thoughts to myself. I only tell people what I think they need to know. Don't forget I wasn't born of royal blood, I had to fight and scheme my way to the Mercian throne. You might think me devious, but my position is precarious. There are others who think that they have a better right to rule than I do. I need to be seen by the Mercians as a successful leader or I could lose everything. Do you understand?'

'Yes, but I don't regard you as devious, just very clever.'

Penda scowled. 'Don't try and flatter me, boy. It won't get you anywhere.'

Peada didn't reply. His father was a difficult man to get close to and he felt he would always fail to measure up to the man's exacting standards. It depressed him and that made him resentful. He wondered if Eowa felt the same about his brother.

CHAPTER EIGHT – THE BATTLE OF GLEN MAIRSON

638 AD

Just when Oswald thought that he had achieved peace, disaster struck. Although the Angles of Northumbria had reasserted their control over most of the Goddodin territory north of the Tweed, Oswiu had failed to capture the near impregnable fortress on the rock called Dùn Èideann. From there the Goddodin continued to control the surrounding countryside to the immediate south and to the west as far as the end of the forth, where it became a river. At this point three realms met: those of the Goddodin, the Picts and Strathclyde.

'Owain has already pushed Domnall's territory back as far as Glen Falloch, now he has allied himself with the Picts and the Goddodin to invade further into Dalriada,' he told Jarlath, who had replaced Hengist as leader of his gesith. 'I dare not take my eye off the Mercians but I need to support Domnall somehow.'

Oswiu, who had been sitting quietly at the high table in the hall at Bebbanburg with the other two, looked at his brother, who nodded, before the former spoke.

'I will return to Dùn Èideann, lay waste the country still held by the rebels, and besiege their stronghold once more. If nothing else, it will prevent them from getting involved in the coalition against Domnall Brecc.'

183

'I need to move to Eoforwīc soon, now that winter is ending, so that I can react to whatever Penda is planning. However, I also want to send some support to help King Domnall. I owe him that much. So Rhieinmelth's father has agreed to launch a few raids into Strathclyde from the south.'

At that moment they heard the sound of voices at the door of the hall, presumably the sentry was telling someone that the king wasn't to be disturbed, not that it made much difference. The door opened and a man entered shaking rain from his cloak.

'Aidan, what brings you here, and in this foul weather?'

'You haven't heard then?'

'Heard what?'

'Ròidh has been taken prisoner and is being held hostage by the Goddodin.'

'What? Where was this and when?'

'A few days ago. He was visiting the vills to the west of Dùn Barra to baptise those who we've newly converted when a raiding party from Dùn Èideann attacked the settlement where he was staying. The thegn managed to beat them off but not before they'd killed five people, run off some of the livestock and captured several people including Brother Ròidh.'

'Presumably they've taken him to their fortress on the rock?'

'We aren't certain but the messenger said that his thegn thinks it likely.'

'What will they do with him,' Oswiu wondered.

'Either execute him as he's a Christian, perhaps even sacrifice him to their pagan gods, or demand a ransom, I imagine.'

'I think tales of human sacrifice by the druids are wild exaggerations, Aidan,' Oswald chided him gently. 'We have only ever found evidence of animal sacrifices.'

'I suppose that's something,' the bishop conceded, 'but what are we going to do to rescue him?'

'Perhaps I need to bring forward my siege of Dùn Èideann? They won't be expecting us to attack so early in the year. Now that the snows have melted it will still be difficult going through the mud, but we should be able to get there in two weeks if I call the muster now,' Owsiu stated.

'You don't sound very certain, brother.'

'I'm not, but we must do something to try and rescue him.'

'Very well, but this needs to be co-ordinated with the raids into Strathclyde as well. I'll send a message to King Royth at Caer Leul to let him know, and you'd better start planning as well, Jarlath.'

~~~

Domangart was practicing the use of sword and shield with Sigbert when the two boys were told that Oswiu wanted to see them. When they got to the hall they found Raulf, Oswiu's body slave there as well.

'Ah, good. I've got a task for the three of you. You're all light and agile. How good are you at climbing rocks?'

The three boys looked at one another and Domangart, being the senior, replied.

'I don't know about Raulf, but Sigbert and I have climbed up the cliff on which this fortress is built a few times. Are we in trouble for it?'

Oswiu laughed. 'You probably should be, but no. The climb up to the base of the palisade around Bebbanburg is

185

quite difficult but the one I want you to scale is much higher, and I want you to do it on a dark night. I suspect that the pitch is about the same though.'

'So you want us to practice climbing up the Bebbanburg rock at night?'

'Yes, start with a night where there is a moon and then wait for a cloudy night and do it again, and as many times as you can between now and two weeks' time when we leave. Oh! And practice it with a thin rope around your waist. You will also have to learn how to sneak up on a man and cut his throat without him making a sound. I'll send you someone to teach you how to do that.'

'May I ask where this rock is you want us to climb?'

'No, you may not. You'll know when we get there.'

'It's Dùn Èideann, I'm sure of it,' he told the other two.

'How did you know? Never mind; sometimes I think you're too clever for your own good.'

'Lord, you didn't ask me if I could climb a rock.'

Oswiu turned to his body slave.

'I know you can climb, Raulf. I've seen you after bird's eggs.'

'Oh, sorry, lord.'

'Don't be. Even Oswald and I went after the nests in the rock faces on Iona when we were boys.'

'This is much harder when you can't see what you're doing,' Sigbert muttered.

'Shhh, use smaller steps than you do in daylight and move your foot up to where your hand is,' Raulf whispered back.

It had soon become evident that he was by far the most experienced climber and, despite Domangart's status as a king's son, Raulf had become their leader. It took them every moment of the time they had to practice and get it right. Several times one of them had nearly fallen and they soon learned not to attempt the climb when it was raining or even when the rock was still slippery after the rain had stopped. They climbed at night and slept during the day.

Because Oswiu had told them not to say what they were doing, the other boys thought that they were just lazy sods and gave them a hard time. However, this just bonded them closer to each other. They became inseparable and, because Oswiu still needed his armour, weapons and horses looking after, the other two helped Raulf with his duties.

Oswiu was making the most of the time he had left with his wife, not just at night, but they went hunting together during the daytime as well. However, just before he was due to leave, Rhieinmelth decided she shouldn't go hunting again.

'I didn't want to tell you until I was certain, but I'm sure now that I'm expecting our first child.'

'Really? That's great news! Do you know when it's expected?'

'You mother thinks it will be born in the late summer.'

'My mother? You told her first?'

'Yes, of course. I needed to be certain that's what my symptoms were.'

'Symptoms?' Oswiu was about to ask what they were, then thought better of it.

'I wasn't vomiting because I'd drunk too much wine the night before.'

'Oh, I see. Well, I don't really, but never mind.'

He had a vague idea that Fianna had been sick quite a lot when she'd been pregnant too.

She laughed. 'Perhaps it's just as well you've going away for a while.'

'I'll miss you. I'd rather be here.'

'Perhaps. But you'd soon get bored and then you'd be insufferable and I wouldn't have the patience to deal with you and pregnancy. No, come back when it's all over; but make sure you come back in one piece.'

'I'll try to.'

He smiled, kissed her and left without looking back.

~~~

'It's a lot further to climb than the rock at Bebbanburg,' Sigbert muttered as he, Domangart and Raulf looked at Dùn Èideann sitting on top of the biggest outcrop of rock that they had ever seen.

Oswiu's army had encamped around it that afternoon after laying waste the land surrounding the fortress.

'There are easier approaches, one of them is quite a gentle slope,' Raulf pointed out.

'Yes, but Oswiu wants us to scale this one,' Domangart replied, 'and I can see why. The Goddodin sentries will feel themselves safe up there, whereas they might well expect an attack up the gentler slopes.'

'Well, I still think it's a long climb.'

'At least it's sunny now and it's close to a new moon tonight, so we can relax for a day or two,' Sigbert added.

'You might be able to, but I've got to look after his horses, sharpen his sword and make him something to eat before I can get any sleep.'

'Don't worry, we'll give you a hand, won't we Sigbert?'

'Of course. You can make us something to eat when you prepare Prince Oswiu's meal in return.'

It stayed fine for the next two days but then it started to cloud over on the third day. However, it rained that night and so it still wasn't possible to launch the attack.

'You seem very eager to get the assault on the fortress started,' Cynhelm said.

He'd joined Oswiu from Dùn Barra with his warband and had been invited to eat with the prince in his tent. Raulf appeared and poured more wine in both their goblets before disappearing again.

'He's my secret weapon, well him and two other boys.' Oswiu said when they were alone again.

'What do you mean?'

'They're going to scale the steepest part of the rock and lower ropes down for the assault party to climb up. The trouble is the conditions need to be correct. We need a cloudy night and the rock has to be dry.'

'Why are you telling me all this? No, don't reply, let me guess. You want me to lead the assault party.'

'It seems you know me only too well.'

'You'd better tell me your plan in detail then.'

Three nights later the conditions were perfect. It was overcast but dry and there was practically no wind. The only problem was sound; it carried a long way on a quiet night. The three boys made their way cautiously to the base of the rock and started to climb. Each had a thin cord tied around his waist with which to haul up the rope ladders once they had reached the top of the parapet and killed the sentries. In addition Domangart, the biggest of the boys, had a short length of rope ladder in a satchel on his back.

The three climbed steadily up the rock. They were each meant to follow a separate pitch but at one point Sigbert couldn't find any decent holds and so he moved over to climb below Raulf. It was a good job he did as the latter's foot slipped off a rounded protrusion in the rock and Sigbert was able to grab it with his free hand.

They reached the narrow grassy ledge at the top of the rock without further incident, but Raulf was promptly sick; no doubt in reaction to nearly plummeting to his death.

"Shhh,' Domangart said so quietly that he could hardly be heard.

'Sorry, I thought I was going to die,' he whispered back.

'You will be if you don't shut up.'

He and Raulf cupped their hands together and Sigbert, taking the satchel from Domangart, put his foot into their hands. He straightened his leg as they lifted him up so that he could reach the top of the palisade. Quickly pulling the short length of rope ladder from the satchel he put the two end loops over the pointed tops of two upright timbers and did a quick scan for any sentries.

At first he couldn't see any, than he heard voices and he saw two men standing at the far end of the walkway. He couldn't see any others so he used his free foot to tap Domangart on the shoulder. The other two lowered him back down. However, as he put his feet down on the grass again his left foot slipped in Raulf's pile of vomit and it slid over the edge.

Thankfully Domangart was quick witted enough to grasp his shoulder to steady him.

'Thanks,' the boy muttered quietly as he broke out in a cold sweat.

Not waiting for him to recover from his shock the other two pushed him towards the rope ladder and he started to climb up it, quickly followed by Domangart and then Raulf. At the top he slid over the top of the palisade and lay in the shadow between the walkway and the palisade trying to quieten his ragged breathing. A second or two later the others joined him.

'Where are the sentries?' Domangart asked in a hushed whisper.

Sigbert pointed to where he'd seen the two men, but they weren't there anymore. He hastily looked around for them and saw one about a hundred yards away leaning on the parapet and gazing out over the surrounding countryside. He taped Domangart on the shoulder and pointed. The other boy nodded and whispered in his ear 'where's the other one?'

No sooner had he asked when they heard the unmistakeable sound of someone taking a piss below them. Evidently the other man had gone down the ladder to relieve himself against the bottom of the palisade. The boys managed to resist the temptation to giggle and Domangart gestured for Sigbert to take care of the man gazing into the distance whilst he and Raulf dealt with the other sentry.

Sigbert tiptoed along the walkway with his dagger in his hand praying that none of the timber planks would squeak. When he was five yards away the man suddenly straightened up and turned to resume his walk along the parapet. It was fortunate that he'd turned away from the boy and Sigbert took his opportunity. The man was wearing a helmet so Sigbert couldn't yank his head back by his hair. Instead he kicked him behind his right knee. As the man tried to keep his balance his legs bent sufficiently for Sigbert to reach his exposed neck and a moment later he'd slashed it open just as the sentry started to cry out.

The sound died in his throat and blood spurted out from his severed carotid arteries. With the blood supply to his brain cut off, the man collapsed onto the walkway with a thump.

'What's the matter Bain? You OK?' the other sentry asked as his head appeared above the parapet as he climbed back up the ladder.

Domangart and Raulf were lying down on the walkway either side of the trapdoor through which the man's head and shoulders had emerged. Raulf jabbed his dagger into the man's mouth and up into his brain whilst the other boy reached down and grabbed his belt to prevent him tumbling back down the ladder.

Together they managed to haul him the rest of the way up onto the walkway, shut the trapdoor and rolled the corpse onto it to make it difficult for anyone else to come up that way. Then they collapsed from mental as well as physical exhaustion.

Five minutes later the three boys had recovered sufficiently to lower the three lengths of twine they had around their waists down the rock face and a few minutes later they'd hauled up and secured the three rope ladders. The first head that appeared was that of Cynhelm. He grinned at the three boys and he clambered down onto the walkway.

'Any problems?'

'No, none at all,' Domangart lied.

~~~

Owain of Strathclyde was unhappy. He glared balefully at the messenger and thought of having him killed for being the bearer of bad tidings. It wasn't the unfairness of such an action that stopped him, it was the knowledge that other messengers would hesitate to come to him and his information would dry up.

The fall of Dùn Èideann and the subjugation of the Goddodin territory to the south of the Firth of Forth by Owsiu had been a severe blow. Now, instead of an ally along part of his eastern border, he had an enemy. With Rheged to the south and Bernicia along the rest of the eastern boundary he was unwilling to concentrate his forces against Dalriada to the north and west.

'Has Oswiu remained at Dùn Èideann?'

The messenger cowered and muttered something.

'Speak up man, where is he?'

'He's gone to Rheged, or so it is rumoured, Brenin.'

Owain mulled this additional piece of unwelcome news over for a moment.

'Who has he left in charge at Dùn Èideann?'

'I understand that it is Eorl Cynhelm.'

'I see. I thought the bloody place was meant to be impregnable. How did the wretched Oswiu manage to capture it in just a few days?'

'The story is, Brenin ....' The man swallowed nervously. 'Well, apparently a few boys climbed the steepest rock face, slew the sentries and lowered rope ladders. The fortress was full of Northumbrians before we knew what was happening.'

'A few boys – are you certain? It sounds so improbable. Go on.'

'Yes, Brenin. Well, they fought their way to the gates and, once they'd captured then, they let the rest of their army in. I barely managed to escape -'

'Yes, thank you. I'm really not interested in how you managed to save your own skin. Any other dire news for me? No? Get out then.'

So far his invasion of Dalriada had gone well. He'd pressed forward into Glen Lochy, recovering the territory to the east of Loch Awe that his father had lost after his failed

193

attempt to storm the Pass of Brander under the brooding bulk of Ben Cruachan, and he'd linked up with the Picts at the junction with Glen Orchy. Now it sounded as if he might have to abandon the invasion of the Dalriadan Kingdom of Lorne in order to protect his own orders in the south-east.

If only he knew what Oswiu was up to.

~~~

Oswald wished that Oswiu was with him. Penda had changed tactics. Now, instead of outright military aggression he had taken a more subtle path and was using pressure to put together what he was calling a *Saxon Confederation*.

'What's he trying to do?' Durston asked.

Oswald had gone to visit Bishop Aidan on Lindisfarne and he'd been accompanied by Durston, Jarlath, Rònan and Cormac. They were sitting with Aidan and Ròidh in the newly built hall that served as both refectory and sleeping quarters for the monks, of which there were now nine plus a dozen novices.

Ròidh didn't contribute much to the conversation but Oswald put his reticence down to the horrific time he'd had whilst a prisoner. When the Goddodin fortress had fallen Oswiu's men had found Ròidh hanging in chains in a small hut which had evidently served as a prison. He'd been tortured, as evidenced by the burn marks all over his chest and legs, but he was alive.

'You can stay here until you're fit enough to return to Lindisfarne. I've already send a messenger to let Bishop Aidan know that you're alive,' Oswiu had told him at the time.

194

'Thank you, Oswiu, but I want to get out of this accursed place as soon as I can. It has too many awful memories for me. I'll try and find a fishing boat to take me down the coast.'

'You'll do no such thing! If you're determined to return to the monastery I'll arrange for a birlinn to take you. I need to send a messenger to my brother in any case.'

'Thank you. I....'

Whatever it was Ròidh was about to say was lost as he dropped back into unconsciousness.

Now, after a prolonged stay in the infirmary on Lindisfarne, he was feeling much better and was nearly back to his old self. He still walked with the aid of a stick but he forced himself to go further and further each day, usually in the company of a novice just in case he had a relapse.

Aidan had tried to make Ròidh prior of the monastery but he had declined. He had no intention of becoming an administrator tied to one place. His role was to accompany Aidan when he toured the kingdom preaching and converting the people and that wasn't about to change if he could help it.

'I'd have thought that was obvious,' Cormac said, responding to Durston's question. 'Sorry, that was rude of me. Presumably he's trying to isolate Wessex?'

Oswald nodded. 'Yes, and eventually built up a large enough army to challenge me.'

'What will you do about it?' Rònan asked.

Oswald sighed. 'Wait until Oswiu returns from the north and then move to confront Penda. I daren't risk embarking on a war with him with just the men I can raise from Deira, Elmet and Lindsey.'

'Surely, if we wait we risk him taking over Hwicce? Jarlath said, looking puzzled.

'Perhaps, at the moment Mercia to the north and Wessex to the east are both trying to take it over. The best we can hope for is that they will end up dividing it between them.'

'How are things going against Strathclyde?' Ròidh asked. 'The last I heard Oswiu was making raids into the south east of the country to distract Owain from his war with Domnall.'

'That seems to be working, up to a point. Owain has remained in the north but he's sent his brother south with a sizeable force to confront Oswiu. Meanwhile he and the Picts are camped at Loch Awe. I'm sure that they won't be so foolish as to try and force their way through the Pass of Brander again, not after what happened the last time.'

'They might try and get around Ben Cruachan to the north,' Aidan said thoughtfully.

'Is that possible? Won't they just find their way blocked by Loch Etive?' Oswald asked.

'Not if they go well to the north.'

'But that will take them into the marshlands on the edge of Rannoch Moor.'

'True, but if they link up with the Picts they'll have guides who know the paths through the bogs.'

'That'll still leave them north of Loch Etive.'

Oswald thought whilst the others were silent, wondering what he was going through his mind.

'That's what Owain will do.' He suddenly exclaimed. 'He might be cut off from the main part of Dalriada but he can still ravage the northern half of Lorne and, if he can capture enough ships, he can even attack Mull and the outer isles.'

'What is even more of a concern is that Iona will then be vulnerable.' Aidan pointed out. 'Owain hates Christians; nothing would give him greater pleasure than to destroy the monastery and kill all the monks.'

196

'But many of my fellow Picts are Christians.' Ròidh exclaimed. 'Aidan and I baptised many of them ourselves. They would never allow it.'

'They might not be in a position to prevent it,' Aidan said quietly. 'If Owain diverts them by suggesting that they complete the conquest of Lorne, he could attack Mull on his own, then cross the narrow Sound of Iona to the Holy Isle.'

'You're right! I must get a message to Oswiu. He's too far away and has too few ships at Caer Luel to go to the aid of Domnall in time, but he could besiege Owain's capital at Dùn Breatainn in the hope that will bring him south in a hurry. I must also warn Domnall.'

'If you send a message directly to Fergus to save time, his fleet could prevent Owain from landing on Mull,' Jarlath suggested.

'Thank you, Jarlath, good idea.'

'A brain as well as a pretty face,' Cormac commented, drawing laughter from the others. Jarlath's features had become more masculine as he'd grown older, but he still looked a lot like his sister, Keeva.

'At least I don't have a face that frightens small children.'

He grinned at Cormac, whose once handsome face was disfigured by a livid scar that ran cross his right cheek to his jaw. He had lost part of his upper lip as well, exposing his broken teeth and giving him a permanent leer.

'At least it shows what an excellent fighter I am.'

'No, it just shows that you were too slow in raising your shield,' Durston said, to more laughter.

Oswald was glad that his companions were in good spirits but, although his smiled at the good-natured banter, he couldn't stop thinking about the situation in Dalriada.

~~~

Fergus had been left behind by Domnall Brecc to guard Domnall's own territory of Kintyre, Arran and Bute and Fergus' Kingdom of Islay and the Isles. When he received the message from Oswald, brought by a currach from Caer Luel, he immediately sent for his sons, Caomh and Judoc. He showed them the message and waited for their reaction.

'What do you propose to do father?' Judoc asked.

His brother gave him a contemptuous glance.

'I'd have thought that was obvious. We need to assemble as many craft manned with warriors as we can, and quickly. We can't let that pagan devil, Owain, ravage Iona.'

'I see.' His father looked disappointed. 'Of course we need to assemble a fleet, but what then? You both need to think this through logically, and stop trying to score points off each other. This isn't a competition. I'm trying to teach you both something.'

'We need to know where Owain is, in what strength and how many ships he has to ferry his army over to Mull.'

'Well done Caomh, now you're using the brain that God gave you.'

'To do that we should send out our fastest birlinns to patrol Loch Linhe.'

'Good, Judoch. Where in Loch Linhe would you use as a base if you were going to invade Mull?'

'Either Lismore Island, or even better, Loch Creran.'

Loch Linhe was the long inlet of the sea that ran from O Ban, opposite the south-eastern tip of the Isle of Mull, up to the northern border between Dalriada and the Land of the Picts. Loch Creran was a sheltered offshoot of Loch Linhe. It was an ideal place to embark an army but it had the disadvantage of having a narrow entrance.

'He'd be a fool to use Loch Creran, where his fleet could be trapped, and why use Lismore Island as a jumping off point? Why not sail straight to Mull? No, my guess is that he'd use Ardmucknish Bay,' Caomh countered.

'Well, there is one way to find out,' their father said with a smile, 'each of you take a fast birlinn and sail up to O Ban. Brennus will be with Domnall Brecc, at the Pass of Brander but there should be someone left in charge at O Ban, the capital of Lorne. They may know more. Then split up and find Owain's base. You're not to fight anyone. Your job is to get back here with the information I need.' He paused and fixed each of his sons with his piercing blue eyes. 'And this time work together. Understand? Now go.'

~~~

In fact neither Brennus nor Domnall were still at the Pass of Brander. Once it became clear that their enemies had moved north to go around Ben Cruachan, Brennus had left some of his men to hold the pass, just in case it was a ruse, and moved off with Domnall to follow the very obvious trail left by the enemy army through the wild, desolate country that led northwards to the top of Loch Etive. Apart from a few shepherds, no-one lived there. It was wild moorland interspersed with numerous streams and small rivers and a lot of bogs below the high mountains. It was bordered by Loch Etive in the west and the treacherous wasteland of Rannoch Moor to the east.

'How does Owain know the way through this wasteland?' Domnall asked Brennus when they camped for the night.

'Although this is part of my domain, it's largely uninhabited. Most of my people who live this far north are in settlements along the sea lochs or in Glen Coe to the north west of us. The Picts tend to leave them alone but, although there are few humans, there are a lot of animals including an abundance of deer, so the Picts hunt here, as do my people. Occasionally they meet and there's a fight, but it's a vast wilderness so it doesn't happen often. Obviously their hunters know the area as well as mine do.'

The next two days were uneventful then the scouts came back to report that the two armies had split, one heading towards Glen Coe and the other towards the headwaters of Loch Etive.

'It looks as if Owain's heading down the west bank of Loch Etive and the Picts are heading to Glen Coe and then presumably back into their own territory.' Domnall said to Brennus after they'd questioned the scouts.

'Where on earth is Owain going then? He'll find himself in a peninsula bounded by Loch Linhe and Loch Etive. There are a few fishing settlements on the coast but a few small boats aren't going to be much good to him.'

'Well, the good news is that they've split their forces. Where are the Picts heading?'

'I'm not entirely sure. Glen Coe will take them to the shores of Loch Leven, another offshoot of Loch Linhe; presumably they'll make their way along the shore heading east, back into their own country.'

'In that case I think we'll leave them to it and follow Owain's trail. If we can bring him to battle we could destroy the threat from Strathclyde for a generation.' Domnall smirked at the prospect and even the dour Brennus smiled briefly.

When they reached Glen Etive the trail they were following turned down the broad valley with its shallow but broad river splashing over rocks. The army crossed it with little difficulty and turned south west along the far bank. However, they hadn't gone far when two of the scouts came riding back on their surefooted mountain ponies.

'Cyning, the Strathclyde men have turned north west up a steep valley that leads between those two big mountains.'

He pointed to where two peaks close together disappeared into the clouds.

'Where on earth are they going?' Domnall asked, bewildered by the change in direction.

'It leads to where Lochs Leven and Linhe meet. Perhaps he aims to meet up with the Picts again, but why would they split up if they are going to re-unite?'

Brennus was as puzzled as his overlord.

Just then a third scout came riding up in a hurry.

'Domnall, the accursed Britons have stopped on top of the saddle between the two mountains. It looks as if they are offering battle.'

Domnall grinned. 'How foolish of them. Come, Brennus, don't let's disappoint them.' He turned back to the scouts. 'What's this valley called?'

'Glen Mairson, so the guide says.'

~~~

Oswiu took one look at Dùn Breatainn and knew that it was going to be even more difficult to take than Dùn Èideann had been. The circular fortress stood on top of a massive outcrop of rock with the sea lapping at three sides of it. The cliffs were sheer and the waves crashing against the base of them made it an impossible climb. Next to it stood a slightly smaller mound of rock and this too was surmounted by a palisade. The only approach was up a path which rose at over forty five degrees from the beach at the bottom to a gateway which linked the two palisades.

He sailed around to the far side of the fortress but this side consisted of a steep scree slope with another length of palisade linking the two parts of the fortress.

'I fear we've wasted our time,' he said to his shipmaster.

'Aye, it looks impregnable right enough.'

Raulf, who was sitting cross-legged nearby trying to scour the rust from his master's byrnie – a daily task in the corrosive salty air - looked across at the two mounds of rock.

'There's a lot of shrubs and small trees in that defile leading up to the gatehouse and it hasn't rained for some time now.'

The shipmaster was about to cuff the boy for his impudence but Oswiu stopped him.

'Well done, Raulf. What made you think of that?'

'I don't know. It just seemed obvious to me. If you could fire it with the wind in the right direction it might just set the gatehouse alight.'

'Yes, it might. It's a pity the wind's coming from the west though.'

'At the moment, yes,' the shipmaster said, 'but it's backing a bit. With any luck it'll soon be coming from the south.'

Oswiu's eyes lit up and he grinned at Raulf.

'How do you and the other two rascals fancy a bit of fire raising?'

An hour later they were ready.

'Now, you know what you have to do?'

'Yes, lord. Build up a pile of kindling and dry wood, wait until the first rays of sunrise then fire the kindling so that it sets the scrub in the defile alight. Wait until we are sure it's burning well and then run and take cover well away from the fire.'

'Good. We'll be coming ashore as soon as the fire dies down, provided it has set burnt down the gate. If not, I'll send a currach to collect you. Now, off you go and good luck.'

That night Raulf, Sigbert and Domangart rowed ashore in a small currach. Luck was with them as clouds obscured the moon until they had landed but, shortly afterwards, the sky cleared and moonlight bathed the area in light. They were frightened that they might be seen as they gathered the material to start their fire, but no shouts of alarm came from above, nor was a patrol sent down to investigate – both something that the boy's over-active imaginations envisaged.

During the night the wind picked up but it didn't change direction all the way to the south as they'd expected. Consequently the defile was still sheltered from it to some extent.

'What do we do?' Sigbert asked anxiously.

'I think we should concentrate on firing the right hand side of the defile,' Domangart replied. 'If you look at the few trees on that side their branches are moving in the wind, although those on the left aren't.'

'Yes, you're right!' Raulf said. 'The wind must be being funnelled up that side somehow.'

The boys took it in turn to keep watch for the dawn but Sigbert was half asleep when the sun's rays bathed the tops of the hills in yellow light, casting purple shadows down the slopes facing him. He awoke with a start and saw with dismay that the River Clyde to the east was now reflecting the rim of the sun that had appeared above the skyline.

'Quick, let's get the fire started,' he yelled loudly and kicked the other two awake.

'You bloody idiot! You fell asleep didn't you?' Domangart accused him.

'Never mind that, you've got the flint.'

Domangart knelt by the small pile of shavings he'd prepared and struck his flint with the sharp edge of his dagger. After a few attempts a few sparks landed in the shavings and it caught fire. He picked up the small bundle of shavings and pushed it into a larger bundle under a pile of twigs arranged like the roofing timbers of a circular hut. Once that was blazing away the boys piled larger and larger twigs and then pieces of wood onto the fire until it was blazing strongly.

They picked up the torches they'd brought with them, lit them and shoved them into the kindling and small branches they'd positioned at the bottom of the defile just where the undergrowth started.

'It's not working,' Sigbert cried in despair as the shrubs and small trees in the defile showed no sign of catching light from their fire.

At the same time shouts from above let them know that the fire had been seen. It wouldn't take long for the men in the fortress to run down the path and catch them.

'Quick, let's get the currach launched before they catch us,' Raulf said in a panic, getting up and turning to head for the beach.

'Wait, it's catching.'

Domangart was right. A gust of wind had caught the nascent fire and it now burned much more fiercely. Slowly the shrubs caught alight and then the wind strengthened and backed further. They could see the men who were descending the path stop, and then start to run back up the hill as the flames seemed to leap from bush to bush and from tree to tree towards their retreating backs. Soon the whole defile was ablaze. The flames leapt across the path and the greenery on the left started to blaze as well.

The boys retreated from the intensity of the heat and watched from the safety of the small beach as the whole defile turned into a roaring inferno. They were so absorbed by the blazing hillside that they weren't aware of the men coming ashore until Oswiu clapped Domangart and Raulf around the shoulders.

'Well done boys. All we've got to do now is wait until it burns itself out.'

Sigbert looked up at Oswiu and smiled, then remembered he'd been dozing on watch. However, it didn't seem to matter now.

It took all morning before the defile cooled off enough for Oswiu to lead his war band up to the blackened remnants of what had once been the gatehouse. He'd left half his birlinns in the river in case someone arrived to investigate. It wasn't the conflagration itself that could be seen from some way away, it was the plume of smoke that streamed away to the north.

When he arrived at the top of the incline he found that the gates were just a pile of blackened timbers and the palisade had been badly charred for some five metres on each side. A group of soot smeared warriors stood in the gap where the gates had been, yelling defiance and waving spears around but, after a volley of arrows, they ran for cover. By the time that Oswiu and his men reached the entrance he found the blackened figure of the custos waiting to surrender to him.

It turned out that the fortress was only defended by ten elderly men and a dozen boys. The rest of the warriors who normally manned it were away with King Owain in the north. Oswiu took the boys as slaves but left the old men behind. After he had carted everything of value, including two chests of gold, several furs and a small box of jewellery, down to his ships, he set fire to the huts and the king's hall and left feeling well pleased.

When he later found out that the youngest of his captives – an eleven year old boy called Guret - was King Owain's only son, he was even more delighted with the day's work.

~~~

The Britons had arrayed themselves across the saddle between the steep slopes that led to the two summits lost in the cloud. Domnall estimated their numbers at about five hundred whereas he had some seven hundred warriors, most of whom had some form of body protection and were better armed that the Strathclyde Britons. He gazed at them in contempt. Most were armed with spears and daggers and carried an oblong shield with rounded corners. A few had swords and battle axes and there were perhaps a hundred archers equipped with hunting bows.

He sent his own archers forward first and a deadly volley rained down on the capering and jabbering Britons. Their own archers responded but most of the arrows thudded into the Scots' large round shields. Then the Britons charged.

Domnall had never seen anything like it. They seemed to almost invite death as they cast themselves at the rows of warriors from Dalriada. Many leaped into the air to land a few rows back in the midst of the Scots, jabbing with their spears and slashing with sword, dagger or axe. They were quickly killed, but not before they had wrought havoc in the midst of their enemies. Meanwhile Domnall and Brennus, King of Lorne, were having difficulty in holding back the

Britons attacking their front rank. The shield wall held, but the warriors there kept giving fearful glances behind them as another cohort of the enemy leapt over them into the men behind.

Gradually the assault petered out and the Britons withdrew, leaving behind them over a hundred men dead and badly wounded. However, Domnall's Scots had also suffered significantly and seventy of his men would play no further in the battle. Worse, his men had been unnerved by the ferocity of the attack. Then he heard cries of alarm from behind him.

One of his men pushed his way through the densely packed army to reach his king.

'The Picts are behind us. What should we do?'

'It was all a trap,' Domnall said to Brennus in despair. 'I've been a fool.'

'No more than me, but I shan't live to pay the price I fear.'

It was only then that Domnall noticed that Brennus had been struck by an arrow which had gone through a tear in his byrnie. It had a barbed point and he'd foolishly tried to pull it out, now he was striving to hold his guts in place as blood seeped through his hands. A stomach wound was usually fatal and it was a painful way to die. Domnall knew then that his only option was surrender.

~~~

'You know what I do with Christians don't you?' Owain of Strathclyde said leering at Domnall Brecc, who lay before him tied hand and foot. 'Perhaps you would like to emulate your White Christ and be crucified? I'm told it can take three days to die that way, and you'll be in agony all the time, especially if I break your knees and elbows.'

Some of Domnall's men had managed to escape by climbing the mountains surrounding the battlefield but most had died there. Owain had ignored Domnall's attempt to surrender and had slaughtered some four hundred Scots without mercy. The King of Dalriada had been captured after his gesith had died around him and he'd been felled by a blow to the head with the blunt side of an axe.

Now his head throbbed, blood still seeped from the wound to his head and he felt faint from hunger. He felt certain that his skull would have been crushed had it not been for his helmet. He was saved from further humiliation by the arrival of a mud splattered messenger wearing soot smudged clothes and whose hair was badly singed.

'Brenin,' the man gasped. 'I got here as soon as I could but I had trouble finding you.'

'What on earth's happened? You look as if you've been in a fire.'

'I have, Brenin. The accursed Northumbrians have attacked Dùn Breatainn and burnt it to the ground.'

'What? How? What about my son; is he safe?'

'They set fire to the defile leading up to the gate and it burnt down. There was nothing we could do when Oswiu of Rheged attacked.'

'And Guret? Is he safe?'

'Oswiu took him prisoner, along with the other boys. He let the men go.'

'Their respite will be short lived when I get back. They will all die for losing me my home and my son.'

'But Brenin, the custos is my father, spare him I beg you.'

'He deserves to die the most; be very careful what you say or you will accompany him to the Otherworld.'

208

'Yes, Brenin.'

'Now get out of my sight. No! Wait.' He kicked the prone King of Dalriada hard in the ribs. 'Go and find this damned Oswiu and tell him that I'll trade his friend here for my son. If he's harmed Guret I'll break every bone in this wretch's body before I hand him over. Clear?'

'Y-yes, Brenin, but where do you want to d-do the exchange,' he stuttered.

'Hmm – tell him to meet me off Toward Point in the Firth of Clyde in one week's time. He's to bring one birlinn, no more. I'll come in one birlinn too. Now go.'

~~~

'If your father has harmed mine in any way I'll cut off your prick before we hand you back,' Domangart whispered in the ear of the unfortunate Guret as he sat tied to the base of the mast of Oswiu's birlinn.

'If I'm hurt your father will be dead meat,' the younger boy replied defiantly. 'In any case you won't live to see the sunset.'

'Brave talk.'

'Do you think my father is going to just sail in, hand over Domnall Brecc, collect me and just sail away? You don't know him very well, do you?'

'Why, what's he got planned?'

'You'll find out.'

'Oh yes, I will.'

Domangart glanced around quickly to make sure no one was watching them before putting his hand under the hem of the younger boy's tunic. He grabbed his balls and pulled on them hard.

209

'Not much to get hold of is there? Now, what has he got planned or I'll leave you speaking like a girl for the rest of your miserable life.'

'I don't know; how could I?' Guret squeaked. 'Please let go, you're hurting.'

'Why say it then?'

'Let go and I'll tell you.'

Domangart relaxed his grip but didn't remove his hand.

'He's not the sort of man to let Oswiu get away with burning down Dùn Breatainn and capturing me. He'll want revenge, but I don't know what he'll do exactly.'

'That's what he said,' Domangart told Oswiu a moment later.

'How did you get him to talk?'

'I threatened him and he retaliated by saying that his father had planned to get his revenge on you. So I grabbed his miserable excuse for a scrotum and pulled and squeezed it until he talked.'

'I see. Remind me never to upset you.'

The two grinned at one another.

'So, what will you do?'

'I see that I haven't managed to teach you to respect your elders yet; your father is going to be disappointed.'

'He'll be furious when he finds out the danger you keep putting me in.'

'Perhaps I won't bother to get him back then. We'll just chuck poor, abused Guret over the side.'

'Good idea; then I'll be king.'

Oswiu looked shocked for a moment until he realised that the boy was teasing him. He cuffed him about the ear and told him to go and give Guret some food and a drink of water.

It wasn't until he had walked away that Domangart realised that Oswiu hadn't told him what he planned to do to avoid Owain's trap.

On the morning of the appointed day Oswiu set out from Rothesay on the Isle of Bute to sail the four miles to Toward Point on the Cowal Peninsula. He suspected that Owain would have ships ready to row out from the opposite shore, which was in Strathclyde, to cut off his lines of retreat. He was not disappointed.

As he approached Toward Point a large birlinn appeared around Cloch Point where the Firth of Clyde turned through ninety degrees and headed east towards the blackened ruins of Dùn Breatainn. The wind was blowing directly northwards up the firth and so Owain's men were having to row hard to make progress.

'What do you think?' Godric asked Oswiu.

He was the shipmaster of the birlinn and stood beside him in the bows studying the approaching craft.

'See anything?' Oswiu called up to Domangart who was perched up on the yardarm from which the sail hung.

He'd put him up there, both as lookout and to keep him out of the way in case he reacted badly when he saw his father. Oswiu would be very surprised if Domnall hadn't been tortured, and even possibly maimed. Domangart had a short fuse and tended to act first and think later.

'Nothing yet, lord.'

'Well, if I were Owain, I'd wait until we were grappled together and had exchanged prisoners, then I'd have my fastest birlinns waiting out of sight, perhaps in Largs harbour, ready to sail across and cut us off from Bute. I'd have more ships waiting around Cloch Point ready to block our escape that way.'

'How would you coordinate them?'

'Perhaps a signal fire on top of Creuch Hill over there?'

As he spoke smoke started to rise from the hill.

'They've lit it too early,'

'No, it's easier to put a fire out that to light it. The signal will be when they douse it.'

Owain's birlinn hove to a mile north of Toward Point, its rowers just pulling enough to keep it in position against the wind and tide.

'They're trying to draw us further away from Rothesay.'

Oswiu nodded. 'Bring the boy here and heave too.'

A few minutes later Godric grinned as he lowered the struggling Guret over the bows of the stationary birlinn so that his father could see the boy with his feet being lapped by the waves. Suddenly a larger than normal one soaked him to his waist and he shook his head trying to clear the few splashes that had got in his eyes.

As soon as he saw the other ship moving towards him again he told Godric to haul him aboard.

'You, you... bastard.' Guret eventually got out as he stood on the foredeck dripping wet.

'Nothing personal, boy. It's just that your father seemed reluctant to come and get you for some reason.'

Guret looked puzzled. 'Why would he do that?'

'Because he wanted to draw us further north. I wonder why?'

'Domangart told you. I shouldn't have said anything, now you suspect it's a trap.'

The boy looked crestfallen.

'Oh, I'm sure it's a trap. I'd expect nothing else from your father. He's even using you and King Domnall Brecc as bait. Doesn't that tell you something about the man?'

Guret nodded, looking miserable. A few moments later the other birlinn came alongside and the crews threw each other a rope to hold them together.

'Why did you dunk my son in the sea?' Owain was plainly furious.

'Because I'm not playing your little games. Now, where is Domnall?'

Oswiu hardly recognised him. He was still covered in blood and he was being held up, unable to stand on his own.

'Father!' Domangart's yell of distress reached the men on both ships and Oswiu looked up sharply.

'Domangart, your father will be fine. Now, do what I told you.'

'Yes Oswiu.' The boy tried to pull himself together and looked around him again. 'The signal fire's gone out. Oh, and there are several birlinns coming around Cloch Point. Oh shit, and several more have appeared from the south of us.'

'Now hand over my son, Oswiu, and you can have this miserable excuse for a man. I wish you joy trying to get away from my fleet though.'

Oswiu smiled at him. 'Domnall first or your son dies.'

'What difference does it make?' he scoffed. 'You won't get away.'

He nodded at his men who carried the King of Dalriata to the gunwale and Oswiu's crew lifted him over the side onto their ship.

'Here's your son, who's a better man than you'll ever be. Guret, I hope to meet you again one day in happier circumstances.'

With that he picked the boy up and threw him into his father's arms. Owain staggered back and would have fallen if it wasn't for one of his warriors steadying him.

'Cut the ropes.'

Guret looked at him as the two ships drew apart, smiled and nodded a farewell. Obviously he'd been pleased by Oswiu's parting comment. A minute later Oswiu's sailors trimmed the sail to make for Rothesay and the rowers started to pull with a will. However, it was evident that the three birlinns approaching from the south would cut them off before they could reach safety.

'Change course and head for the Kyles of Bute.'

Godric acknowledged the order with a grin and the birlinn picked up speed now that they were sailing on a broad reach. Instead of heading to intercept their course towards Rothesay, the Strathclyde ships were now on their stern quarter and had no hope of catching them before they passed Ardmaleish Point and entered the narrow straight that separated Bute from the mainland.

The three enemy birlinns continued to pursue them, as Oswiu had hoped, but as they sailed passed Kames Bay north of Rothesay four more birlinns appeared. However, these belonged to Fergus, King of Islay.

'Right, Godric, bring her about and head back down towards those three birlinns.'

As they did so two more of Fergus' ships appeared from the top end of the narrow straits and joined them. The three enemy birlinns were now trapped by seven Dalriadan ships. They took the wise course and surrendered.

It was only then that he noticed that Domangart had deserted his post up the mast and was gently washing the blood from his father's face and body. He smiled to himself and looked around.

'Sigbert, up with you lad. Take Domangart's place as lookout.'

Owain couldn't see what was happening around Toward Point but, when his three birlinns didn't re-appear with the

214

captured Oswiu he began to worry. Signalling to his other four ships he set off to find out what had happened. As he cleared the point he could see into Rothesay Bay but there were only a few fishing boats there. Puzzled he carried on around along the southern tip of the Cowal Peninsula and, as he came opposite Kames Bay, he could see eight Birlinns coming towards him, three of which were his. They were in amongst the others and he came to the inescapable conclusion that they had been captured.

Cursing he turned around as quickly as he could and headed back to the Clyde, vowing to be revenged on Oswiu and Domnall Brecc someday.

Domnall slowly recovered as they voyaged back to Dùn Add. Domangart had asked to return to his father and Oswiu realised with surprise that he would be sorry to lose the boy's company. However, the news that awaited him there soon drove all other thoughts from his mind. His father-in-law, Royth, had died. He was now King of Rheged.

CHAPTER NINE – THE SAXON CONFEDERATION

639 AD

'What do you make of the events in Wessex?'

Oswald was sitting with Aidan, Ròidh, Jarlath and Cormac in his hall at Yeavering. Aidan and Ròidh had just returned from Lindsey where Hengist, formerly one of Oswald' gesith, was effectively the ruler. Bubba, who Oswald had put on the throne as sub-king when he deposed his father, had been killed when he was thrown from his horse whilst out hunting. His son was just eight and so Hengist had been appointed as regent until the boy was older. No one was taking a wager on the boy reaching maturity though.

'Cynegils was devastated when Cwichelm died,' Aidan replied. 'As you know, his father made him sub-king of southern Hwicce when he became fourteen and had finished his training as a warrior. Then, barely three months later, he died of a mysterious illness. Not surprisingly everyone is pointing the finger at Penda, saying that the boy was poisoned on his orders.'

'What do you think?'

'It's possible of course, and his death suits Penda. Not only does it leave South Hwicce without a king but Cwichelm had the makings of a strong ruler. The other son, Cenwalh, is only eleven and is said to be, how can I put it tactfully?'

'Particularly stupid and has poor judgement?' Oswald suggested.

'A trifle harsh, perhaps, and not very Christian, but that seems to be the general consensus.'

'I suppose we have to hope that Cynegils lives to be an old man then.'

Cormac stopped what he was saying as Cyneburga walked in with Keeva.

'What were you saying about my father, Cormac?'

Oswald got up and went to his wife, taking her by the arm and leading her into the curtained off area that formed their private chamber.

'I'm afraid I have some very bad news from Wessex.'

'My father?' Cyneburga clutched at the cross hanging around her neck.

'No, not Cynegils, it's Cwichelm. He's dead, my love. No one knows how but I understand that it was very sudden.'

'Oh! Cwichelm? But he was only young; and only recently made sub-king. Fourteen is very young to die, unless he was killed.'

'Some are saying that Penda poisoned him, but it's only a rumour.'

Suddenly the news hit her; her brother was dead. He was a year younger and, as small children, they'd been quite close.

'Promise me one thing,' she said quietly. 'Kill Penda for me.'

~~~

'Cyning, wake up. The Mercians have invaded Hwicce.'

Cynegils blinked the sleep from his eyes, untangled his naked body from that of his wife, and sat up. Blearily he saw one of his gesith standing inside the leather curtain than screened his private chamber from the main hall at Wintan-ceastre. He pushed the sheepskins off him, stood up and pulled the tunic that the man offered him over his

217

head. Wrapping a fur trimmed woollen robe about him he pushed his feet into a pair of leather shoes and pulled the man roughly outside into the hall.

He grimaced at the sound of snoring and the smell of foul air that was a mixture of smoke, body odour and stale farts, and made his way outside. The sentry followed him, beckoning the mud-splattered, weary messenger to follow them.

'Now what's this about Hwicce?'

'This man will tell you, Cyning. He's just come from Gleawecastre.'

'Yes, Cyning. The Mercians arrived from the north without warning and laid siege to the town. It fell quickly but the king's hall behind its tall palisade is holding out. The custos sent me to warn you and I was lucky to slip through the Mercians and steal a horse. Oh, and the eorl is dead.'

Gleawecastre was the capital of southern Hwicce, the small kingdom over which his son Cwichelm had ruled for such a short time. Cynegils had reached an agreement with Penda to partition the old kingdom with one of Penda's eorls ruling the north and Cwichelm the south. Now it seemed that either the eorl or Penda had broken that agreement.

'How many Mercians?'

The question caught the messenger off guard.

'How many, Cyning? I'm not sure. Many more than we have to defend the hall. Perhaps three hundred or so?'

'And were they all warriors or did they contain members of the fyrd?'

'Not the fyrd, Cyning. They were all dressed in chain mail or leather jerkins with helmets.'

It wasn't just the Eorl of Northern Hwicce then, Cynegils thought. Only Penda could provide that number of trained warriors. He turned to the member of his gesith.

218

'We'll need to muster the fyrd and gather as many warriors as we can quickly. Send messengers to all the eorls; oh, and to Oswald in Northumbria too. He won't be in time to help us, but he should know what's going on.'

Three days later Cynegils marched north-west towards Gleawecastre but he hadn't gone more than ten miles before a messenger from Oswald found him. He was surprised, there hadn't been time for his letter to reach Yeavering, where he expected Oswald to be as it was now late April, let alone for a reply to find him. After he had read the missive he halted the column and summoned his war council.

His eorls gathered around him at the side of the road out of earshot of the army. Cynegils unfurled the parchment and, skipping the usual pleasantries at the beginning, he read out the contents.

Aidan had a message from James the Deacon a few days ago. So important were the contents that Aidan contacted me immediately. James has received a warning from Paulinus, who you will recall fled with Edwin's queen, Æthelburh of Kent, when the latter was killed. It appears that her father has received overtures from Penda to join what he termed a Saxon Confederation. This is the first I have heard of this, but you may already have knowledge of it. Just in case you haven't, this is what had reached me, albeit at third hand.

Penda and his son, Peada, have put pressure on the Middle Saxons, the East Saxons and the South Saxons to join him in invading East Anglia. He wanted Kent to join as well but Æthelburh's father, Æthelberht, has refused him.

You don't need me to tell you that, if Penda succeeds, he will control all of southern and middle England except for Kent and Wessex.

219

The only good tidings are that Oswiu seems to have checked Strathclyde's ambitions in the North for now. However, Dalriata grows ever weaker and my strategy now is to try and set the Christian Picts against the pagan Owain.

At least that leaves me free to come to your aid, should you need me. It strikes me that control of Lundenwic may be crucial, lying as it does in the middle of the Saxon kingdoms, and so I'm preparing to bring as many warriors by sea as I can to take the city. If you could strike east to link up with me we may yet frustrate Penda's plans.

He stopped reading and looked around him.

'Well, what do you think?'

'What about Hwicce? If Penda is involved in this so-called Saxon Confederation and preparing to attack Ecgric of East Anglia, then that gives us the perfect opportunity to recover Hwicce, and perhaps take over the whole kingdom,' one of his nobles suggested.

'That may not be such a good idea,' another said. 'I wouldn't be surprised if Penda is using his son's army from Middle Anglia with those of the other Saxon kingdoms to attack East Anglia while he keeps his Mercians back. If we attack Hwicce he can go around us to attack Wessex,' another said.

'Or Hwicce might be a trap.'

'But if we don't advance towards Lundenwic Oswald will be unsupported. After all, he can't bring that many warriors with him by sea.'

Cynegils nodded. 'We need to know more. We'll send messengers to the three Saxon kingdoms to try and find out what they intend; another to Kent to see if Æthelberht will move on Lundenwic to support Oswald and one to East Anglia to warn King Ecgric. Meanwhile we'll march on

Tamworth, ravaging the country as we go. Penda won't expect that. We can return via Gleawecastre and re-capture it.'

~~~

'Cynegils is doing what?'

Penda was with his son Peada in Leicester preparing for the invasion of East Anglia. He had brought a hundred men with him but he was relying on the Saxons and Peada to provide the bulk of the invasion force. He had several hundred warriors in Mercia itself, but they were scattered and, in any case, three hundred of them were at Gleawecastre waiting to repel Cynegils' army. Now it seemed that he was already no more than thirty miles south of Tamworth, about the same distance away as Leicester, but most of his forces were mustering twenty miles further east.

'You'll never reach Tamworth with a large enough force in time, unless the fortress can hold out for several days.'

'I don't think that there's much chance of that, do you? The garrison consists of the old, the ill, the disabled and boys training to be warriors. The fyrd hasn't been called out and the warriors who aren't with me or in Hwicce are in no position to resist the bloody West Saxons. Cynegils will have burned Tamworth to the ground before we can start moving towards him. Doubtless he'll capture Hwicce on the way home too. Damn him! He's outwitted me.'

'What about East Anglia?'

'Well there is nothing I can do to save my capital, southern Mercia – which he is bound to ravage – and Hwicce, so we might as well continue to invade East Anglia and then press on north into Lindsey and Elmet. That will give Oswald something to worry about instead of coming to Cynegils'

221

aid. Then we can think about teaching Wessex a lesson they won't forget in a hurry.'

'You're not going to allow him to burn and pillage our people, surely?'

'What other choice do I have?'

'You could negotiate.'

'That's for weak rulers. We will recover, but it will take time.'

'You're wrong, father. It's not weak to minimise the damage and give yourself time to regain the advantage.'

Penda looked at his son with new eyes. He'd always tended to think of him as a little slow on the uptake but what he'd just said seemed to make sense, much as he hated to admit it.

'Very well. You can ride to Tamworth with your gesith. Just make sure you get there before Cynegils. Let's see what you can salvage from all this.'

'What can I offer him?'

'Hwicce. All of it. Provided he withdraws to Wessex. We can always take it back later.'

'And what will you be doing?'

'Continuing with the original plan. With Wessex out of the game we should soon be able to ride from the River Severn to the German Ocean in Mercian territory.'

'And what about Oswald?'

'I'll offer to stay out of Elmet and Lindsey provided he doesn't interfere. Once we've consolidated our hold of East Anglia I'll be too powerful for him to resist me.'

~~~

'It's a good deal, Cyning. We not only recover Gleawecastre and southern Hwicce, we also get the northern half as well.'

'Are you really so short-sighted?' Cynegils said, trying to keep the contempt out of his voice. 'He's in a very weak position now, but if we agree to this treaty it will give him time to finish his expansion of Mercian territory to the east. If he does that he will be too strong for Wessex to challenge. Not only will he take Hwicce back, he could even invade Wessex and take that over as well.'

The eorl who had spoken looked at his king angrily for a moment, then nodded to indicate the truth of what Cynegils had said.

'Have we had any reply to your letters to your fellow Saxon kings?' another asked.

'Not yet. Nor have I heard where Oswald is. I think the safest thing to do is to play for time until we know more.'

'Are you certain that Peada's offer of peace isn't a smokescreen whilst his father gathers an army to trap us here?'

The speaker was Bishop Birinus, who had accompanied the army with several priests. Not everyone was a Christian but the majority of Cynegils' men were and those who were still pagan were becoming more interested in converting as time wore on.

'Our scouts who are keeping an eye on Leicester say that he had moved east towards Stamford, so I think he is still intent on the invasion of East Anglia.'

'If he's committed to this war, then we could move south to Oxenforda. It would look as if we are heading back to Wessex but from there it's only a three day march to Lundenwic. By then we should know where Oswald

223

is.' Ceolwald suggested. He was Cynegils' half-brother and Eorl of Dorset.

'Yes, thank you, brother. Let me think on that. We'll meet again later.'

The meeting dispersed whilst Ceolwald and Cynegils went to discuss the idea further.

'Peada, I accept your father's offer. Withdraw your men from Hwicce now and I'll sent my brother Ceolwald to garrison Gleawecastre and Weorgoran-ceastre.'

Weorgoran-ceastre was the capital of northern Hwicce.

'And you'll return to Wessex?'

'We'll leave Tamworth and march south towards Oxenforda tomorrow,' Cynegils promised.

'And you will cease your despoliation of Mercia?'

'I have to feed my men, but I swear we'll confine ourselves to just taking what we need and we'll not lay waste the country as we go.'

'Very well. I'll send messengers to Weorgoran-ceastre and Gleawecastre now. Like you they will only take from the people of Hwicce what they need to feed themselves.'

'Good. I understand that you're a Christian, unlike your father?'

'Yes, why?'

'Then we can both attest to the truth of what we have promised on the Holy Bible. This is Bishop Birinus. He will take our oaths.'

Both kings swore to do as they had promised but Cynegils was very careful not to undertake to do more than to retreat via Oxenforda.

~~~

Oswald wished that Oswiu was with him as he sailed down the East Coast in his birlinn, the Holy Saviour. The sky was as grey as the sea and occasional drops of water splattered him as he stood on the aft platform, though whether this was sea spray or rain he wasn't certain. Jarlath, the captain of his gesith, stood next to him and Beorhtwulf, who had replaced the now dead Alaric as steersman of the king's personal birlinn, was training one of the ship's boys – a thirteen year old called Hrodger – to steer and to set the sails in the prevailing wind to get the best speed out of the ship. Not that they could go as fast as possible as they needed to remain in contact with the rest of the fleet. Oswald had managed to gather a total of fifteen craft - a mixture of birlinns, pontos and large currachs – to convey his war band of over four hundred warriors south.

Beorhtwulf looked to the north east, where the wind was coming from.

'There's a squall coming, Cyning. Quite a vicious one by the look of it and the speed at which it's approaching. Put three reefs in the mainsail,' he yelled at his crew.

Hrodger handed the steering oar over to him as several men hastened to take in the sail, scrambling up the rigging to the yardarm to do so.

'Boy, signal the rest of the fleet to close up to us and reef their sails.'

Hrodger rushed to where the halliard by which Oswald's personal banner was raised to the top of the mast was fastened. He lowered and raised the banner several times to get the attention of the other shipmasters then he ran to the bows. He climbed up and stood on the gunwale hanging onto the carved figure of Christ on the prow and waved at the other ships, then pointed towards the squall, then beckoned the ships to come closer.

225

Most of the other craft got the message straight away and started to reef their sails whilst steering towards the Holy Saviour, but two ships to the lee of him continued blithely on their way. Evidently they hadn't been paying attention.

'Those two haven't got the message,' he panted to Beorhtwulf after running back to the stern.

The steersman nodded and put his oar over, changing course towards the two ships. That woke them up and Hrodger signalled them again from the prow. This time he saw men clambering up the rigging to the yardarm and the two ships – a birlinn and a ponto – changed course to move towards the rest of the fleet. Beorhtwulf muttered 'dozy swine' to no one in particular as he moved back to his original course.

A few minutes later the squall hit them. The vicious wind pressed against the reefed sail, making the birlinn heel over and increasing her speed through the water. One man, slower than the rest to reach the deck, was caught still climbing down the rigging and was carried overboard. His cries quickly faded as the birlinn swept on leaving him to his fate.

Almost horizontal rain lashed the crew as they scrambled for something to hold onto. Hrodger felt himself swept up in Oswald's powerful arms as the king pushed him against the base of the mast and tied him there. A large wave broke over the windward side of the birlinn and cascaded down into the bilges. A few seconds later the pressure of the wind brought her into the wind and she broached. She nearly capsized but the additional ballast provided by the water in the bilges helped to stabilise her and the mast, which had leaned over until it was at an angle of forty five degrees to the vertical, whipped back upright again as Beorhtwulf and two other men wrestled with the steering oar to bring her head round again.

Oswald was amazed that the mast hadn't snapped and he fell to his knees to thank God for their safe delivery as the squall moved on towards the distant coast. He stood up again and scanned the sea for the rest of his ships. One had lost her mast and another, a currach, had capsized. He later learned that a dozen men and three boys had been swept overboard and drowned and another man's head had been smashed in when he'd been thrown across the deck by a wave. A few more had broken bones but altogether they'd got off comparative lightly.

He sent the birlinn with the broken mast back to the nearest Northumbrian port with a skeleton crew and those too injured to fight or row. It reduced his fighters to four hundred but, he reflected, it could have been an awful lot worse.

Five days later they turned into the estuary of the River Thames. A few boats had come out from the shores of both Essex and Kent to investigate, but had beat a hasty retreat when they saw the size of the fleet. That night they anchored in the middle of the first bend in the river which his pilot, a sailor who had visited Ludenwic several times before, told him was called the Lower Hope.

'How long will you stay here, Cyning? Jarlath asked him nervously.

He was a lot happier on dry land and he worried that they could be trapped here without sufficient sea room to fight a naval battle.

'I want to find out more about the local situation before I go any further,' Oswald replied with a smile. 'If I'm going to put my head into a wolf's mouth I need to know how many teeth it has first.'

To his surprise the first craft to appear was a small birlinn which had set out from the Kent coast. Three men climbed aboard, two of whom looked like monks except their tonsure was circular and worn on the crown of their heads instead of the forehead, like Celtic monks. He recalled that James the Deacon had this type of tonsure and so he concluded that these were Roman clerics. The man they accompanied was dressed in a similar manner except that his habit was cream and he wore a red cloak embroidered with white crosses over it. His tonsure was covered by a red skull cap.

'Greetings my son, I'm Paulinus, Bishop of Rochester. Am I right in thinking I'm addressing King Oswald of Northumbria?'

Oswald nodded before replying.

'Paulinus? I knew you had been Bishop of York during the reign of the usurper Edwin, but I haven't heard of Rochester or knew that it had a bishop.'

'I was recently enthroned as bishop by Archbishop Honorius of Cantwaraburg as we spread the true faith ever eastwards.'

'I gather I have to thank you for the timely warning about the plans of the pagan Penda of Mercia.'

The expensively dressed cleric nodded. At that moment another cleric approached. Unlike Paulinus, this one was dressed in a much worn habit of undyed coarse wool tied around the waist by a rope girdle with a plain wooden cross hanging from it. His tonsure identified him as a Celtic monk.

'Ah, this is my brother and chaplain, Father Oslac. This is Bishop Paulinus.'

'Greetings in Christ, bishop. I know you by reputation, of course. It's a pleasure to meet you.'

It was obvious to Paulinus from the disdainful way that Oslac regarded his rich attire that he didn't approve.

'There is something troubling you, Father Oslac?'

'No, bishop. I was just thinking that if my own bishop, Aidan of Lindisfarne, had owned such fine raiment he would have sold it and given the proceeds to the poor.'

If Paulinus was offended he hid it well.

'I was told that both Oswald and Oswiu tended to speak their mind somewhat bluntly. It seems that it runs in the family.'

'Enough, Oslac. Each to his own,' Oswald interrupted. 'I was hoping to see King Æthelberht and find out what has happened since you sent your missive to James the Deacon, but no doubt you can tell me.'

'The king will be on his way but his hall is at Cantwaraburg, some thirty miles away. Rochester is a mere five miles from here. It lies on the River Medway and you had scarcely dropped anchor before someone docked there to tell me of your arrival.'

Two ships boys appeared with two small barrels over which they threw wolf skins for the king and the bishop to sit on, whilst the three monks, Jarlath and Beorhtwulf stood behind them on the small aft deck. Hrodger appeared again with a flagon of mead and, after another boy had handed round goblets, he poured out the amber liquid. He was about to leave but Oswald motioned for him to stay. Two minutes later Oswald repressed a smile as the boy re-filled Paulinus' empty goblet. The aesthetic Aidan would have been dismayed by what he would have regarded as gluttony.

'Penda is still in Middle Anglia but he is believed to have moved closer to the border with East Anglia. His son Peada has gone to Tamworth for a reason that is not entirely clear; however, there are rumour that Wessex had mobilised. The three small Saxon kingdoms have sent war bands to join Penda but they have done so unwillingly.'

229

'Thank you. What is the situation in Ludenwic?'

'Ludenwic?' Paulinus seemed surprised by the question. 'Its ownership is disputed between the Middle Saxons, the East Saxons, the South Saxons and ourselves. Penda has given it to one of his nobles, Eorl Toland, to settle the dispute.'

'Tell me about Ludenwic and this Toland. How many men does he have? What are the defences like?'

Paulinus shrugged. 'I know nothing about Toland except that he is from Oxenforda. Presumably his lands are in that area. I understand that he has a war band of fifty trained warriors but he can call on the local fyrd, which must number a couple of hundred, I suppose. They are mostly Saxons and it's rumoured that they don't like having an Anglian imposed on them. The old Roman city and its fortress have been abandoned. It's said that the city is full of ghosts; all rubbish no doubt but it's what people believe. The Saxons have built a new settlement about a mile or so to the west. The place has no palisade, or so I'm told, except around Toland's hall.'

'That's most helpful, bishop. Thank you.'

'Why are you so interested in Ludenwic?'

'It is an important trading port for three of the four Saxon kingdoms. Whoever controls it can exert pressure on them. That's why Penda has installed Toland there. If I can wrest control of the port from Mercia, then I might have a chance of persuading the surrounding Saxon kingdoms to break their alliance with Penda.'

'If you do succeed in capturing it, how will you, a Northumbrian, hold it?'

'That's why I want to talk to King Æthelberht.'

~~~

230

'Why do you want to make a present of Ludenwic to me, Oswald? What do you gain?'

Æthelberht and Oswald were sitting alone in a chamber in Paulinus' hall at Rochester. Each had stationed two sentries from their respective gesiths at the door to ensure their privacy as well as their safety.

'Penda is my enemy and Cynegils is my father-in-law as well as being my ally. Penda is trying to take all of Hwicce and, for all I know, he has succeeded by now. His so-called Saxon Confederation is aimed at the conquest of East Anglia. Once he has that he'll move against my sub-kingdom of Lindsey. Then he will control all of Anglo-Saxon England except for Kent and Wessex. You and Cynegils won't be able to resist him and we'll have a pagan bretwalda ruling all of England south of the Humber. Is that what you want?'

'Of course not! No more than I'd want you as Bretwalda of All England. From what I hear you are well on your way to making yourself Bretwalda of the North and here you are seeking my help to capture Ludenwic.'

Oswald sighed. 'What can I do to assure you that all I desire is to frustrate Penda's ambitions?

Æthelberht grunted but said no more.

'Very well, but the longer we delay the more time we give to Penda to reinforce Ludenwic.'

'Let me consult with my council. We'll meet again this afternoon.'

Oswald glared at the King of Kent before stomping out of the chamber. He couldn't understand why the man was so reluctant to commit to the obvious course of action.

'Well what do you make of Oswald? You're the only other one who has met him.'

Paulinus looked at Æthelberht warily before replying. He, Archbishop Honorius and a three of Æthelberht's eorls were sitting in the bishop's hall later that day.

'He's a barbarian with no diplomatic skills but he has a clever mind. I've no doubt he can be devious enough to deceive his enemies, but he has a reputation for honesty that makes me believe he would never pretend to a friend when he was not, if that's what you fear, Cyning.'

'Honorius?'

'I am a simple churchman, Cyning.' A statement which elicited a disbelieving snort from one of the eorls. 'My task is to convert the pagans to the path of the true faith, I claim to know nothing of politics,' he continuing, ignoring the eorl's reaction.

In fact, he was a very clever and astute Gregorian missionary who had risen from a humble monk to become the leader of the Roman Catholic Church in England. Although he was a Roman, he was a great admirer of Aidan, who he had met when he travelled to Lindisfarne two years previously.

'Nevertheless you have been to Northumbria and you have met Bishop Aidan. You must have formed some opinion of his king from what he said.'

'I suppose so,' he said at last. 'Oswald is undoubtedly a gifted military commander, a brave fighter and he is ambitious. His brother, Oswiu is the same, and they are both devout, albeit as members of the wrong church.'

'You say he is ambitious, how far does that extend?'

'I would say that he seeks to consolidate his position in the North but he would be a fool if he sought to become Bretwalda of England, if that's what you fear. His priority seems to be to counter Penda's expansionist aims.'

232

'Thank you, archbishop. My thoughts exactly. Good. Do any of my eorls wish to add anything?'

'He has a reputation as a fearless fighter. In my experience dishonest tricksters tend to hang back and let others do the fighting for them,' the one who'd snorted said.

At that moment one of the king's servants appeared hovering in the doorway. When Æthelberht waved him in he came and whispered in his ear.

'There is a messenger here from King Cynegils. He asked me to give you this immediately.'

As soon as he'd handed the sealed scroll in its waxed leather pouch to the king he withdrew. Unlike Oswald and Oswiu, Æthelberht had never learned to read, either in Latin or in English. He handed the pouch to Honorius who took out the scroll and unfurled it.

'It starts with the usual greetings and then he goes on as follows:

Having persuaded Peada to surrender Hwicce to me by threatening to burn Towcester and most of Mercia to the ground, I have now moved to Oxenforda. I gather that their eorl is in Ludenwic and so they were in no position to resist me. I have sent messengers to the Middle, South and East Saxons but none have replied to me as yet. I hope that they can be dissuaded from the folly of allowing the pagan Penda to conquer East Anglia. That would make him too powerful for us to resist.

My son-in-law, Oswald of Northumbria, is heading for Ludenwic by sea, if he has not already arrived there. He believes that, if he can capture it, it will apply pressure on the other Saxons kings to desert Penda's side.

I am well aware that we haven't always been friends in the past but I pray you, assist Oswald in his endeavours. I

leave Oxenforda tomorrow heading for Ludenwic with my
war host. I pray that we can join forces with Oswald as
allies. I have no desires on Ludenwic, provided it doesn't
remain in the hands of Penda.

It concludes with the usual good wishes.'

'Well, I think that makes my mind up for me. Send someone for Oswald; we'll join forces with him, summon our men and be ready to join Cynegils war host when it arrives.'

~~~

'There is a messenger here from Toland, father. He has surrendered Ludenwic to Æthelberht.'

'What? Why? Has the man gone mad? Surely he could have held out against Kent, especially as the place is surrounded by our allies.'

'Apparently he brought nearly two thousand men against it.'

'Two thou.... Where he get than number from, even with his fyrd I doubt he could raise much more than a thousand.'

'Apparently he was supported by war bands from Northumbria and Wessex, or so the messenger says.'

'Where is the snivelling cur, he must be mistaken. Bring him in.'

His disbelief faded away when he saw that the messenger was Toland's eldest son. He was unlikely to be wrong.

'What happened?'

'Æthelberht, Oswald and Cynegils attacked at dawn, Cyning. We were outnumbered by nearly ten to one. We didn't stand a chance. I saw my father fall to Whiteblade's sword and, knowing that the situation was hopeless, I seized a horse and escaped the slaughter to bring you word.'

234

'You did right, boy. Thank you. I'm sorry about your father. Wait! You say Cynegils was there?'

'Yes, Cyning. At least I saw his banner and a man who looked very like him on his distinctive white horse.'

He turned to Peada.

'You fool, he tricked you. He swore on the Bible that he would retreat via Oxenforda. What he obviously didn't swear was to return to Wessex.'

'We can march south and re-capture it, father.'

'What with? I've been outwitted and I've lost Ludenwic. Moreover there is an army two thousand strong facing us if I try to go south.'

'We have the same number here,'

'Yes, with the South, Middle and East Saxons. They joined us through fear. Now that I've been made a fool of and there is a powerful army sitting threatening all three of their kingdoms not one of their men will still be here as soon as this news spreads. Do you still fancy fighting an army over three thousand strong led by the accursed Oswald with one a third its size? No, of course not.

This fiasco has cost me Ludenwic and Hwicce, Mercia has been ravaged by the West Saxons and what have I got to show for it? Nothing, not a bloody thing. One day, Oswald, I'm going to take great delight in taking your head from your shoulders. In the meantime we go home and lick our wounds.'

CHAPTER TEN - WAR ON TWO FRONTS

641 – 642 AD

Oswiu lay on the bed made of layers of furs and played with his son, Ehlfrith. He'd been born in Caer Luel eighteen months ago and now Rhieinmelth thought that she might be pregnant again. Ever since he had given up Fianna and she'd married Jarlath he'd missed his first born son. He hadn't seen the boy for years and he now had a real desire to do so. Aldfrith must be seven now. He knew that Jarlath and Fianna had two boys of their own and he wondered whether they would agree to him coming to live with him. He decided to write and ask.

'I've written to Jarlath,' he began.

'Jarlath? The commander of Oswald's gesith? Why?'

He realised that his wife must have forgotten that Jarlath had married his concubine.

'Because Aldfrith is now seven and I want him to be brought up in my hall.'

'Aldfrith? Oh, you mean the bastard you sired before you married me. I'd thought you'd forgotten all about him. I certainly had, until you unwisely reminded me, that is.'

Oswiu had been in love with Rhieinmelth when they wed. He thought that she was the prettiest girl he'd ever seen and he'd enjoyed making love to her. However, Oswald had noticed a definite cooling in their relationship in recent

236

years. The two brothers didn't see much of each other but the last time they'd met Oswald had asked him if the couple were having problems.

'Rhieinmelth doesn't seem as happy as she used to be these days; is something wrong between you.'

'If anyone else had asked me that I've have brushed it off, but you know me too well.' Oswiu sighed deeply. 'Once the initial novelty of our marriage wore off we discovered that we had little in common. I despise the Britons in Strathclyde and did little to hide it, forgetting that she and her people were Britons too. It drove a wedge between us.'

'But Strathclyde has always been the enemy of Rheged.'

'I think she saw my attitude towards Strathclyde, and the Welsh come to that, as indicative of a bias against her race as a whole. But that hasn't been the only difficulty. I see so many problems with the way that her father rules Rheged and want to improve matters, but she defends her father every time I suggest some change. That frustrates me and things keep getting worse between us.'

'What will you do?'

'I know I can't put her aside, at least not yet. My claim to a throne of my own depends on my remaining as her husband. Once her father dies and I become king, then I might be able to do something, but even then putting my wife into a convent, which would be the easiest way of divorcing her, would alienate me from her people.'

The two brothers had gone on to talk about other things.

Over the past two years the arrival of their son Ehlfrith had brought Oswiu and Rhieinmelth a little closer together, but that just meant that they tolerated each other a little better.

Then the sudden death of her father had hit Rhieinmelth hard. She had withdrawn into herself and left Oswiu alone to rule Rheged.

Her attitude to his announcement about his eldest son hadn't come as a surprise, but the arrival of Aldfrith had turned her antipathy towards her husband into outright animosity. Now she wasn't even polite to him in public. Then came the news that drove all concerns about domestic disharmony from his mind.

Oswiu was amazed when an envoy arrived from Talorc, the paramount king of the Picts.

'Brenin,' the man began, speaking in the Brythonic tongue, 'King Talorc sends you his greetings and a wish that our two countries might be reconciled.'

'I find that hard to credit when he was instrumental in the defeat of my ally, King Domnall, barely two years ago.'

'Our quarrel was with him, not with Rheged, King Oswiu.'

'I'm not sure it's that simple, but you mentioned something about reconciliation?'

'As I'm sure you know, my people and Owain of Strathclyde are fighting over the area of Lorne north of Loch Etive that we conquered together. King Talorc was wondering whether you might assist him by invading Manau. It would mean that Strathclyde would be fighting on two fronts and you would gain a province to add your brother's province of Goddodin.'

'Before Strathclyde captured it, Manau was part of Dalriada. Don't you think that Domnall Brecc might be a trifle upset if I now captured it?'

'Perhaps,' he conceded. 'I don't suppose that Talorc minds who invades it, just so long as Owain has to weaken his forces in the north in order to defend it.'

'Very well. Let me think about it and we'll meet again tomorrow.'

He considered going to discuss the situation with his wife but he knew that she would just tell him not to get involved. If something didn't affect Rheged directly she wasn't interested; whereas Oswiu had a loyalty to Oswald and Northumbria as well. If Domnall could regain Manau it would give Dalriada a border, albeit a short one, with Goddodin just south of the point where the Firth of Forth became a river. That would make co-operation between Northumbria and Dalriada much easier.

'I've given King Talorc's proposal much thought. I'm going to suggest to my brother that he and Talorc become allies. That will give Owain pause for thought and may help to contain his expansionist ambitions; that is, provided Talorc is willing, of course,' Oswiu told the Pict the following day.

'I suspect that he might not be averse to the idea,' he replied cautiously. 'What of Manau?'

'I don't want to get involved. War between Strathclyde and Northumbria would inevitably drag Rheged into the conflict as we border Strathclyde to the south. However, I will write to Domnall Brecc and suggest that he might like to take the opportunity war in northern Lorne offers for him to regain Manau.'

'Very well. It is less than we had wanted, but let's hope he feels strong enough to act on your suggestion.'

'Before you go, you are evidently no ordinary messenger. You haven't told me your name.'

'No, I didn't, did I? I'm your nephew.'

'My nephew? I didn't know I had a Pictish neph-. Ah! You must be Talorgan, my late half-brother Eanfrith's son. You made a wise choice when you decided to stay with your

239

mother's people instead of returning to Northumbria with your father.'

'It wasn't a difficult choice. Remember I'm three-quarters Pict and only a quarter Northumbrian.'

Rather than send a messenger, Oswiu decided to travel to Yeavering himself to see Oswald. It was some time since the two had met and he'd take Aldfrith with him so that the boy could see his mother.

Fianna had hardly been overjoyed when Jarlath told her that Oswiu had sent for his son. She had wept and Jarlath wished that there was something he could do, but Oswiu was a king and the boy's father. He couldn't gainsay him. Over the past six months Fianna had got used to his loss, helped by the fact that she had two children with Jarlath. However, re-uniting her with her eldest for a brief period wasn't likely to help anyone. Had Oswiu and his wife been on speaking terms she could have pointed this out to him, but she wasn't interested in the slightest when he told her he was going to visit Oswald. Her only reaction had been relief that she wouldn't have to put up him for a while.

It galled her that her husband still expected to sleep with her whenever the fancy took him. She only wished that he'd followed his brother's example and kept Fianna around for sex. She'd once asked him why he didn't take a mistress but he had looked at her with horror.

'Adultery is prohibited by God,' he'd replied. 'I still pray for forgiveness for taking Fianna to my bed out of wedlock.'

As he'd grown older Oswiu had become more devout and had even founded a monastery near Care Luel in expiation of his sins.

'Oswiu, it does my heart good to see you,' Oswald cried when his brother dismounted outside the king's hall at Yeavering.

Oswald was now thirty seven and was a little stouter than when Oswiu had last seen him. He also had a few grey hairs at his temples. Oswiu, on the other hand, was much as Oswald remembered him. At twenty nine the King of Rheged was in his prime and was, if anything, a little thinner now.

Oslac came forward to embrace his brother as soon as Oswald stepped back. He had changed the most. He was four years younger than Oswald but looked older. He had developed a distinct paunch and he was rapidly losing his hair; so much so that his tonsure was barely discernible now.

When he stepped back Oswiu saw his mother waiting for him to greet her. She was in her late fifties and looked it. The odd strand of hair that had escaped from her head cloth was quite grey and her face was lined with deep creases. She stooped a little now and walked with the aid of a stick.

'Mother.' He bowed slightly but made no attempt to embrace her. Her smile faded but she had expected it. They had never been close and had fallen out too many times for him to pretend that he loved her. 'I trust you are well?'

'Apart from the pains in my joints and the lack of teeth to chew my food, I'm fine thank you, Oswiu. You remember your sister?'

For the first time Oswiu noticed the woman standing slightly behind Acha. At first he didn't recognise her. His sister, Æbbe, had been a girl when he'd last seen her, now she was twenty five and dressed as a nun. He grasped her hands and kissed her on the cheek.

'What are you doing here? I thought you were at Ebchester.'

'It's good to see you too, Oswiu,' she replied with a laugh. 'Oswald and Bishop Aidan have agreed to found a new monastery at Coldingham. It'll be for nuns to complement the male house on Lindisfarne. I'm to be the abbess.'

'But that's marvellous. Have you found any girls to join you as novices?'

'Well, only one so far.'

'And I'm far from being a girl,' Acha added. 'I've decided to spend what few days remain to me in quiet prayer and contemplation preparing for the afterlife, so you won't have to see me again. You should be pleased,' she said with a touch of bitterness.

'Oh, mother. It was never my wish for there to be such rancour between us. It was just that we seemed to argue whenever we came together. Perhaps we're too alike?'

'Perhaps. However, I gather that there is similar acrimony between you and Rhieinmelth. Have you ever thought that you might be at fault and not the women in your life?'

Oswiu stiffened and bit back an angry retort.

'I gave up Fianna, who I loved deeply, for Rhieinmelth. It might have been politically sensible, but it was a grave mistake for me personally. I haven't been happy since. At least I know have Aldfrith by my side.'

'Yes, it was another mistake, to bring the boy here I mean. Seeing his mother and the only father he's really known will be upsetting for him. It'll be hard on Fianna and Jarlath too.'

'Jarlath?'

'Yes, he was man enough to accept your by-blow as his own and when you decided you wanted the boy after all, he sent him to you without protest. In my eyes that makes him much more a man than his real father is.'

No one had remembered that Aldfrith was listening to all this. Suddenly he gave out a wail and, kicking his heels into his pony, he galloped off down the valley heading westwards.

'Oh shit,' Oswiu exclaimed. 'Well done mother. This is your fault, as usual. If I never see you again it'll be too soon.'

He jumped onto his own horse and, before anyone realised what was happening, he set off after his son. His gesith had dismounted and set their horses free to graze on the lush grassland whilst the family were greeting each other. No one was therefore ready to accompany their king and by the time that they had gathered their wits, Oswiu and his son had disappeared around a bend in the river.

The first person to recover was Jarlath. He'd been standing with Oswald's gesith at a distance, but not so far away that he couldn't hear what was being said. When Aldfrith bolted in shame he'd reacted without thinking and ran forward, vaulted into the saddle of the nearest horse and set off in pursuit.

'What a bloody family,' Œthelwald muttered quietly, but not so quietly that his father hadn't heard. His son had returned from Iona to start his training as a warrior no more likeable than when he'd left. Now he'd finished his training and his father didn't know what to do with him.

It didn't take Oswiu long to catch up with Aldfrith but the boy refused to stop. Oswiu solved that problem by moving his horse alongside his son's pony and, putting an arm around the boy's slim waist, he lifted him bodily off the pony and sat him in front of him. He pulled his stallion to a halt with difficulty and then dismounted before lifted the sobbing boy down and clutching him to his chest.

'You grandmother had no right to say those things. She's a nasty, spiteful, vindictive old woman. I love you very much.'

'Then why did you go away and leave me?'

'Because he didn't want the burden of children when he had a new wife to entertain,' a quiet voice said from behind them.

Neither had noticed Jarlath ride up. He now sat there looking down at them with conflicting emotions.

'Do you really love Aldfrith, Oswiu?'

'I swear by Christ's Holy name that I do.'

'What about Ehlfrith?'

'Well, I love him too, of course. But he is still a baby.'

'I mean which one will succeed you as King of Rheged?'

Oswiu's flushed with anger.

'That's got nothing to do with you.'

'Don't argue,' Aldfrith almost screamed at them. 'You're as bad as one another. You both say you love me, but you never think about me. When I see my father and my foster-father arguing like this, how do you think it makes me feel?'

'The boy's right,' Oswiu said wearily. 'You're not some chattel to be disposed of as your elders see fit. What is it you want, Aldfrith?'

It was not something the seven-year old boy had thought much about. At that age he wanted to be safe and comfortable and to be loved. He liked a bit of adventure too and he'd enjoyed travelling the country to Rheged and back again. He did know he wanted to be a warrior when he grew up and he knew that Jarlath was one whereas Oswiu was a king. He supposed that meant he was like his uncle Oswald. He didn't see much of him though, he was always away.

'I don't really know as yet,' he said after a while. 'I want to be a warrior when I grow up, not a monk, I do know that.'

'What about your mother?'

'Of course I miss her but I'm seven now, I love her but I don't need her like I did when I was small.'

That make both men smile.

'Very well,' Oswiu broke the silence. 'You asked me who will succeed me as King of Rheged. The honest answer had to be Ehlfrith as he's the direct descendant of the previous kings. However, I'm prepared to formally acknowledge Aldfrith as my son and make him my heir in all respects, except for Rheged.'

'In that case I think you should stay with King Oswiu, Aldfrith.'

'Why?'

'This is something you're too young to understand but kings die in battle all the time. Your father is King Oswald's choice as heir so someday you might be King of Northumbria. He can train you for that, I can't.'

'What about my cousin though?'

'Cousin?

'Œthelwald. He's King Oswald's only son and he's a warrior now.'

'As I said, Oswiu is Oswald's choice as heir to Northumbria, not Œthelwald. Although the Witan elects the king from eligible æthelings, his nomination will hold great sway.'

'Good! I don't like Cousin Œthelwald very much.'

'Nor do we,' both men said together, then laughed.

~~~

245

Domnall Brecc had taken Oswiu's hint and was mustering as many men as he could in order to invade Manau. At first their progress was easy. The Strathclyde Britons fled before him and the native inhabitants welcomed the return of the Dalriadans as most of them were Scots settlers. He deliberately stayed south of the River Forth, which divided Manau from Pictland, until he came to Stirling.

'Brenin,' a voice called from behind him as he was thinking of camping for the night. 'Domnall, stop.'

The breathless rider was one of the rearguard and he'd evidently ridden hard to catch his king up at the head of the army.

'What is it? Why the urgency?'

'We've been tricked, Brenin. King Owain's war host is behind us and the Picts are streaming out of Stirling to trap us between the Forth and the Carron.'

Domnall cursed long and hard. He'd brought every warrior who could be spared from Kintyre, Arran, Bute, Cowal, Islay and the Isles. If he lost this battle Dalriada would be anyone's for the taking. For the moment he wondered whether Oswiu was in on the conspiracy but he couldn't see what advantage the fall of Dalriada would have for him, or his brother Oswald. Having stronger neighbours on their northern borders hardly helped them. No, Oswiu had been duped as he had.

~~~

Whilst Domnall Brecc was trying to recover Manau, Oswiu was launching an invasion of his own.

'Why do you put up with these raids from the Isle of Man,' his wife chided him soon after his return from Yeavering.

246

Man lay in the middle of the Irish Sea with Strathclyde to the north, Rheged to the east and Ulster to the west. It was inhabited by Scots and had once been part of Dalriada. Now it was ruled over by Penda of Mercia and he'd encouraged the pirates who used it as a base to raid the Rheged coast.

'For once you have a point. However, before I act I need to know more about the island and, in particular, what numbers of ships and men I'd be facing.'

'Then, for once, I may be of some use to you, husband.'

She beckoned to an elderly slave woman who shuffled forward and bobbed awkwardly to king and queen in turn.

'This is Wynda, she was born on Man and grew up there. '

'How long ago was that?' Oswiu scoffed.

'I don't suppose that the island has changed much, Brenin, even though I haven't been there for over thirty years.'

'Very well. Tell me about it, but briefly.'

'Most of the isle is quite mountainous and few people live in the interior. The highest mountain is Snaefell in the northern half. Below it the northern tip of the island is relatively flat and this is where most of the cultivated land is. There are three main settlements: Douglas and Ramsey on the east coast, and Peel on the west.'

'Thank you, Oswiu said, surprised at the conciseness of the old woman's statement.

'My pleasure, Brenin,' she cackled before shuffling off.

'Now all I have to do is to find out how big these settlements are today and how many warriors there are.'

'How will you do that?'

'Send someone up Snaefell to watch and learn. Sigbert and Raulf both have excellent eyesight.'

Both were now warriors and part of Oswiu's gesith. A small fishing currach landed them on a small sandy beach on

the east coast where a stream ran into the sea. According to
the old hag the spring that fed it was near the summit of
Snaefell so the two scouts made their way up the stream a
little way and settled down for the rest of the night.

At dawn they set out to follow it upwards, munching on a
piece of hard cheese to assuage their hunger. In addition to
their swords they had both brought a hunting bow and a few
arrows in the hope that they could kill something to
supplement the cheese, dried meat and porridge oats that
they had brought with them.

The source of the stream was a few miles up the narrow
valley but it was a stiff climb and it took them the best part of
three hours. The area was boggy and they had to climb
upwards to get around it. From there they could see the
largest settlement, Douglas, below them. There was a large
hall and thirty or so huts. The bay on which the settlement
sat had a few of fishing boats pulled up onto the narrow
shingle beach and ten or so more were out at sea, but what
interested them were the seven birlinns. They were all small:
perhaps ten to fifteen oars a side, but it meant that there
were around a hundred and fifty to two hundred men in their
crews.

They continued their climb, this time up the bare slope of
Snaefell itself until they reached the summit. From there they
could just make out the coast lines of Ireland, Strathclyde
and Rheged. Peel on the east coast was too far away to
make out any details but it appeared to be just a small fishing
hamlet. Ramsey was barely four miles away and the details
were quite clear in the chilly but fine day in early
autumn. The fifteen huts clustered around a hall and the
settlement was protected by a palisade with just one gate on
the inland side. There was another leading out onto the
narrow sandy beach. This beach wasn't as sheltered as the

one at Douglas and there were no birlinns there. Several boats appeared to be fishing to the north of the island and these had presumably come from Ramsey.

As they watched a wide beamed trading vessel appeared from the south heading to pass Man to the west. There was a flurry of activity below in Douglas and they noticed for the first time a plume of smoke from the top of a mountain five miles or so away in the middle of the island. Evidently it was a lookout station. Three of the birlinns were pushed off from the beach, one heading south and two to the north.

The merchantman was about level with the hamlet of Peel when the Mercian birlinn rounded the Calf of Man – the small islet at the southern end of Man. There was only a light breeze and the merchantman was travelling slowly as it had no oars and was solely dependent on the wind. The rowers in the birlinn put their backs into it and were catching their quarry slowly but surely. By the time that the merchantman had reached a spot due west from Snaefell their pursuers were no more than four miles behind them. Then the trading vessel had a stroke of luck. The wind picked up and the merchantman speeded up. Soon it was beginning to pull away slightly from the birlinn.

The chase continued, however, until the ship being pursued had nearly reached the northern tip of the island. It was then that the other two birlinns appeared heading straight for the unfortunate trading ship. The ship changed course towards the Ulster coast, sailing as close to the wind as it could, but the birlinns turned to intercept her. They had been sailing but now hauled up the sail and started to row. Ten minutes later, the merchantman turned through ninety degrees and ran with the wind almost behind it for the northern tip of Man.

The two birlinns had been wrong footed and were now desperately trying to rig their sails again as the rowers turned her onto the new heading. The merchantman had nearly made it when the wind dropped again. Now she was helpless as the three birlinns closed in on her, each set of rowers trying to be the first to reach her. The outcome wasn't in doubt.

That afternoon Sigbert and Raulf descended to the beach where they had landed and just after nightfall the currach appeared to take them back to Caer Luel.

~~~

Domnall Brecc knew that his position was serious. However, Strathcarron, through which the River Carron meandered, was bounded by a range of high hills on the north side of the river and he decided to make his stand below one of the tallest near a bend in the Carron. Whilst the Picts remained north of the Forth he might still have a chance.

'Where is the nearest ford across the River Forth?'

'Not for some distance upstream, but there is a bridge a few miles from here,' one of his guides who was born in Manau, replied.

'Good.' He turned to his cousin, Dúnchad mac Conaing. 'Take a hundred men, all I can spare I fear, and hold the bridge - destroy it if you have to - but keep the Picts on the far side of the River Forth. I'll take the rest of the army and face Owain and his pagan horde.'

Dúnchad nodded. He had taken over as Thegn of Arran and Bute when Oswald had departed for Northumbria seven years previously. As soon as he reached the bridge he realised that it would be difficult to demolish. It had been well built from thick tree trunks that would take time to chop through with axes. He looked towards the advancing Picts and calculated that he had less than twenty minutes before they got there. Then the horsemen galloped ahead of the mass of warriors on foot, trying to get to the bridge before he could damage it.

'Archers,' he yelled. 'Take up position along the banks either side of the bridge and keep the horsemen from interfering. Those with axes chop at the supports this end of the bridge. The rest of you prepare to hold the bridge.'

With that Dúnchad picked up his own axe and started work on one of the supports. Standing thigh deep in water he couldn't see much but he heard the whirr of arrows followed by the screams of wounded men and the whinnies of dying horses.

Three other men joined him and they got into a rhythm, each chopping in turn as the chips of wood flew thick and fast. Finally he heard the support creak and the four men stepped away from it just as it snapped under the weight of the logs above it which formed the roadway. The near end of the bridge sagged into the water but it was still passable.

Dúnchad clambered back up the bank and looked towards the Picts. There were perhaps seventy horsemen on the far bank of whom half had been unhorsed, killed or incapacitated. However, his archers were running low on arrows and their arms were tiring. A group of eight horsemen had reached the far side of the bridge and charged recklessly across it. Three were hit before they got halfway and, as the rest were about to charge into the warriors massed on the other side, the other support gave way with a loud crack and the horsemen plunged into the fast flowing river.

By now the rest of the Picts were approaching the river bank with their own archers running in front of the rest. Dúnchad decided that there was no point in wasting the lives of his men; it would take the Picts hours to repair the damage enough to cross the river safely.

One or two brave – or foolish – men tried to cross the river but either they couldn't swim or the current was too strong and they were swept away. The leaders could be seen arguing what to do; presumably some were in favour of repairing the bridge and others on marching further upstream to the next crossing place. Suddenly there was a tearing and grinding sound as the decision was made for them. The water pressure on the part of the structure in the water had swept it away and half of the rest of the bridge was pulled into the water. Dúnchad turned to two of his scouts.

'Go and find out what's happening further up the valley.'

As they galloped away he ordered his men to follow them and they set off to retrace their steps. They had crossed the hills between the two rivers via a saddle which was the lowest part of the range of hills but, if he returned that way it would bring him out behind Domnall's army. Instead he headed west in order to cross via much higher col which he calculated should bring him out either behind the men of Strathclyde or on their left flank. Either way, he should be able to surprise them.

It took his men two hours to reach the saddle, but Dúnchad had ridden ahead to see what was happening. Just as he reached the saddle his scouts re-joined him.

'As you can see, lord, the king is outnumbered but he is holding his own. The enemy seem loathe to press home an attack though.'

252

'No doubt Owain is trying to lose as few men as possible whilst he waits for the damned Picts to join him. Had they been able to cross the Forth, they would have been able to attack Domnall in the rear by now.'

As soon as his men had laboured their way up to join him he led them down the other side aiming at the rear of the left flank of the enemy. At first he kept his banner hidden. For a while Owain might be fooled into thinking it was his allies, though he would realise it wasn't as they drew closer. Picts fought half naked with painted torsos. Few had much in the way of armour. In contrast many of the men from Arran and Bute owned a leather jerkin or a chainmail byrnie of some sort and most had a helmet. Even the few who didn't own a helmet were dressed in leggings, a tunic and a sheepskin to give them some protection.

After they had successfully negotiated the first part of the descent, which was littered with boulders, they started to run whilst trying to keep together. It was at that point that someone realised that they weren't Picts. Dúnchad's banner man waved it aloft and the men started to cry their leader's name as they quickened the pace.

Whether their arrival would have turned the tide in their favour was something that would never be known. When they were still three hundred yards away from the enemy a wail went up from the ranks of Dalriada. Domnall Brecc had been killed.

The heart went out of his men and they started to fall back. Then those at the rear started to flee, most heading towards the route through the hills that Dúnchad had originally take to reach the River Forth. A few with less sense fled onto the open plain behind them where they would be trapped at the junction between the Firth of Forth and the place where the River Carron joined the Firth.

Dúnchad watched impotently as Owain's men pursued the routed Dalriadans. There was no point in trying to attack the enemy now. His duty was clear: to save as many of his own men as he could.

'What do we do now, lord?' one of his horsemen asked.

'We save ourselves. We head northwest back to Dalriada and hope we can get out of Manau before the Picts cut us off.'

Two days later Dúnchad reached Dùn Add and was made high king by Fergus of Islay, the only remaining sub-king. Domangart, as Domnall's eldest son, might have expected to inherit, but he was an inexperienced youth of seventeen. As some form of consolation Dúnchad made him King of Arran and Bute as his vassal. It was not a wise move. It gave the boy a power base from which to challenge Dúnchad later; a challenge that would be successful.

However, it remained to be seen how much of Dalriada would be left for either of them to rule over after the catastrophe at Strathcarron. Of the hundreds of men that Domnall had led to disaster, barely a hundred and sixty had made it home again. The rest were either dead or enslaved.

Oswiu was furious when he'd heard. Evidently the High King of the Picts, Talorc, was a man with no honour and he wondered whether his own nephew, Talorgan, had been aware of the plan. It was possible, of course, that he'd been an innocent dupe. Oswiu hoped so.

That question was answered a little later when he heard that Talorgan had accused Talorc of duplicity and then had to flee for his life into the far north where the high king's writ didn't run.

~~~

The report from Sigbert and Raulf about the Isle of Man had given Oswiu an idea. It was now early October but, September having ended cold, wet and windy, the new month had started fine and warm, during the day at least. The clear skies meant that the nights were chilly but what worried Oswiu was the lack of wind. He needed some for his plan to work.

The news of the massacre at Strathcarron had reached him as he prepared to invade Man. At first he thought he'd have to call it off and prepared his defences – both in Rheged and Goddodin -against Owain but then he received news that changed everything. Owain had been wounded in the battle and, although it wasn't serious, he'd neglected the wound and it had become infected. A month later he died from septicaemia.

The new King of Strathclyde was his fifteen year old son, Guret, the boy who Oswiu had captured at Dùn Breatainn three years previously. He had liked Guret then and knew that the boy wasn't a fanatical pagan like his father had been. Being so young, he'd be far from secure on his throne and Oswiu decided to try and make him an ally.

However, his priority was the Isle of Man. It would stop the raids on the coast of Rheged and it would deprive Penda of territory. He nearly decided to delay as Rhieinmelth was due to give birth any day now, but it was late in the season for sailing and so in the end he decided to go. He only expected to be away for a few days and his wife probably wouldn't care less if he was nearby or not when the time came.

The two big merchantmen sailed down close to the coast of Rheged and the signal fire was lit. This time five birlinns sailed out of Douglas with the wind behind them. Three

255

headed to cut the ships off whilst the other two headed north in case their quarries decided to turn and run for it. The merchantmen seemed to take alarm and there was a flurry on deck as they trimmed their sails to head closer inshore.

'And a fat lot of good that's going to do them!' yelled one jubilant Mercian shipmaster across the sea to another.

Two of the pirate ships had flung grappling irons across to pull the merchantmen close to them so that they could board when a cry of alarm reached them faintly. However, they ignored it and swarmed across the gunwale onto the decks of the two merchantmen. As they did so armoured warriors appeared from under the aft and forrard decks and more jumped out of the cargo holds. The fight was brief and bloody. The pirates were outnumbered, unarmoured and taken completely by surprise.

Some tried to surrender but they were given no quarter. A few minutes later both boarding parties were dead and the Rheged warriors had captured the two Mercian birlinns.

The cries of alarm had come from the two pirate birlinns to the north. They had been watching what they thought was the capture of two easy prey when one of the crew shouted a warning as six large birlinns appeared from a cove to the east. Whilst the pirates had ten oars a side the new arrivals had between fifteen and twenty. Furthermore their crews were rowing hard whilst the Mercians still had their sails up.

In their panic it took them longer to get their sails furled and their oars in the water than usual and then the rowers had to get their static ships to move up to full speed, which took time. By then four of Oswiu's birlinns had almost reached them. When they came alongside they didn't bother to send away a boarding party but groups of men strained to swing out a boom carrying a net full of rocks. When it was over the Mercian vessels the net was opened and the rocks crashed down and stove in the planking below the water line.

Oswiu's ships sped on to chase the one remaining Mercian birlinn which was heading back to Douglas as fast as it could go. It was heading into a strong breeze with twenty rowers to power it. It should have been much lighter than the larger ships but it was crammed with warriors and probably didn't weigh much less than larger birlinns with their extra rowers.

They had nearly reached Douglas when another birlinn appeared from around a point called Little Ness a mile and a half south of Douglas. It had been waiting there since the previous night and now, sailing on a broad reach with a strong wind behind it and its thirty rowers adding to its speed, it was closing on the hapless Mercian ship fast.

The smaller birlinn knew that it was caught and the rowers stopped rowing. However, it didn't save it. A third birlinn drew alongside and swung out it deadly boom with its net of rocks and another Mercian ship slowly sank beneath the choppy waters of the Irish Sea.

Leaving the crews of the two merchantmen to deal with the two captured birlinns, Oswiu swept on and into Douglas Bay. The large settlement sprawled around the bay with no thought to defence. When Oswiu's fleet beached their ships and three hundred well-armed men leapt ashore the remaining Mercians decided not to put up a fight. A few fled into the interior where they were hunted down and killed by the locals. Man had been part of Dalriada before its capture by Penda and so the majority of its people were Scots from Ulster.

Oswiu was a popular conqueror and especially so when he announced that Man would now return to Dalriada. He sent a birlinn to let Fergus know what had happened and then, leaving the crews of two birlinns behind until Fergus could take over his new domain, he departed with nine birlinns, including the two captured ones, for Dùn Breatainn. The merchantmen that he'd borrowed returned to Caer Luel to load their cargo of wool, furs and gold before embarking on their last trading voyage before winter made sailing inadvisable.

~~~

Oswald had moved his base to Eoforwīc. He'd found that both Yeavering and Bebbanburg were too far north for him to keep track of what the wily King of Mercia was up to. Besides, Oswiu was now effectively his sub-king of the northern half of his extensive realm.

'You've heard the latest tidings I suppose,' he asked his wife, who was sitting sewing with Keeva in the hut that he'd built for them at Eoforwīc.

The king's hall had no private space, just a curtained off corner that did nothing to hide the sounds of forty warriors who lived in the hall carousing, farting and snoring.

'What? That Æthelberht of Kent had died? Yes. What do you know of his successor, Eorconberht?'

'Not much. I'm told he's a devout Christian and he's married to Sexburga of Ely, King Anna of East Anglia's daughter, so that alliance should strengthen the opposition to Penda.'

'But I thought that Eormenred was Æthelberht's eldest son?'

'And so he is, but the Witan of Kent chose the younger son; they must have had good reason.'

At that moment the sentry outside announced that Jarlath wished to enter.

'Jarlath, what brings you to see me? I thought you were watching the young warriors train.'

'I was, Cyning, but something has happened which I needed to discuss with you urgently. I apologise for interrupting, Síþwíf,' he added looking at Cyneburga.

'Well, what's happened,' he asked Jarlath as soon as the two of them had walked outside.

The captain of the king's gesith looked around him to make sure there was no one within earshot.

'King Cynegils is dead, Oswald.'

'No! How do you know?'

'A messenger has just arrived. He'd ridden hard and was nearly out on his feet so I said I'd tell you.'

'This is very bad news, especially on top of Æthelberht's death. Not only was Cynegils the queen's father, but he was our most powerful ally against Penda. I can't imagine that the pagan Cenwalh will be such an asset.'

'No. There's worse news. Cenwalh has agreed to become betrothed to Edith, Penda's sister.'

'You jest. She must be twenty years older than he is.'

'Yes, hardly a love match.'

'Obviously not. Cenwalh will have acted to secure his throne. With Penda as his father-in-law none of the other Æthelings will challenge him. It won't last of course. He's not very bright but he won't like being treated like a vassal, which is what Penda will do. The lad is too headstrong to accept that. And he'll want a wife to give him a son. Edith must be too old for childbearing by now, if she ever could. She never gave her first husband any.'

259

'I have a bad feeling about this. First I lose Kent as an ally and now Wessex. It's time to prepare for war.' He sighed. 'You had better summon the Witan.'

~~~

The arrival of Oswiu's fleet off Dùn Breatainn caused something of a stir. He noticed with a wry smile that a small fort was being built at the bottom of the defile which had been set on fire when he was last there. It wouldn't be so easy to capture the fortress next time. There were four birlinns drawn up on the beach when they arrived and one of these now made its way towards his ship. He hove to awaiting its arrival and signalled for the other birlinns to do the same.

'What do you want here, Oswiu of Rheged. Have you come to try and burn us out again? You won't find it so easy this time.'

'My quarrel was with Owain, not with his son. I've come to negotiate with King Guret.'

'Negotiate? Negotiate what?'

'Peace. If you give me safe conduct I will come ashore to speak with him, if he's here.'

'I see. I'll return shortly. Remain here.'

'We'll move a little closer inshore so that we can drop anchor.'

An hour later the birlinn returned. This time Guret was aboard.

'I seem to remember that you once threatened to drop me overboard, Oswiu. I assume that if I come aboard again you won't do that?'

Oswiu laughed. 'It's good to see you again Guret. I'd say that I was sorry about your father but you know I'd be lying.'

'At least I can't blame you for his death.'

'Come aboard so we can talk properly.'

'I won't ask for a safe conduct because I know you are a man of honour.'

'Yes, but your advisors might not be so trusting.'

As he spoke he could see three men begin to argue with the young king.

'If it makes those three any happier I'll swear on the Holy Bible not to harm you and to allow you to return once we have finished speaking, or I can come aboard your ship.'

'That won't be necessary. I know you, they don't.'

The smaller birlinn came alongside Oswiu's ship and Guret leapt nimbly from one to the other. His three nobles followed, rather less nimbly.

To Oswiu's surprise Guret came and embraced him with a smile. He took the opportunity to whisper in his ear 'I could do with a friend just at the moment. Don't trust these three,' before stepping back to introduce his companions.

'This is Brandon, Cunobelinus and Nechtan.' He introduced each in turn. 'They are my council of regency who are to advise me until I am old enough to rule on my own.'

His tone of voice told Oswiu exactly what Guret thought of the arrangement.

'What do you want here, Oswiu? What tricks are you planning this time?' Cunobelinus asked.

'No tricks,' he replied, trying to hide his annoyance. 'This is Beorhtric, Eorl of Dùn Èideann and the captain of my gesith, Ceadda. Shall we sit?'

The ships boys brought them a few empty barrels and covered them with animal pelts so that they could sit down, then Oswiu continued.

'Strathclyde is exhausted by war and Dalriada even more so. Rheged and Bernicia, in contrast, have prospered over the past few years. My army is strong, well trained and well equipped. I could, if I chose, march into Manau and even Lorne and restore it to Dalriada, as I have just done with the Isle of Man.'

'You've captured that nest of pirates from Mercia? How?' Nechtan asked.

'It must have cost you a lot of men. Was it worth it if you gave it away to Dalriada?' Brandon commented, almost at the same time.

'I lost precisely two men and a few wounded, but I'm not here to talk about that.'

'Anyone who has the cunning to capture Dùn Breatainn and Man with scarcely any losses is a man worth listening to. What do you propose, Oswiu?'

With one sentence Guret had put his council in their place and asserted himself as the person who would do the negotiations. Oswiu had to hide a smile as the others realised what had just happened.

'Thank you, Guret. I propose a treaty between us which establishes our borders as they are now and by which you undertake not to engage in any further conquest of Dalriadan territory, or indeed any incursions into either Rheged or Goddodin. Nor will our ships engage in combat with each other at sea.'

'That's all very well, but such an agreement is worthless unless the Picts agree to something similar,' Cunobelinus pointed out.

'Talorc sent my nephew, Talorgan, to me some time ago proposing an alliance between Northumbria and the Picts, to which Oswald has agreed, so I don't think that will be a problem.'

The three advisors looked at each other nervously. They didn't like the way that this was going.

'How do we know we can trust you?' Nectan said. 'You could be luring us into a false sense of security just so you can invade and take us unawares.'

'That's enough,' Guret snapped. 'I trust Oswiu and that's what matters.'

'You're still a boy,' Nechtan sneered. 'You have no experience. Leave these matters to older and wiser heads.'

'Older yes, but not wiser,' Oswiu murmured. 'You have a choice. Either you support your king and show him proper respect or Strathclyde will be torn apart through weak rule.'

'Yes, you were out of order Nechtan.' Cunobelinus agreed. 'We are the king's advisors, not his rulers. You should apologise.'

Nechtan went red in the face and Oswiu thought that he was going to refuse, but then Brandon put a warning hand on his arm and the man made a visible effort to calm down.

'I'm sorry, Brenin. I spoke out of turn,' he said formally.

'Thank you Nechtan. I know that was difficult for you.'

'However, Nechtan has a point, Guret. Strathclyde and Rheged have never been friends, nor have we and Northumbria,' Brandon said.

'That doesn't have to continue,' Oswiu replied. 'In the past Rheged and Strathclyde have fought over who owned Galloway. It has been part of Strathclyde for decades now and I'm content to accept that.'

The three nobles looked pleased at that but Guret decided to try and resolve another bone of contention from the past.

'What about the borders with Goddodin and the rest of Bernicia? Our eastern border has never been well defined.'

'I suggest that we each nominate five commissioners to inspect the border and agree where it should run. Is that acceptable?'

Guret looked at his three advisors and then each nodded.

'That seems very sensible. I am grateful to you for what has been a most useful meeting.'

'If it brings peace to my borders, then it was time well spent.'

He didn't add that he had a feeling that Oswald might need his services in the not too distant future and he needed to make sure the North was at peace first. There remained the problem of the duplicitous Picts but there was nothing he could do about them for the moment.

CHAPTER ELEVEN – THE WAR CLOUDS GATHER

Summer 642 AD

Oswiu returned to Rheged well pleased with himself. However, his mood changed as soon as he landed. An agitated servant ran to meet him as soon as he'd disembarked at Caer Luel.

'Brenin,' the man cried. 'Thank heavens you've returned. We sent a messenger in a currach to find you several days ago.'

'Well, he didn't find me. What is it? Spit it out.'

'It's the queen, Brenin. She's very ill.'

'Rhieinmelth? What's wrong with her?'

'She gave birth to a healthy daughter but her attendants haven't been able to stop her bleeding. She's very weak now.'

Oswiu gave a cry and ran towards the hall. They might not love each other anymore but he didn't want her to die.

'You mustn't go in, Brenin,'

'Get out of my way woman.'

The king brushed past the servant and rushed into the bedchamber.

'Oswiu, I think you may have come just in time,' his wife said weekly, gasping for each breath. 'Just in time to say goodbye,' she managed to finish before she closed her eyes.

'No, don't go. I'm so sorry for not trying harder to love you.'

'Me too. Don't worry. I'm close to dying, but I can last a little longer I think.' This came out in gasps interspersed with long pauses for Rhieinmelth to gather her strength. 'Isn't she beautiful?'

Oswiu hadn't noticed the cot and went over to look at his daughter.

'She is. What shall we call her?'

'Alchflæd I thought,'

'Yes, I like it.'

He went back over to the bed and kissed his wife's deathly pale forehead.

'Is there nothing anyone can do for you? If only Aidan or Ròidh were here. They both trained as infirmarians.'

'Oswiu, hold me. I think my time is near.'

'Have you been shriven?'

She nodded weekly. 'Yesterday,' she whispered.

He was still holding her tightly when he felt her body go limp as she exhaled her last breath.

He stayed with her for a long time, quietly weeping, before Ceadda came in and gently led him away so that her women could prepare her body for burial.

It was only then that he thought of Elhfrith. The boy was too young to have been completely weaned, and he'd obviously need a wet nurse for Alchflæd. He needn't have worried. An hour later a woman came up to the hall who had just given birth to twins and volunteered to nurse his children.

Oswiu went to find his other son, Aldfrith, and found the boy sitting disconsolately outside the hall looking at the distant hills.

'Is it true father? The queen is dead.'

'Yes, I fear so.'

'What will happen to me now?'

'What do you mean?'

'I lived in the queen's chamber with Elhfrith.'

'Ah, I see. Well, he and your baby sister will be going to live with a wet nurse until they are both weaned. You can stay on in my wife's chamber for now and I'll find you a slave to look after you. Would you prefer a boy or a girl?'

His son looked thoughtful for a while.

'Well,' he said, 'a girl would look after me well but I might enjoy the company of a boy.'

'He's there to look after you, not be your friend.'

'But Jarlath used to be King Oswald's body slave and he's his closest companion now.'

'Yes, you're right.' Oswiu smiled. 'You've given me an idea.'

Jarlath and Keeva were brother and sister and they had both looked after his brother until Keeva became Oswald's lover. Perhaps the answer would be to find a pair of siblings to serve his son. He went to see Ceadda.

'How many children did we bring back from Douglas?'

The families of the Mercians who were killed or who surrendered had been captured and, together with the surviving men, were destined to become slaves.

'We captured about sixty but all of the men and women were either sold on the island of sent on the two merchantmen for sale in Frankia. I think we brought no more than a dozen or so children back here because no-one wanted them. They're all too young to work in the fields or the mines. Why?'

'I need slaves to look after Aldfrith.'

'What about the queen's women?'

'She had left instructions that they were to be freed and nearly all want to become nuns to pray for her soul. Besides, I grew up with body slaves near my own age and it worked well. I learned how to get the best out of people without just giving orders, which were then resented. I'm sure I was happier than if I'd had slaves who were much older than me too.'

'Well, we'd better go and see what's left at the market.'

Ceadda had been correct; there weren't many slaves left. There was a boy of about twelve and two siblings, a boy of ten or eleven and a girl perhaps a year older. The two siblings looked undernourished but the other boy caught Oswiu's eye. He was well fed, wore the remains of what had been an expensive tunic and, unlike the cowed, snivelling majority of children in the slave market, he looked at the crowd with haughty distain.

'I'll buy all three, go and have a word with the auctioneer,' so saying the king handed Ceadda a heavy gold arm ring.

Ceadda looked at him with surprise. The arm ring was one that Oswiu wore most days. He'd taken it from an Irish chieftain he'd killed in battle when he was sixteen and it was his favourite. It was worth many times what the three children would have cost him if he'd bid for them.

He went up to the auctioneer on the platform in the middle of the market which was set up each week outside the walls of Caer Luel. Anglo-Saxons didn't have the skills to build walls of stone and so the gaps where the Roman walls had collapsed had been filled with lengths of palisade. The rostrum had been built backing onto a length of the infill palisade. Oswiu frowned. It was a stupid place to put it because it made it easy to scale the defences at that point. He made a mental note to get it moved.

Ceadda whispered in the auctioneer's ear and handed him the arm ring in a sack. The man was about to protest until he looked inside it; then he couldn't conclude the sale quickly enough.

'What are your names?' Oswiu asked them once the crowd had dispersed.

'I'm Ealswith and my brother is Ludeca.'

'And you?'

Wigmund,' the older boy said sulkily.

'No it isn't,' Ludeca said. 'It's Alweo.'

'Alweo,' said Oswiu in surprise. 'The only Alweo I know of is Eowa's son.'

The boy who had pretended to be Wigmund gave the younger boy a venomous look but said nothing.

'What was the eldest son of King Penda's brother doing on Man?'

Alweo sighed. 'I was spending time with my cousin, who was the son of the King of Man.'

'King of Man? I didn't know Penda had a brother, apart from your father.'

The boy mulled over whether he should reply, but in the end he sighed and then answered.

'He was the husband of my aunt. She died a few years ago but Wigmund was her son. He and I were good friends and my father thought it would be good for us to spend the summer together on Man; not his most brilliant idea as it turned out. '

'Where is this Wigmund now?'

'He was sold this morning.'

'And his father?'

'He was drowned when you sunk his birlinn.'

Oswiu turned to Ceadda.

'Find out who he's been sold to and bring him to my hall.'

269

'Yes, Cyning. What about these three?' Ceadda asked.

'What? You think I can't manage three children without help?'

'No, I just thought it a trifle undignified for the king to walk through Care Luel leading three slaves by the ropes tied to their wooden collars.'

'Well, we can solve that one. Take their collars off.'

'But they'll run away.'

'Where to? The sentries won't let them back through the gates, and in any case they know that they would be hanged for trying to escape.'

He turned back to the children.

'Right, just so you know what your future holds. Ealswith and Ludeca will be body slaves to my seven year old son, Aldfrith. You'll live in the king's hall and will be well treated if you work hard and behave yourselves.'

'What about me?' asked Alweo, now not quite so certain of himself.

'That rather depends on how much your father wants you and Wigmund back.'

~~~

Oswald usually found a solution to most problems but his son was different. He had made love to Cyneburga several times by now but she showed no signs of pregnancy. He'd long ago come to the conclusion that Keeva was barren. Now he wondered if the problem was his, but he'd managed to get Gytha, his first wife, pregnant twice. He resigned himself to the fact that Œthelwald was likely to be his only child but the thought depressed him.

Any father should want his son to succeed him, but Oswald shuddered at the thought of Œthelwald on the throne of Northumbria. His son was selfish and self-centred. He had no love for the people, nor any idea how to manage them. He didn't even seem to regard his father with any affection and Oswald feared that, had he more of a power base, he might even be dangerous. As it was, the type of young men he attracted to him were mainly drunkards and wastrels.

'Father, it's time you gave me a land of my own to rule. Even your brother has Rheged and seems to run Goddodin for you as well. Can't you give me Deira or Elmet or even Lindsey?'

'They are not mine to give you, as I've told you many times before Œthelwald. Their Witan elects the king from the eligible æthelings. I can't impose you on anyone.'

'Oswiu wasn't elected.'

'No, but he married the only surviving member of the royal house. In any case Rheged isn't Anglo-Saxon; the Britons have different ways of doing things.'

He wondered why he was bothering to explain all this to his son. They'd been over this ground several times in the past. Œthelwald was now nineteen so he, not unnaturally, considered himself old enough to be given significant responsibility. However, Oswald didn't think him suited to any form of leadership role and he didn't know what to do about him. For now he'd made him a member of his gesith, but he thought himself above the others and wasn't popular. Then he had an idea.

'There is one thing you could do, but I'm not sure you are suitable for the role.'

'What is it,' his son asked cautiously.

'You know that Kent has a new king, Eorconberht, and that he's married to Anna of East Anglia's daughter? Good. I want you to go to Eorconberht and see if you can negotiate an alliance with him. Then go and see Anna at his capital of Blythburgh and try and persuade him to ally himself to us as well. Do you think you can manage that?'

'I'll do my best, father. Thank you for entrusting this important task to me.'

His gratitude seemed genuine and Oswald smiled at him.

'It'll be safer and quicker to travel by sea. I'll lend you the Holy Saviour and one other birlinn as escort.'

'Who'll be my shipmaster; I assume you'll want Jarlath to remain with you?'

Knowing that the two didn't get along Oswald thought for a moment about who to send with Œthelwald. Both Cormac and Durstan were experienced sailors and would be good advisors for his son and, furthermore, were the only members of his gesith not to have quarrelled with Œthelwald.

'I was thinking of either Cormac or Durstan. Which would you prefer?'

'Thank you for giving me the choice father. I suggest that Cormac takes charge of the Holy Saviour and Durstan brings his own birlinn as the escort.'

'That seems sensible. A lot rides on this; don't let me down.'

'I won't. Thank you for exhibiting some faith in me at long last.'

~~~

Oswiu anchored in the estuary of the River Dee and waited for Eowa to appear. A few hours later five birlinns approached from the direction of Legacæstir; the number matched Oswiu's small fleet, as they had agreed.

'I can see my father,' Alweo yelled and even the normally taciturn Wigmund got excited.

272

Oswiu assumed that it was the tall man dressed in a polished byrnie with a red cloak and an open helmet with a circlet who was standing in the bows with one foot on the gunwale as if he was about to leap overboard.

The leading Mercian ship slowed as they approached Oswiu's birlinn and the crew backed their oars, then shipped them neatly and together. Oswiu was impressed as the other craft slowly inched alongside and the sailors on both lashed them together. It had been such a perfect manoeuver that the normal grappling irons weren't needed.

As the two hulls gently rubbed together in the swell sailors ran cables from the aft of both ships to the bows of the other, which stopped the to and fro movement of the two hulls.

'Are you coming aboard or am I?' Eowa called across.

'I'll come over to you, but the boys can stay here initially.'

Eowa gave him a grim smile. 'Very well. I hope that when we've spoken you will be able to trust my word a little more.'

'Oh I trust you, Eowa. I'm not sure I trust all Mercians, however.'

The man laughed. 'I'll see you shortly, Alweo, and you too Wigmund. I'm sorry about your father.'

Oswiu clambered across onto the other ship followed by Beorhtric, who had come with Oswiu to represent Goddodin.

After introductions the three men and the captain of Eowa's gesith, a man called Bergred, sat down on chairs that Eowa had brought with him; much more comfortable than barrels Oswiu thought.

'Your messenger said that you wanted to discuss something to our mutual advantage. What I'm unclear about is whether my agreement to whatever you are about to propose is connected to the release of my son and nephew.'

At that moment one of the ship's boys from the Holy Saviour jumped aboard and came to whisper in his king's ear. Oswiu nodded and the boy went back to the other ship.

'It seems that you don't trust me all that much either, Eowa. I understand that there are another four birlinns which are just rounding the Wirral to cut off our escape to the sea. Well, I can't say I blame you but what you don't know is that the rest of my fleet, which outnumber yours, is hove to on the horizon. No doubt the boys up their masts will have seen your ships and even now my fleet is moving to join us. Now I suggest that we avoid a stupid bloodbath. If you signal your ships to retreat, mine will do the same.'

'Just a precaution, you understand. Very well. I'd be stupid to engage you without hearing you out.'

He signalled to one of his crew who went to the bows and vigorously waved a banner to and fro. The approaching ships furled their sails, turned around and their rowers began to propel them back whence they had come. Oswiu's fleet had just appeared over the horizon but, when they saw the Mercians retreat, they stopped where they were.

'Now, what is it you have to say?'

Oswiu lowered his voice and checked that there were no sailors or warriors in earshot.

'I am led to believe that you are a Christian who doesn't always agree with your pagan brother.'

When Eowa didn't react, he continued.

'Oswald and I would like to bring peace to England but your brother seemed obsessed with conquest. We think that you would make a much better king of the Mercians and one with whom we could work to bring Christianity to everyone and unite the country under one bretwalda.'

'You want me to depose my brother and seize the Mercian crown myself?'

'As a first step, yes.'

'And what makes you think that I'd be so disloyal?'

'Isn't loyalty to God and His Son, Jesus Christ, more important?'

'My brother isn't anti-Christian in the way that that rabid dog, Owain of Strathclyde, was. He tolerates the worship of Christ but doesn't choose to abandon the old religion himself.'

'I see, so you have never dreamed of becoming King of Mercia instead of being one of his vassals? After all, you are the elder.'

'Perhaps, but whether I'm prepared to take the risk involved is another matter.'

'If you did rise in revolt, would your men follow you?'

'Most, yes. They've never even seen Penda. He has stayed in the south ever since Heavenfield.'

'Oswald seeks to unite Northumbria with Easy Anglia and Kent. I've reached agreements with Strathclyde and the other Saxon kingdoms are unlikely to get involved after their last experience of alliance with Penda.'

'What about Wessex?'

'If Mercia is divided, my guess would be that Cenwalh will decide to stay out of it. Who would your sister support?'

'She's closer to me than Penda, but I don't know how much influence she has with her husband. I gather that Cenwalh is considering divorcing her.'

'I don't suppose that would please either you or Penda.'

'Especially my brother, as he arranged the match.'

'Very well. Apart from Middle Anglia, who else would support Penda at the moment?'

'He has close ties with some of the Welsh kings.'

'Gwynedd and Powys you mean?'

'Yes, especially Powys. I think we can exclude Gwynedd. Its king isn't called Cadafael Cadomedd for nothing.'

Cadomedd meant *Battle Decliner* in Welsh.

'I need to think about this. It's not a decision to be taken lightly, and I need to consult with my nobles and commanders,' Eowa went on.

'I wouldn't want word of this to reach Penda.'

'Don't worry. I'll only talk to men I can trust. What about my son and nephew.'

'As a gesture of good faith I'll return them to you now, but we'll meet aboard my birlinn tomorrow. Send your chairs across though.'

The two men smiled at each other.

'Until tomorrow.'

In the end Eowa agreed to join Oswald's attack on Penda and Oswiu went back to Caer Luel to send a messenger to Oswald.

CHAPTER TWELVE – THE BATTLE OF MASERFIELD

August 642 AD

Oswald, Oswiu and Eowa sat around a table in the latter's hall in Legacæstir. The area around the old Roman town was covered with leather tents belonging to their three war hosts. In all they had mustered a total of nearly four thousand men. Oswald had left part of his fyrd behind in case Peada led his men into Elmet, Deira or Lindsey to take advantage of his absence. It was an unnecessary precaution as it turned out.

'According to my scouts, Peada has moved north west towards Derby with some fifteen hundred men,' Oswald said.

'My brother seems to be mustering his men at Shrewsbury. I'd have expected them to link up but perhaps they are attempting a pincer movement?' Eowa looked puzzled, a sentiment shared by the other two.

'Presumably he intends to draw you towards him, Eowa, to defend your lands.'

'Perhaps. Or maybe he will try and catch us in the flank by turning towards Shrewsbury when he reaches Uttoxeter.'

'Either way, we need to stop him in his tracks.' Oswiu said.

'Do we have an estimate of how many men Penda has?' Oswald asked.

'About two thousand. I'd have expected more, but perhaps he doesn't trust Cewalh and has left men behind to counter any move Wessex makes.'

'Very well, can I suggest that Oswiu takes his army to deal with Peada whilst we move south towards Penda? When you have defeated the Middle Anglians, come west to join us as fast as you can.'

Oswiu nodded. 'That seems sensible. It shouldn't take me more than four days to reach Peada and deal with him. I'll then make for Shrewsbury, so expect me on the seventh.'

~~~

Oswiu watched from the cover of the woods above the road from Uttoxeter to Legacæstir. Peada had obviously sent out raiding and forage parties to range either side of his line of march because he could see several fires burning to the south and east. At the moment Peada seemed to have no more than a thousand with him. When the middle of the Anglian column was level with his position he gave a signal and a hunting horn blared forth.

Immediately a shower of arrows hit the unprepared Middle Anglians and perhaps sixty of them fell dead or wounded. They had been taken completely by surprise. It was a hot day and most who possessed armour had decided to march without wearing it. Whilst the warriors scrambled to pull on their byrnies and helmets and the unarmoured fyrd pulled their shields round from their backs, another volley hit them and more men fell. Peada's men were well disciplined however and, by the time the third volley rose into the air, all had their shields in position. Only a few fell this time.

278

With a roar Oswiu's warriors, mostly from Rheged and Goddodin but with a sizeable warband from Bernicia as well, ran out of the woods on both sides of the road and down the slight slope. They smashed into the enemy column and their opponents were pushed into a narrow line facing both ways. Oswiu's men then proceeded to cut the line in numerous places and surrounded small knots of the enemy. Although they fought desperately, the Middle Anglians were disorganised and effectively leaderless.

Those who could slipped away and fled back the way they'd come. The rest prepared to sell their lives dearly.

Oswiu had led a wedge to cut through the enemy line and, whilst his men widened the gap, pushing the Anglians into tight groups which had difficulty in wielding their swords and spears, he picked out a giant of a man who had already slain three Rheged warriors.

He was armed with a battle axe and a spear, both of which he used to keep his opponent at a distance before jabbing with his spear and, when the other man moved his shield to defend against the thrust, he swung the heavy axe as if it were a feather and chopped his adversary down.

Oswiu's gesith surrounded him and the giant to keep anyone from interfering as their king went onto the offensive.

'You're slowing down, getting tired, old man?' he taunted the big Anglian.

With a roar the man forgot about his spear and tried to chop his axe into Oswiu's side. The King of Rheged stepped back and the axe whistled harmlessly by him, unbalancing the big man. Oswiu took advantage and stepped in, chopping his sword down on the wrist holding the spear. It cut most of the way through the joint and the hand flopped uselessly, hanging by a few tendons and a flap of flesh from his arm. The spear dropped to the ground.

It took a moment for the Anglian to realise what had happened; then he screeched in a mixture of rage and agony. He swung his axe again but Oswiu ducked under it, straightened his arm, and pushed his sword up under his ribs. The point lodged in his heart and a second later the big man crashed to the ground.

His gesith cheered and he looked around for another adversary, but Peada had fled, taking what was left of his army with him. Some groups had been unable to extricate themselves and they fought on to the last man. Only a hundred or so, all of them from the fyrd, surrendered.

'What's the casualty list?'

'For us, not too bad, Cyning,' the Eorl of Dùn Èideann replied. 'Under a hundred dead and eighty wounded. Of those fifty will either die of their wounds or are too maimed to fight again.'

'And the Middle Anglians?'

'Over four hundred dead. Two hundred more badly wounded and seventy prisoners.'

'So Peada has lost half his army?'

'So it would seem. There are still those out foraging and raiding but I don't think we need to worry about them now.'

Oswiu nodded. 'We need to get on the road to Shrewsbury.'

'The men are tired, Cyning. Can I suggest we delay until dawn tomorrow?'

'Can we reach Shrewsbury in two days?'

'It would mean a hard march and the men would be in no state to fight when we get there; better to allow three days.'

'Hmmm, I promised my brother we would reach there by the seventh. I don't suppose that one day will make much difference.'

In fact, it was going to make all the difference in the world.

~~~

Oswald rode forward with Eowa and three members of his gesith: Jarlath, Rònan and Beorhtwulf. Two had been his body slaves when they were boys and the third he'd known since he was sixteen. He knew they'd die for him. He was less certain about the warriors who accompanied Eowa. They seemed uncomfortable in his company and hadn't spoken a word to his three so far. Despite the Mercian's assurance that his men were loyal to him, Oswald wasn't so sure.

The scouts had reported that there was no army encamped at Shrewsbury. The settlement was surrounded on three sides by the broad River Severn and by a palisade on the fourth. As Penda obviously wasn't there anymore, he decided not to waste time and men capturing the place, though it was a risk leaving it in Mercian hands as it would be across his lines of communication.

The army took the road to the north of the settlement, where the Severn curved to the west, where there were the obvious signs left by a passing army.

'Do you know where this road leads,' Oswald asked Eowa.

'A hamlet called Maserfield and then into Powys, if I remember correctly.'

'Aye, Maserfield,' one of the Mercian's escort said with an unpleasant grin, and then spat into the dust.

281

'Why would he go there?' Oswald wondered, ignoring the man.

'Once in Powys he can disappear into the mountains and we'll never find him.'

'That doesn't sound like your brother to me, does it to you?'

'Perhaps he needs to gather more men to his side. The Welsh fight half-naked but they're doughty warriors.'

'Yes, I know. I fought Cadwallon.'

'What do we do? Wait for your brother?'

'Oswiu said he'd be here today but there's no sign of him and no messenger even. He might be days yet.'

'Or he might have lost the battle against Peada.'

'I doubt it. My brother hasn't lost a battle yet, and he had more men than the Middle Anglians. No, it's just taking him longer than he thought.'

'My brother has two thousand men, at most, and we have over three thousand. I say we attack him before he can escape,' Eowa said.

'Very well. I'll send the scouts forward to see if they can find out exactly where Penda is.'

~~~

Œthelwald arrived at Cantwareburg without any problems. He'd sailed into Ludenwic and then hired twenty horses for himself, an escort of fifteen and for use as packhorses before setting out for the capital of Kent.

As soon as he saw it, he was impressed with the church. Originally a Roman church built some three hundred years previously, it had been repaired and extended by masons from Frankia and Rome. All the other Anglo-Saxon churches he'd seen had been built of solid timber or a timber frame filled with wattle and daub.

He had been sent off to Iona as an unwilling pupil but, to his surprise, he had enjoyed the simple life of the monks and, when it came to leave when he was fourteen, he'd been sorry. However, he'd enjoyed training to be a warrior, but after that his life had been without purpose, for which he blamed his father.

He had immediately liked Eorconberht and the archbishop, Honorius, and started to attend services in the church with the monks. This had impressed Eorconberht and his squally devout queen and after a while he obtained his assurance that he would continue his father's policy of alliance with Northumbria and opposition to Penda.

Œthelwald should have moved on at that stage to visit Anna of East Anglia but he couldn't bring himself to leave Cantwareburg. He spent his time hunting and in theological discussions with Honorius and the monks.

Cormac had accompanied him to Cantwareburg whilst Dunstan remained with the two birlinns and most of the crews at Ludenwic. Both men were getting worried at the passing of time and in early August Dunstan send a message to Cormac urging him to bring Œthelwald back to Ludenwic.

Cormac had tried but failed to persuade Œthelwald to return to Ludenwic, but then a messenger arrived which made him all too eager to get back to Eoforwīc.

~~~

'He's occupying the old hill fort to the north of the settlement, Cyning,' the scout told Oswald later that day.

'How far from here?'

'About seven miles or so,'

283

'How many men?' Eowa cut in.

'It's difficult to say. The old fort is circular in shape with several rings of earthen mounds protecting the top. As far as I could tell that's flat but we couldn't see over the top ramparts. There could be thousands inside.'

'I suggest we camp three miles away and attack at dawn,' Eowa said, turning to Oswald.

'Yes, that makes sense, but I'd like to see this old fort for myself.'

Once more he rode forward with Eowa and the same escorts as before. Oswald had learned that the name of the Mercian who'd spat in the dust when he confirmed the name of the settlement as Maserfield was Eadgar, the son of one of Eowa's eorls called Leofric. However, in addition to the five warriors he took another fifty mounted men who remained concealed in edge of the woods half a mile from the fort, just in case they ran into trouble.

The hill fort sat in the middle of open countryside so the only way they could get a closer look at it was to ride around it in the open. It consisted of four concentric rings of earthworks and had two entrances, each protected by a series of three gateways. As they rode around it out of range of the archers on the top, more and more warriors came to jeer at them until the topmost rampart was crammed with men.

'How many do you think?' Oswald asked Eowa.

'At least two thousand, maybe more. Most are Mercians but I estimate that there are at least five hundred Welshmen up there as well, presumably from Powys.'

'Yes, I agree. This is going to be a difficult place to attack.'

'We need to get up to the top under cover of darkness, I think, then storm the place at dawn.'

284

'Perhaps, but they are bound to hear us.'

'Does that matter? If they decide to attack us at night the battle will take place on the approaches instead of at the top. We have more men and can use wedge formations to break through their lines.'

'Very well. We'll move into position under cover of darkness.'

It wasn't until just before dawn broke that Oswald found out that he'd been betrayed. A messenger came looking for him as he waited in the midst of his warriors for the first rays of the sun to appear over the eastern horizon.

'Oswald, where are you? Where's the king?'

'Over here, quietly now. What is it?'

'Eowa has been treacherously slain, some say by Eadgar. Eorl Leofric has led the Mercians back down the hill.'

Oswald immediately knew what that meant. No doubt Leofric expected Penda to raise him to replace Eowa as a reward. How little he knew Penda, he thought with a chuckle. Then his mood grew sombre when he realised his own plight. He was now trapped with two thousand men between a thousand Mercians at the bottom of the hill and another two thousand at the top, together with who knew how many Welshmen.

'Pass the word, we're retreating to the bottom to attack Leofric.'

As the sunshine slowly crept over the ground towards the base of the hill fort, shining off the helmets of the Mercians waiting below, black clouds began to scud across the sky, obscuring the sun and replacing the illuminated earth with dark shadows. Oswald had never seen anything like it. It was if Heaven had suddenly gone into mourning.

As he reached the last of the four ramparts he yelled 'charge' and he and his men swept down the last slope and headed for the waiting Mercians. The momentum of the Northumbrians hurled the first row of the shield wall back into the second and they, in turn, were forced back into the third and final rank of warriors. Chaos ensued and the battle deteriorated into a series of individual fights. However, as the Northumbrians had the superior numbers there could only be one outcome and the Mercians started to die by the score.

Just when Oswald thought he'd won he heard a roar behind him and saw Penda's men running down from the final rampart.

'Shield wall,' he yelled but there was no time to form up before the enemy crashed into them. Oswald never knew but there were a thousand Welshmen with Penda and so now it was Oswald's turn to be outnumbered. That, coupled with the casualties he'd already suffered and the momentum of the attack meant that his men had little hope of winning. He grabbed Rònan's arm.

'Sound the retreat, quickly now.'

Rònan put the hunting horn to his lips and blew the short repeated blasts that told everyone to withdraw. At first the Northumbrians just stood there stunned.

Then Oswald yelled, 'get out of here, for the sake of Christ Our Saviour, run. Save yourselves to fight another day, and may God go with you.'

They took one look at the Mercians and nearly naked Welshmen, who were now no more than two hundred yards away, and they fled. All but Oswald's gesith and perhaps another two hundred of his war band, who were not about to desert their king, no matter what he said.

By now rain had been falling heavily for a little while and the ground was becoming slippery underfoot. This worked in the Northumbrians favour as several of the enemy who were charging down the final slope slipped and fell, only to be trampled on by those behind them, some of whom also went sprawling. It was not enough to make any difference though.

Oswald hefted his shield and with Rònan on one side of him and Jarlath on the other he waited for the oncoming tide. Suddenly he felt a piece of bread being pushed into his mouth as Oslac stood behind him and muttered the words 'in the name of the Father, the Son and the Holy Ghost, this is my body, eat this in memory of me.' He moved on down the line and then Penda's army hit them.

Oswald was forced back as a Mercian banged his shield into his and tried to stab his sword into his neck. Rònan got there first and thrust his spear into the man's side just as another enemy warrior crashed into his own shield.

Then Oswald saw Oslac standing in front of him holding his crucifix on high and cursing the Mercians in the name of Jesus Christ. Miraculously no-one cut the chanting priest down until Penda appeared and, with a laugh, swung his sword and chopped Oslac's head from his body.

'So much for the protection of your God, priest,'

'No!' Oswald cried as he saw his brother fall and, barging the warrior facing him aside, he charged forward determined to kill Penda. He never got there. The man he had knocked out of the way turned and thrust his spear into Oswald's back. It broke the links of his chain mail but the blow didn't have enough force to break through the padded leather jerkin underneath. It did, however, jar Oswald's spine and two of his discs were dislodged. He was crippled and fell face down into the churned up mud.

Penda went to pin him to the ground with his sword but Jarlath got there first, standing over Oswald to protect him. He was quickly joined by Rònan, Beorhtwulf and the few remaining members of the king's gesith. By now most of those who had stayed behind with Oswald were dead, but they had succeeded in delaying the pursuit for long enough to give their comrades a reasonable chance of escaping.

Two hours later the fleeing Northumbrians ran into Oswiu's advance guard and, when the pursuing Mercians realised that they were now facing another army, they quickly lost their enthusiasm for the chase and started to run back to Maserfield.

When they got there Penda decided not to face Oswiu, who probably had as many men as he had, and moreover were fresh, so he withdrew to the east for now. It was not an easy decision. He didn't know if his son had survived; it was obvious that Oswiu had won though. For now he had to be satisfied with killing Oswald and one of his brothers, but the temptation to wipe out the whole brood was strong. He discounted Offa as a pitiful anchorite living on one of the small islets off Lindisfarne; he was no threat to anyone. Oswiu was quite different though.

An hour later Oswiu surveyed the battlefield and wept. No more than five hundred Northumbrians had died, compared to three times that number of the enemy, including Leofric, Eadgar and the other turncoat Mercians, but it was the sight of his brother's dismembered torso nailed to a crudely made cross that caused him to despair. Oslac's headless corpse lay beneath his brother with his head a few feet away. There was no sign of Oswald's head or limbs, presumably Penda had taken them away as grisly trophies of his pyrrhic victory. Nine members of his gesith, including Jarlath, Rònan and Beorhtwulf, lay around him; every single body riddled with arrows. Evidently Penda had decided not to waste more lives and had his archers kill them from a distance.

288

He wondered what had happened to their supposed Mercian allies until one of his men came and told him that he'd found Eowa at the top of the hill. He'd been stabbed in the back and then had his throat cut. The last had been unnecessary. Practically no blood had run from his severed throat, indicating that his heart had already stopped.

Oswiu's men gathered the bodies of the Northumbrians together and buried them with due ceremony in a mass grave, but he left the Mercians and the Welsh where they lay for the crows and buzzards to feast on.

Wrapping his brother's bloody torso in a leather tent and sewing it closed, he loaded it onto a pack horse and, as he began the dismal journey back to Bebbanburg, Ceadda came to his side.

'I know how deeply you are grieving for Oswald, but you should send some men to Legacæstir to bring Eowa's son and nephew to Bernicia, unless you want Penda to kill them. And you need to get to Yeavering and call the Witan together to elect you as king.'

'Why, what's the urgency? They won't know of my brother's death yet.'

'Word will spread quicker than a man can ride, believe me.'

'Even so, I want to bury what's left of Oswald first.'

'I suspect that you won't have time for that.'

'Why not?'

'Because Œthelwald thinks he should be his father's successor.'

THE END OF WARRIORS OF THE NORTH

TO BE CONTINUED IN

BRETWALDA

DUE OUT IN EARLY 2017

Historical Note

In the early seventh century AD Britain was divided into over twenty petty kingdoms. I have listed them here for the sake of completeness, though only a few of them feature significantly in the story. A few others get a passing mention. From north to south:

Land of the Picts – Probably seven separate kingdoms in all in the far north and north-east of present day Scotland at this time. Later they became one kingdom.

Dalriada – Western Scotland including Argyll and the Isles of the Hebrides. Also included part of Ulster in Ireland where the main tribe – the Scots – originated from.

Goddodin – Lothian and Borders Regions of modern Scotland – then subservient to Bernicia and so was part of Northumbria.

Bernicia – The north-east of England. Part of Northumbria.

Strathclyde – South east Scotland.

Rheged – Modern Cumbria and Lancashire in the north-west of England. A client kingdom of Northumbria.

Deira – North, East and South Yorkshire

Elmet – West Yorkshire

Lindsey – Lincolnshire and Nottinghamshire

Gwynedd – North Wales

Mercia – Most of the English Midlands

East Anglia – Norfolk, Suffolk and Cambridgeshire

Powys – Mid Wales

Middle Anglia – Bedfordshire, Northamptonshire and Warwickshire

Dyfed – South-west Wales

Kingdom of the East Saxons – Essex

Hwicce – South-east Wales, Herefordshire and Gloucestershire

Kingdom of the Middle Saxons – Home counties to the north of London

Wessex – Southern England between Dumnonia and the Kingdom of the South Saxons

Kent – South-eastern England south of the River Thames

Kingdom of the South Saxons – Sussex and Surrey

Dumnonia – Devon and Cornwall in south-west England

Little is known for certain about Oswald's life in exile. Much more is known about his life once he became King of Northumbria in 634 AD at the age of thirty.

Following the victory at Heavenfield, Oswald reunited Northumbria and re-established the pre-eminence of Bernicia in the North, which had declined under Edwin's reign from 616 to 633. Bede says that Oswald held *imperium* for the eight years of his rule and was the most powerful king in Britain. In the 9th-century Anglo-Saxon Chronicle he is referred to as a Bretwalda. Adomnán describes Oswald as "ordained by God as Emperor of all Britain".

Oswald seems to have been widely recognized as overlord, although the extent of his authority is uncertain. Bede makes the claim that Oswald "brought under his dominion all the nations and provinces of Britain", which, as Bede notes, was divided between the Angles, Saxons, Jutes, Britons, Scots, and Picts. An Irish source, the Annals of Tigernach, records that the other Anglo-Saxons of England tried to unite against Oswald early in his reign; this may indicate an attempt to put an end to Oswald's power south of the Humber, which presumably failed. Other evidence would suggest that it was only Mercia who opposed him.

Oswald apparently controlled the Kingdom of Lindsey, given the evidence of a story told by Bede regarding the moving of Oswald's bones to a monastery there; Bede says that the monks rejected the bones initially because Oswald had ruled over them as a foreign king. In the north it may have been Oswald who conquered the Gododdin. Irish annals record the siege of Edinburgh - thought to have been the royal stronghold of the Gododdin - in 638 and this seems to mark the end of Gododdin as a separate kingdom. That it was Oswald, or perhaps Oswiu on his behalf, who captured Edinburgh (or Dùn Èideann as it was then called) is supported by the fact that it was part of Oswiu's kingdom in the 650s.

Oswald seems to have been on good terms with the West Saxons: he stood as sponsor to the baptism of their king, Cynegils, and married Cynegils' daughter Cyneburga. Although Oswald is only known to have had one son, Œthelwald, it is uncertain whether this was a son from his marriage to Cynegils' daughter or from an earlier relationship as Œthelwald would have been too young to be chosen as King of Deira in 651 had he been Cyneburga's son. He was most probably the child of an earlier marriage during Oswald's exile, and this is what I have assumed.

Apart from a list of their names, nothing is known about four of Oswald's brothers. Only Oswiu, who became King of Bernicia after Oswald's death, is mentioned in various records of the time. I have therefore invented the story of their lives and deaths as monks from Iona.

Although Edwin had previously converted to Christianity in 627, it was Oswald who spread the religion in Northumbria. Shortly after becoming king, he asked the Abbot of Iona to send a bishop to facilitate the conversion of his people. Initially, a man was sent who did more to alienate people from Christ than he did to convert them. Aidan, who proposed a gentler approach, was subsequently sent instead and Oswald gave the island of Lindisfarne to Aidan as the seat of his episcopal see. For the purposes of this story I have ignored the earlier, unsuccessful, bishop. In contrast, Aidan achieved great success in spreading the Christian faith.

Bede puts a clear emphasis on Oswald's saintliness as a king. Although he could be classed as a martyr for his subsequent death in battle, Oswald is normally praised for his deeds in life and his martyrdom wasn't the primary reason for his elevation to sainthood. He was renowned for his generosity to the poor, the austerity of his life despite his wealth, and his ceaseless struggle to promote Christianity.

Oswald was killed by the Mercians in 642 AD at the Battle of Maserfield - a place generally identified with Oswestry - and his body was dismembered. Bede mentions the story that Oswald prayed for the souls of his soldiers when he saw that he was about to die. The traditional identification of the battle site with Oswestry, probably in the territory of Powys at the time, suggests that Penda may have had Welsh allies in this battle, and this is also suggested by surviving Welsh poetry which has been thought to indicate the participation of the men of Powys in the battle. If the traditional identification of the site as Oswestry is correct, Oswald must have been on the offensive in the territory of his enemies. This could conflict with Bede's saintly portrayal of Oswald, since an aggressive war could hardly qualify as a just war, perhaps explaining why Bede is silent on the cause of the campaign. He says only that Oswald died "fighting for his fatherland". Nor does he mention other offensive warfare Oswald is presumed to have engaged in between Heavenfield and Maserfield.

Oswald may have had an ally in Penda's brother Eowa, who was also killed in the battle, according to the Historia Britonnum and Annales Cambriae; while the source only mentions that Eowa was killed, not the side on which he fought, it has been suggested that Eowa was an ally of Oswald's and fighting alongside him in the battle, in opposition to Penda.

Oswald soon came to be regarded as a saint. Bede says that the spot where he died came to be associated with miracles, and people took dirt from the site, which led to a hole being dug as deep as a man's height. Reginald of Durham recounts another miracle, saying that his right arm was taken by a bird (perhaps a raven) to an ash tree, which gave the tree ageless vigour; when the bird dropped the arm onto the ground, a spring emerged from the ground. Both the tree and the spring were, according to Reginald, subsequently associated with healing miracles. The name of the site, Oswestry, or "Oswald's Tree", is generally thought to be derived from Oswald's death there and the legends surrounding it.

Bede mentions that Oswald's brother Oswiu, who succeeded Oswald in Bernicia, retrieved Oswald's remains in the year after his death. Initially his remains were interred at Bardney Abbey in Lindsey, where it was credited with performing several miracles. In the early 10th century, Bardney was conquered by the Danes, and in 909, following a combined West Saxon and Mercian raid led by Æthelflæd, daughter of Alfred the Great, St Oswald's relics were moved to a new minster in Gloucester, which was renamed St Oswald's Priory in his honour.

The cult of St. Oswald was not confined to England. Saint Oswald's church, Bad Kleinkirchheim, Carinthia, one of many churches and place names which commemorate Oswald on the Continent.

Oswald's head was interred in Durham Cathedral together with the remains of Cuthbert of Lindisfarne (a saint with whom Oswald became posthumously associated, although the two were not associated in life; Cuthbert became abbot and bishop of Lindisfarne more than forty years after Oswald's death) where it is generally believed they remain, although there are at least four other claimed heads of Oswald in continental Europe. One of his arms is said to have ended up in Peterborough Abbey later in the Middle Ages. The story is that a small group of monks from Peterborough made their way to Bamburgh, where Oswald's uncorrupted arm was kept, and stole it under the cover of darkness.

The Church of Saint Oswald at Heavenfield stands near the location of the wooden cross erected by Oswald just before the decisive battle. However, there is no evidence that his brothers Osguid and Oslac were present at the battle, or that Osguid died there.

His brother Oswiu became King of Bernicia, possibly as Penda's vassal, after the death of Oswald. However, Oswine was made king by the Witan of Deira until deposed by Oswiu seven years later. The early part of Oswiu's reign was defined by struggles with Oswine and then Œthelwald to assert control over Deira, and his contentious relationship with Penda.

In 655 Oswiu's forces killed Penda at the Battle of the Winwæd, despite being betrayed by Œthelwald, which established Oswiu as one of the most powerful rulers in Britain. Œthelwald fled and Oswiu made his son Elhfrith Deira's king, but as his vassal.   For three years after the battle Oswiu's control also extended to Mercia, earning him recognition as bretwalda over much of England.

Oswiu was a devoted Christian, promoting the faith among his subjects and establishing a number of monasteries, including Gilling Abbey and Whitby Abbey. He was raised in the Celtic Christian tradition, rather than the Roman Catholic faith practiced by the southern Anglo-Saxon kingdoms as well as some members of the Deiran nobility, including Oswiu's queen. In 664, Oswiu presided over the Synod of Whitby, where clerics debated which of the two traditions - Celtic or Roman Catholic - should prevail and decided that Northumbria would follow the Roman Church, a momentous decision which would affect England for the next millennium.

Oswiu is thought to have had children as follows:

1. Out of wedlock by Fin (Fianna in the novels):
   Aldfrith. King of Northumbria 685 – 705.
2. By Rhieinmelth:
   Elhfrith. Sub-king of Deira 655-664.
   Alchflaed (dau). Married Peada of Mercia.
3. By Eanflaed:
   Ecgfrith. Sub-king of Deira 664 – 670. King of Northumbria 670 – 685.
   Osthryth (dau). Married King Æthelred of Mercia.
   Ælfflaed (dau). Abbess of Whitby.
   Ælfwine. Sub-king of Deira 670-679.

Oswald's only son, Œthelwald, was Sub-king of Deira from 651 to 655 when he was deposed by Oswiu for treachery.

Other Novels by H A Culley

The Normans Series

The Bastard's Crown

Death in the Forest

England in Anarchy

Caging the Lyon

Seeking Jerusalem

Babylon Series

Babylon – The Concubine's Son

Babylon – Dawn of Empire

Individual Novels

Magna Carta

The Sins of the Fathers

Robert the Bruce Trilogy

The Path to the Throne

The Winter King

After Bannockburn

Constantine Trilogy

Constantine – The Battle for Rome

Crispus Ascending

Death of the Innocent

Macedon Trilogy

The Strategos

The Sacred War

Alexander

Kings of Northumbria Series

Whiteblade

About the Author

H A Culley was born in Wiltshire in 1944 and entered RMA Sandhurst after leaving school. He was an Army officer for twenty four years, during which time he had a variety of unusual jobs. He spent his twenty first birthday in the jungles of Borneo, commanded an Arab unit in the Gulf for three years and was the military attaché in Beirut during the aftermath of the Lebanese Civil War.

After leaving the Army, he became the bursar of a large independent school for seventeen years before moving into marketing and fundraising in the education sector. He has served on the board of two commercial companies and several national and local charities. He has also been involved in two major historical projects. He recently retired as the finance director and company secretary of IDPE and remains on its board of trustees.

He has three adult children and one granddaughter and lives with his wife and two Bernese Mountain Dogs between Holy Island and Berwick upon Tweed in Northumberland.

43476124R00185

Made in the USA
Lexington, KY
28 June 2019